THE
WATER
UNIVERSAL
SOLVENT

THE UNIVERSAL SOLVENT

Beth Fowler

Copyright © 2001 by Beth Fowler.

ISBN #:   Softcover   0-7388-9945-3

All rights reserved. No part of this book may be reproduced or transmitted in any form or by any means, electronic or mechanical, including photocopying, recording, or by any information storage and retrieval system, without permission in writing from the copyright owner.

This is a work of fiction. Names, characters, places and incidents either are the product of the author's imagination or are used fictitiously, and any resemblance to any actual persons, living or dead, events, or locales is entirely coincidental.

This book was printed in the United States of America.

To order additional copies of this book, contact:
Xlibris Corporation
1-888-7-XLIBRIS
www.Xlibris.com
Orders@Xlibris.com

This book is dedicated to you, dear reader, whose body is mostly water.

PROLOGUE

The comfortably disheveled second-story bedroom, dark but for the blue glow from the computer screen, was tinged orange for a second when a cluster of sparklers flew past Rusty Sinclair's window.

"I don't believe this!" Rusty blew a plume of cigarette smoke at the computer screen.

"Yeah, you'd think those yobbos could wait until tomorrow night to welcome in 1998," Kim said, referring to the people outside on the streets shooting off rockets and lighting sparklers. She was sprawled on his bed, dribbling habanero sauce on a cracker. His flannel shirt on her body assumed her shape pleasingly.

"I'm not talking about them. C'mere. Look." He read from the *U.S. Water News* website, "'The Clean Water Act is one of the most successful pieces of federal legislation ever crafted. In 1997, more than 60 percent of the nation's waters now support fishing and other uses, and while the U.S. population grew considerably since 1972, modern wastewater treatment facilities helped pollutant levels in the nation's waters fall 36 percent."

"Isn't that true?" she asked.

"Yeah, but poison is poison," Rusty said. "Having less pollution in our water doesn't make it less pernicious. PCB and DDT were outlawed in the Seventies, yet they're still found in people's blood—people who were born since then. The poisons are in our water table. Our rivers and streams look cleaner, but they're deadlier. You've got your atrazine and your benzene. You've got your cancer and your tumors. You've got your Arctic polar bears with pollutants concentrated in their fat. Now how did that happen?"

Kim groaned.

Ignoring his girlfriend's bored groan, he ranted. "I'll tell you how. Water's the universal solvent. Contaminants dissolve in water on contact and are distributed via rain, the oceans, the water tables. There are 80,000 chemicals—"

"In the environment." Kim's voice overlapped with his. "I know, I know. Think global. Act local. For instance, you could quit smoking."

"I will." He lit another cigarette and logged onto the Millennium Institute's website. "'Humans currently use half of the world's available fresh water,'" he read, "'and 26 percent of the water is used by plant and animal life. At our current rate of growth, by 2025 we will be consuming 100 percent of available fresh water supplies.'" He scrolled to a list of forty contaminants found in water meeting U.S. Government drinking water standards and said, "Yeah, yeah, yeah. Tell me something I don't know."

"Must you do that now, Rusty?" Kim asked. "I've got to go to work soon. Third shift."

"I'll tell you why people are apathetic." His pique filled the bedroom, penetrated the dark corners.

"OK. Rusty, you tell me why," Kim said flatly. She handed him a cracker drenched in habanero sauce.

He set the cracker aside. He hadn't missed her sarcastic tone. Sometimes he could be overzealous, he knew, a perfect son of a bitch, but he went on ranting. "They crank their taps on, water flows out the spigot, tastes all right. The fact is, people are scared shitless to face the truth."

"Don't yell at me."

"I'm not yelling at you." Rusty pushed himself away from the computer and swiveled his chair to face her. He wrapped his arms around Kim's waist and rested his head against her warm stomach, her inviting smells. He slid his hands under the shirt and traced his fingers along the vertical hollow of her spine. Trying to push away the image of his late wife being bathed by a hospice worker was impossible. They'd placed her bed in the Florida room where she could watch sparrows playing in the birdbath outside. She'd found joy in simple things then. A lone cloud. A dragonfly. Sun rays slanting across the room. "I'm not yelling at you," he said softly.

"I know." Kim stroked his hair.

Shouting and a sputter of popping noises erupted from the street. A red flare sailed past the black windowpanes.

"Tell me, honey. Tell me," she said. Her strong fingers massaged the taut tendons at the back of his neck. She had every right to be sick of hearing him go on and on about water, even so, he gently removed her hand from the nape of his neck.

"See this map," he said. A map of the United States titled "Community Water Systems Violating Maximum Contaminant Levels or Treatment Standards in 1997" glowed on the screen. He'd signed an employment agreement with Statonics forbidding bringing proprietary data home, but they'd never find out he'd copied the map.

"This is that project you guys are doing for the EPA," she said from behind him. He could hear Kim packing her makeup bag.

"Yeah," he said over his shoulder. "The white states had zero to six percent violations of drinking water health standards. The light blue states: six to eleven percent and the dark blue: more than eleven percent."

"Our region is white. What's the problem?"

"I fucked up. After I'd entered our region's data and gave it to the project leader, I realized the formula was incorrect. The formula's been incorrect for the past three years." Saying it made his throat close.

"Someone else wrote the formula. You didn't even work on the project the last three years. Why are you taking this all on yourself?" She thought a moment and said, "What do you plan to do?"

"Did. I gave the project leader the correct formula and the revised map. But I saw a copy of the report Statonics submitted to the EPA. It's this one, the erroneous one." Firecrackers exploding outside again brightened the bedroom with an eerie light. Her eyes flashed.

"You're kidding!" she said. "But why would your supervisor send the wrong report?"

"So the government can write more happy-grams like the one about the Clean Water Act. Election year coming. Keep the mobs ignorant and placated. I don't know!" He was yelling again. He grasped her arm and said, "Sorry, sorry."

"Now what?"

"I told the project leader I'm going to inform the EPA the numbers are wrong. Have been wrong."

"What'd he say?"

"He threatened me."

"Oh, Rusty."

"My supervisor was the one who let the incorrect data slide through all this time. Well, screw him and his reputation. I'm going to the regional EPA director on Monday. I've got to explain this in person." Rusty returned to the screen and hit the keys. "This is what the truth looks like." The states in the region turned dark blue, indicating contaminated drinking water.

"Sometimes I wonder if this is exaggerated millennial doomsday stuff," she said breezily. "The boy who cried wolf."

He shut his eyes, and collected restraint by counting: one, computer; two, bed; three, I love her. "You've forgotten how the fable ends."

"I'll go to the EPA with you on Monday."

"I'll probably lose my job."

They looked into each other's eyes for a long moment. Complete understanding. She pulled him to his bed and fed him crackers with habanero sauce. "You've got a few silver hairs right here on your sideburns." Her fingers danced on his face. "I better examine you for more silver hairs." She slid between the sheets down to the middle of the bed.

"Um-m," he said, "an oral exam." He surrendered willingly to the melting feeling, and floated out the window, gazing down at those yobbos who thought you only found true love once in a lifetime.

When Kim came out of the shower, a perfumed cloud rolled into the bedroom. "I'm going to call Cindy for a ride into work," she told him.

"Why?" He stared, unseeing at the computer screen.

"My car's at the station. Inspection."

"Take my car." He fished his car keys out of his pants pocket.

"I'll get a lift. Cindy lives near here. She's on third shift too."

"Why can't you take my car?" His voice was rising. He couldn't help it. "Take my car." He tossed the keys at her. She let them fall to the floor.

"Why are you yelling again?" She pulled the towel tighter around her.

"You can leave your stuff here."

"And that means what?"

"Bring some clothes and keep them here. There's room in my closet."

"What about Tiva?"

"Bring your cat," Rusty said, "She can move in too." Kim narrowed her eyes, fighting a smile. "Why not?" he said.

"Are you ready for a live-in girlfriend? Tubes and bottles of girl goop in the bathroom? Cat hairs clinging to your black jeans?"

He rose from his chair and walked slowly to her. "You're right. I'm not ready for a live-in girlfriend."

"Well, then," she said, obviously trying to sound stoic.

She was too important to him to let slip away on hints and sideways proposals. His heart swelled in his chest. "I want to marry you. That's what I'm saying."

"I never thought of myself as someone's second wife. It sounds, oh, I don't know."

"Not my second wife, Kim. My forever wife."

He watched her face clear, her smile widen. He slipped his hands under the towel and cupped her buttocks.

She said, "Third shift sucks. Yes. My answer's yes. I gotta get going now."

They laughed and shook hands as if they'd made a business

deal. When he tried to pull his hand away, she wouldn't let go. "Happy New Year, Rusty."

"Happy New Year," he said, convinced that with her as his partner, life promised to be nothing but happy. After she left, he returned to the blue map on the screen. The map indicating actual water contamination violations dissolved. He pounded keys, trying to retrieve the map. "Hey! Somebody's hacking me!" A black skull appeared against a background of flame images on the screen. An explosion outside shook the walls and reverberated off the other houses in the neighborhood. The entire bedroom was washed in hellish orange. A vacuum of silence, then screaming.

CHAPTER 1

The truck driver pulled away from the curb and asked him if he'd been on the road for long. Every lift asked that question or a variation of it.

"Depends," the hitchhiker replied, *on what you mean by long.* Was seven years and some spare change long? His hip flask poked his buttock. He removed the flask from his back pocket and put it in his jacket pocket.

The driver's eyes had followed the path of the thin, silver flask. "Can you spare a hit?"

"It's mean stuff," the hitchhiker warned.

"Hunh," he snorted. "One for the road."

"You sure?"

"Sure, I'm sure."

The hitchhiker unscrewed the lid off the flask and handed it to the truck driver. "Take it easy," the hitchhiker said. "I'm warning you."

The truck driver leered and knocked back a swig. His leer metamorphosed into bewilderment and then into a mask of agony. His complexion flushed red. Sweat broke out on his forehead and streamed down his temples. Tears gushed from his eyes. He wiped his tongue on his nylon jacket. After a full ten minutes of driving while under the influence of red-hot hell, he handed the flask back to the hitchhiker and said gruffly, "A little dab'll do ya."

The hitchhiker maintained a blasé expression and said, "Habanero." One of these days, a brute was going to knock his teeth out for playing a trick like that. He deserved it.

"Read to me, why doncha," the trucker said. "Passes the time."

The hitchhiker picked up the "U.S. Today" newspaper lying between them on the seat and read: "President Flores' popularity plummeted sixteen points when federal troops she'd sent failed to quell the Egyptian-Sudanese Water War. Meanwhile, Republican Congressman Yung lauded her for deploying the National Guard to restore order when water riots broke out simultaneously in Tucson, Arizona and Austin, Texas."

"Read sumpin else." The trucker sounded peeved.

"A prominent college professor stated unequivocally, 'Water can not be synthesized.'"

"Sumpin else."

"'The UN's Comprehensive Assessment of the Freshwater Resources of the World is seriously flawed.'"

"Sumpin else. Any crime?"

"'The FBI is trying to collar racketeers who thrive by exploiting people's basic need for drinkable water.'"

"This water crisis snuck up and bit us in the ass," the trucker said as if it were the punch line to a joke.

"Don't you remember 1993 in Milwaukee?" His question carried an unmistakable chiding tone. He collected restraint and evenly said, "More than 400,000 people got sick and about 100 people died from water contamination. Haven't you heard of 'blue baby syndrome' caused by nitrite in drinking water? MTBE carcinogens in drinking water? How about male impotence linked to pollutants?"

"Sure, sure, I hearda that." The trucker gave the hitchhiker a sidelong glare. "What are you? A scientist or sumpin?"

"Or something." Sitting high in the passenger seat of the semi, he watched the scenery spin past, drawing out his thoughts. He was thinking about the mountains and how they looked blue no matter whether they were the Rockies, the Smokies or the Catskills, no matter whether the trees were winter naked, sprayed with buds, lush with green leaves, or fiery with golden foliage as they were today. It saddened him that, at times, he'd forgotten to remember the mountains, for he was sure they remembered him. They fit the contours of his mind pleasantly as if he were more whole with the dusty blue perimeter as his companion.

A sign painted in tipsy red letters nailed onto an abandoned corncrib proclaimed "The Future IS Now! PrePare to meEt JESUS." Some things hadn't changed much, he thought morosely. His reflection in the sideview mirror showed him a man whose red hair was shot with silver filaments, a man whose sorrow could be read in the wrinkles around eyes and mouth, a man whose future could rewrite his past. Or so he hoped.

And he was thinking about the people he used to work with. Back in the late Nineties they'd referred to the imminent second millennium as Y2K. Why two kay. Slick with a technical, yet questioning ring to it, but after the millennial bash hangovers subsided, everybody simply said two thousand or two thou'. Now, five years after the turn of the century no one mentioned Y2K or fax machines or Alzheimer's, except in a historical context. People still got the sniffles, and they still feared the unknown, whether the unknown was the foreigners living next door or the outcome of a policy change at work. Buzzing to work or to the corner liquor store via a personal jet-powered backpack was the stuff of vintage cartoons, not reality.

"I got a load of cable to deliver in Fort Trust." The trucker checked the GPS. "Ain't but across the Mason-Dixon Line a piece."

That was, he knew, his cue to prepare to disembark.

They traveled in silence until the driver said: "Ain't many jobs in this town, if that's what you're hunting for. This was a working town that quit."

"Yeah, I see what you mean."

The truck rolled into the crumbling edges of a small town. They passed an abandoned factory. Rust bled off the roof onto the walls. Vines choked the doorway of a food processing plant maybe. The kind she used to work in. After the accident, that's what he called it, he'd packed his backpack, withdrew all his money from the bank, told his parents he was going on a business trip and left on the last day of 1997. His fantasy, his dad's too, had been to drive around the country like John Steinbeck did in "Travels with

Charley." They didn't have a dog and for some reason they never drove farther than the foothills of Mount Rainier, which wasn't all that bad. He hadn't planned to travel this way, under these circumstances, meandering across the nation like an underground stream, surfacing then going under again.

The trucker lifted his left hand off the wheel and thrust his thumb toward the next intersection where people were clustered around a red, white and blue portable tank to fill their jugs with government-approved drinking water. "Potable Water: Boil Before Use," the familiar sign on the water tank said. The tanks could be found everywhere across the country, wherever there were people.

"You can drop me off at the water tank."

The driver shrugged, shifted into gear and pulled away. The hitchhiker adjusted his black cowboy hat and carried his backpack in his hand. A weak sun nailed up cold clouds. He sat on a weather-silvered park bench and traced his broad thumbnail in a carving of two parallel lines with a curved line like a sidewinder snake between them: the hobo glyph meaning poor water. He'd be spending another winter sleeping in cars, in factory warehouses, in airport lounges, in roadhouses. A gust snatched leaves off the gingko trees and agitated the pond. He resisted flipping his collar up. The trouble with stopping was his mind started up. He felt guilty, responsible for her death. Nighttime was worse. He had no one to talk to, no cadre of friends to retell his story to, shading the emphasis here and highlighting a detail there until the disaster made sense, seemed forgivable. He was stuck with working it over by himself. The explosion, the fire. Blowing the whistle on his employer had been a rash act. Risky. Stupid. Selfish.

It was almost five o'clock. He would hunt for a bakery or produce store that sold stale bread or bruised bananas for pocket change this late in the day. He would hunt for a hidey-hole to sleep in. And tomorrow, a job. He snugged his black cowboy hat down low and set off.

A week later and he still hadn't found a job. He approached a low slung, white brick building. The sign out front had a green and white triangle logo on it and the words Shatz Company. Through the front plate glass window he saw that the reception area was filled with men and women applying for jobs, by the looks of it. A woman, the receptionist perhaps, accepted papers from each person before he or she left and came out the front doors. She looked out the window and smiled abstractedly.

He removed his black cowboy hat, strode through the glassed in entrance hall and pardoned his way past blue-collars, white-collars and no-collars to her desk in the reception area. He asked for an application to fill out. With a dancer-like rotation of the left wrist and artfully poised fingers, she pointed to a stack of papers on a table. He filled in the application truthfully, to a point, yet he knew she'd dwell on the gaps in his employment as if he were only worthy and extant when he'd contributed to Social Security and FICA. He signed a name using the penmanship he'd begun affecting when he'd last changed his identity.

He could hear her, Miss Ray the simulated wood nameplate declared, behind him making coffee, answering the phone, tapping at the computer keyboard, consoling a woman applicant who was crying because her grandma's medical bills wiped out their life savings. The receptionist listened sympathetically while simultaneously collecting completed applications. She was of slight build and wore a pink dress that seemed childish with its ruffled collar. Her movements were close, contained, and quintessentially feminine. Sometimes she sighed.

"Here's my application, Miss Ray," he said.

Shatz Company's secretary seemed too young to fathom why he wasn't making a play for her, as the other male applicants were feeling inspired to do. She swept back a lock of blond hair with her small hand. "Please, call me Lucinda. Miss Ray sounds too similar to misery for my taste." She looked at his application and said, "Wade R. Rhodes." She dragged the name through a bog of insignificance implying that he, standing there in scuffed boots and threadbare black jeans, didn't have a rat's chance for a job. They always twisted some reason 'round making it sound as if the company were doing him a favor. ("Dear Mr. W.R. Rhodes," the laser-printed, watermarked, oatmeal stationery would state, "We regret to inform you that we presently don't have an available position to best maximize your skills and experience," or similar corp-speak.) Hell, he thought, I wouldn't hire me.

"Everybody, I'm sorry," she announced surprisingly loudly for as small as she was. "It's ten o'clock. The application process is concluded. Come back tomorrow if you're not finished filling in your apps or mail them in." The people in the reception room grumbled and shuffled out the front door. "Hold it, you," she said. "Hold it, Mr. Rhodes." It took him a moment to realize she was referring to him. The name was so new to him. Lucinda Ray crinkled her nose at his application. "This is a P.O. Box. We need a home address."

"I don't have a home address." He'd been crashing in different motels or the Y each night.

"May I please see your driver's license?" Boredom or fatigue weighed down her words. She studied his photo. If she saw the slice mark in the lamination where he'd removed the other man's photo and had inserted his, she wasn't letting on. At length she said, "You looked better without that beard."

"So do you."

"Oh, har, har. Your work history is highly irregular," she said, scanning his application. "Can you account for the gaps?"

"I traveled abroad. I didn't start working in the States until Ninety-eight."

"I can see that. What did you do with your whole life up until then? You didn't fill in the education section."

He chose the words carefully, hoping she'd infer that his father had died recently, and due to misplaced sympathy, she'd lighten up. The stratagem shamed him, but he said, "My father was a freelance photographer. I was educated overseas. I worked with him until recently."

For the first time, she looked at him with a modicum of interest. "Might I have seen any of his work?"

"I don't know, Miss Ray. Tell me every photograph you've ever seen, then maybe I can answer your question." He grinned apologetically. She didn't deserve this.

"Look. We don't need," she glanced at his application, "an orchard laborer, an auto technician or a delivery truck driver."

"What do you need?"

She cocked her head, challenging him. "A data analyst."

"I can do that."

"While tuning up cars you picked up a little data analysis on the side?"

"Something like that. Give me some numbers. Give me a test. Don't you have an applicant screening test?" His eagerness, his betrayal of desire dismayed him. He was old enough to know the world had a cruel way of curing you of desire by altering what you desired into a source of grief.

She rifled through papers and pamphlets and pulled out a folder. "Analyze this." She winged the folder at him. It carried a wisp of perfume: Samsara. He'd bought it as a Valentine's gift once.

"You expect me to crunch these numbers in my head?" he asked.

She stepped away from her desk so he could sit in her chair in front of the computer. The seat was warm. She stood behind him. Her voice came from overhead. "Look on the main menu and choose any program you like."

He did so. "You have a lot of neat software in here for—"

"For a secretary?"

"For a small company." He made a mental note to steer clear of this tetchy woman. Neo-feminists were more prickly than their predecessors. He set up the X- and Y-axes. The data to be entered pertained to water filtered through a polymeric membrane. From what he'd seen of the photos and product literature in the reception area, Shatz Company built recycling systems for plastics, organics, paper, glass. Maybe these numbers about water were dummy data for applicant testing purposes only.

"Where did you and your dad travel?" Lucinda asked conversationally.

"Asia, Australia…"

"Were you in Japan?"

"Briefly." He'd read plenty of novels set in Japan anyhow.

"What did you think of it?"

"I was too young to remember." The facility with which he lied amazed and shamed him. Lying was a habit too easily adopted and honed. He hit a key to create a line connecting the points on the chart.

"Did you travel in Taiwan?"

"Yeah."

"How about Formosa?"

"Yeah."

"How does Taiwan compare to Formosa? I've been thinking of signing up for a package tour to one or the other."

"It's hard to say. Asian countries are similar in obvious ways, but different in ways too subtle for most Westerners to notice." He hoped his adlibbed answer satisfied her as much as it disgusted him. He printed out the graph he'd designed using the water data.

She grabbed the graph as the printer spit it out. "Our chief engineer made a pie chart with this same data. You made a line graph."

"A pie chart is good for illustrating proportion. I think for this data, the engineer is more interested in a trend. I made a line chart so you can get the overall picture of the relation between the sets of data on the X and Y axes." She'd mentioned an engineer, so the data must be real. "Is this from an actual project?"

"We're dabbling in water purification, a sideline you could say."

How should he play it with this woman? Innuendoes never got him anything, nothing that he'd wanted anyhow. "Lucinda," he said. He waited until she was looking at him. Her light gray eyes with the black pupils reminded him of aluminum nails. "Lucinda, I really want this job. Give me more numbers to crank."

She did. After he'd entered data and created graphs for an hour, she said, "It's a part-time position." She smiled in a generous way that warmed him. He discouraged his natural inclination to respond in kind and tamped down his smile.

CHAPTER 2

Clete Shatz pounded the center of his chest with his fist. His chronic heartburn had been acting up since he'd laid off ten percent of the workers in all departments, save for research and development, which in his mind was the key to the future. He took a deep breath, trying to open up his chest so the acid could find its way out of his system, but it was wedged in his esophagus, burning, pulsating. It's the price one must pay, he thought, for success.

This leather chair, this huge desk, the artsy photograph on the wall behind the credenza, the couch, the mahogany conference table with its set of matching chairs, the smell of his office reminded him he'd made it, he'd arrived. He was on top. In some ways, on some days, though, he yearned for the times back when he'd clung to the back of a garbage truck and leaped off, the wheezy brakes waking people up in neighborhoods as different from each other as tarpaper from terrazzo. Operating a garbage collection service, and now building recycling systems had been recession-proof enterprises for so many years, but you had to stay ahead of the pack. Too many companies were in the recycling business these days. His competitors had caught him napping and slapped him awake with his company's sinking sales figures. That's what he'd let them think. Lull them into complacency.

He was on the brink, he just knew it. He was on the brink of solving the water problem. He was going to make a killing with the Aquamira, the special research and development project Henry and the lab rats were working on. To keep creditors off his back and meet the payroll until the Aquamira was operational, he bid on stinking penny ante shit—customized material recycling systems, subcontract work and sub-subcontract work. He got up from the chair and went out to the reception area.

His executive secretary turned in her chair and smiled at him, apparently mistaking his grimace as the beginnings of a smile. She was holding an application form. "I didn't think I'd be saying this," Lucinda said, "but I think we ought to hire this applicant."

"Hire who?" Shatz tightened his tie and buttoned his suit jacket.

"Whom. We'd hire whom."

Her bemused smile was one of the reasons he let her get away with correcting his grammar.

"Wade Rhodes," Lucinda said. "He applied for the data analyst job yesterday. Along with three hundred forty-seven others."

"Christ. That many." The upside of a soft economy was a talented pool of overqualified, underemployed applicants to choose from. The downside was, he wasn't hiring today. Never hurts to build up a pool of qualified apps, though, for the boom times. "What's his app say?"

"Place of birth: Boise, Idaho." She read the sporadic work history.

Shatz studied the early morning traffic passing by on Point Street. He pressed his palm on the cold plate glass window. Chilly air outside caused condensation to form a handprint. It disappeared when he lifted his hand to fondle a golf tee in his pocket. "Why are we hiring a no-hoper?"

Lucinda joined him at the window. "I know what you mean. He does look like a no-hoper, but he took a data analyst test. This is the graph he prepared. Looks good to me. Besides, all the other apps want three times as much pay and full benefits. Show the application and graph to Henry. See what he thinks. He's the one who requisitioned a data analyst." She returned to her computer. "An h-mail came from your wife."

"Pop her out," Clete said. He jabbed his thumb with the golf tee and hoped against reason for good news from his wife, or at least not bad news.

Darla's hologram materialized in the reception room. She'd transmitted the call earlier that morning when she'd been applying makeup at her vanity after Clete had left for work. Her seated figure, sheathed in an ivory kimono, wavered before them. She opened her mouth most unattractively as she applied lip liner.

"Clete," the hologram writhe said, "Sorry about h-mailing."

"Sorry like hell," Clete said. He knew her, her ways.

Lucinda pulled at the drawstring on her collar and suggested, "This is personal. Maybe we should switch to text mode."

Sales and accounting staffers on the other side of the glassed in entrance foyer stood up at their cubicles and craned their necks to get a gander of Clete Shatz's wife curling her eyelashes at her Louis XIV vanity, although the vanity didn't transmit because the h-camera was positioned on the vanity top with her perfume bottles, makeup bottles, lipstick tubes and whatnot.

"Switch, switch," he said, chopping the air with the blade of his palm. Both Clete and Lucinda relaxed when Darla's hologram dissipated.

Lucinda brought Darla's message, in text, up on the computer screen. Clete saw his secretary's face congest as her lovely features prepared to manufacture tears. "Read the stinking message!" he said.

Lucinda read, "'I'll cut to the chase. I'm filing for divorce. My attorney will contact you regarding the disbursal of my half of our assets. If you can buy out my half of Shatz Co., so much the better. Sorry so blunt. I'm moving my personal effects out today. You can live in the Oak Heights house until it's sold. Warmest regards, Darla.'" Tears threatened to spill over Lucinda's eyeliner.

"'Warmest regards,'" Clete echoed dryly. He peered into the cars driving past. Darla always got what she wanted. And one time, she had wanted him. So much so, that she'd convinced him that he'd wanted her too. Women didn't know what they wanted, he supposed.

"Where is everybody going? If they're going to work, they're late." He swiped Wade Rhodes' application off Lucinda's desk and jovially asked, "How's *your* love life?"

"Actually," she said into her empty Love Me Love My Cat coffee mug, "my love life's nonexistent."

Clete returned to his chair and propped his feet up on the credenza behind him. Darla's h-mail hadn't surprised him. Very much. She'd left four days ago, taking cold war tensions with her to New Orleans allegedly to attend an attorneys' conference. "A grownups' pajama party in the Big Easy," she'd snipped. Some sense of humor, Clete thought. When she'd returned last night, they didn't pretend to be glad to see each other. "Absence makes the heart grow fonder," she'd said, "of someone else." She used her edgy wit to slice profits away from companies who'd lost to her clients' product liability claims. Judges either admired her or despised her. Now she was holding the blade of malice to the jugular vein of his assets. But he wasn't going to let her carve up his company, his life, as part of their divorce settlement.

To make enough money to buy out her half of the company and their joint assets and still come out on top, the profits from the Aquamira would have to be in telephone number-sized sums. Long distance.

The security manager barged into Clete's office. "Hey, chief. Fire up your security monitor screen and get a load of Henry. He's late again."

Clete glared meaningfully at Jack Funk and said, "I'll have to get better locks installed on my office door." He switched on the monitor and they watched Henry Healy, Shatz Company's chief R & D engineer, fumble out of his car and kick the door shut. He plodded up the back steps two at a time and swung the lab door open, crashing it against the cinderblock wall. He slammed his satchel and thermos onto his desk and leaned against a cluttered workbench. He panted.

Funk gloated. "I bet ol' Henry's gonna wish he was back in England after you rip him a new asshole."

"Go on, Funk. I'll deal with Henry." Shatz turned off the security monitor screen and muttered, "It's Maalox time." He opened his desk drawer and cracked open a new bottle of chalky liquid, knowing as he guzzled it that the true causes of his heartburn weren't what the Maalox chemists had in mind when they'd come up with this new improved formulation.

Entrepreneurs have vision, yes, vision. One of the marks of captains of industry was their ability to see into the future and share their vision with employees so everybody on board was rowing in the same direction. Although Henry Healy, the chief research and development engineer, shared the vision to create a solution to the water problem, Clete knew he was going to take it hard, take it personally when Clete told him the six requisitions for new hires were on hold, for now.

As he walked from his office to the lab, Clete hoped he could think of a way to convince his most important employee that not hiring more engineers and technicians was in their best interests and at the same time inspire him to remain motivated, keep his morale pumped up. Christ, he thought, not only did you need vision, you needed a damn psychology degree.

He unconsciously ran his fingers along the corners of his mouth to remove chalky white residue. Consciously, he lifted his cheeks until it felt as if he were smiling. He opened the lab door. Lab personnel, wearing blue coveralls, exchanged wary glances with each other over their computer monitors and workbenches. None of them greeted him or glanced at him. He let his cheeks fall. No doubt the lab rats thought their heads were on the chopping block. People seemed to think he enjoyed laying off employees. Before he could dwell on the whys of this unfair assumption, he killed the thought.

In the late Sixties, the lab had housed his one garbage truck. He and his first wife had shared a battered desk right over there in the corner where now a door lead to the offices, which had been added on later. As he'd augmented his route with more neighborhoods and hired additional garbage collectors and married his second wife, he pulled enough clout to get a major discount on a fleet of garbage trucks at the Mercedes dealer. Ah, those were the days.

You could see the ghosts of oil stains on the concrete floor if you knew where to look. Clete knew where to look.

Back then as now, the walls were plain gray cinderblock. After he'd sold the garbage collection business and had pocketed profits grand enough to change his lifestyle, he'd had heating, shelving, cabinets and workbenches installed in the garage and he hired assemblers to build systems that separated metals, glass, organic matter and plastics. At first, few customers wanted to buy recycling systems. Business sagged and Darla pumped her personal bucks into it. He even turned his old garbage dumps into a tourist site to scrounge up capital. As his business grew, he extended the front of the building to house sales and accounting staff, his executive office and the reception area. Another extension was added where production workers assembled material recycling systems. Sufficient land, zoned for industrial use, skirted the building for further expansion. He'd planned it that way.

These days, the clanks and rumbles that normally emanated from the factory on the other side of the lab's walls were disheartingly subdued. The walls retained a chill in spite of the heaters. Membranous windows along the ceiling diffused sunlight into cottony rectangles.

Clete shot out his arm and checked his watch. Only moments ago, he was all set to ream Henry out for reporting to work late. Again. In the scheme of things, Henry's tardiness this morning was small potatoes. A different sort of lateness stoked Clete's heartburn.

Henry Healy was seated on a metal stool, scrutinizing a supplier's catalog and blowing smoke through his lipless mouth. Lucinda had once joked that small-headed, heavy-bottomed Henry looked like a bedraggled pigeon. She was being kind.

"Henry," Clete said.

He jumped and stuffed a rolled up paper into the top desk drawer. "Yes! What?"

Clete rolled his tongue along his molars and tried to think of the best way to broach the subject. Employee relations, he knew, was his short suit. About that Lucinda had not been kind. "Is the Aquamira prototype ready yet?" No point in beating around the bush. We're all men here.

"Er...no...I'm trying to locate a vendor that sells pump mechanisms fitting our revised specifications and tightened budget. Sorry, but the budget and the deadline are impossible. If I had more time and help. I need more men." Henry petered out.

"The requisitions are on hold." Still no point in beating around the bush.

The tip of Henry's hawk nose nearly met his upper lip, such as it was. "Give Rafferty and his crew a secondment from production."

"Speak English."

"That was English."

"I mean Yankee English."

"Transfer Rafferty to the lab to help me with the prototype. I need more men."

"I laid Rafferty and his crew off." An executive decision he'd just as soon forget.

"What do you want, then?" Henry ran tobacco-yellowed fingernails along his scalp.

"I want to build the best water remediation system the world has seen."

"We see eye to eye on that. But with all due respect, you're handcuffing me with this moratorium on hiring."

Clete called Lucinda and asked her to bring that application she'd shown him. Within a few minutes she walked briskly into the lab and handed Wade Rhodes' application to Henry. When she walked out, Clete noted that the technicians looked up, eyes bright, smiles squirming on their faces.

Henry looked at the application and tossed it aside. "What? You havin' me on?"

"Do you want him or not?"

"What ever for?"

"You're the one who requisitioned a data analyst."

"With all due respect, sir," revealing snaggly teeth, "I submitted not one, but six personnel requisition forms."

Clete pounded his chest, hammering gastric acid into words. "Throwing additional men at the Aquamira isn't going to help."

"There's the off chance that you're right." Henry seemed oblivious to how insulting his choice of words was.

"You don't have a man-hour capacity problem."

"You sound just like Ingle," Henry said.

Clete almost rose to the bait of being compared to the director of accounting, but stopped himself. "It's... What's that saying about perspiration and inspiration?"

"I'm sure I wouldn't know," Henry replied.

"I'll have Lucinda tell this applicant thanks but no thanks." Clete sauntered around the worktable; kicked empty potato chip bags. He ignored Henry's offer of a Benson & Hedges. Clete sat on one of the stools. Maybe a pep talk was in order. "Shatz Company is going to develop the best water recycling and purification system on the market: the Aquamira."

"Spot on, you are!" Henry Healy said.

"Research is the only the first step. You've researched it to death, Healy. Now develop!" He jutted his chin toward the worktable strewn with tubes, drawings and metallic debris.

"One can only do one's best in these circumstances." Henry bent, knees cracking, to open a file drawer. "Will you look at the engineering drawings?"

"Not now." He'd seen them plenty of times.

"They'll prove we're making progress. I've got the old drawings and if you look at the old ones compared to the revised one we're working with..." The sentence floated in midair twisting itself with cigarette smoke.

Christ, Clete thought, *more revisions*.

Henry rattled the file cabinet drawer. It stuck. He hit the drawer with his fist, sucked in air and shook his arm. The lab technicians smirked, ostensibly immersed in their work.

Pushing Henry aside, Shatz kicked the file drawer with his Gucci heel. Henry blanched. The cabinet rocked back an inch, but the drawer still wouldn't open. Shatz bunched his cheeks in his idea of a smile and steered the conversation along a different stream. He thought perhaps showing concern for Henry's personal life might remind him what was at stake, motivate him to bust ass to complete the project. "How is your wife?"

"Er, not too bad." Henry looked pensive for a moment. "She's due for another gene therapy treatment before Thanksgiving. They're so bloody expensive."

"Do you still own property in England? Sheffield was it?"

"I sold our house last year. We lived in the Peak District."

As Henry described the various hues of purple heather and the brilliant sunsets that colored England's hills, Clete recalled how he'd lured Henry away from a British conglomerate. Shatz Company had sponsored Henry Healy's work permit, a matter of dictating mumbo jumbo for Lucinda to wordsmith into a job ad they ran in classified sections and then when all American job applicants failed to meet the tight specs, she typed more mumbo jumbo onto Henry's work permit application. It was a win/win situation because Henry was well known in the field of wastewater remediation and he could help Shatz Company make the transition from material recycling system manufacturer to water remediation system manufacturer. He had a proven track record for bringing high-tech products to market. He had patents and patents pending. He'd pulled down a laughably low salary over there "across the pond." Clete had clinched the deal when he explained Shatz Company's health benefits to Henry. You would have thought, though, that after five years in the States, Henry could have found a decent dentist.

"Did you buy another house in England?" Clete asked.

"No. No need for a house there."

Shatz took this in. Henry, like other employees with access to proprietary information, had signed a confidentiality agreement barring him from working for a competitor for two years after leaving the employ of Shatz Company, which meant he was practically married to Shatz Company.

"Every manager thinks he needs more staff," Clete began loudly, convincingly for the lab rats' benefit, "but you've got to understand the market we're in. We have an advantage larger companies don't have. We're small enough to be agile, agile enough to change our strategy to capture the moving market. Today it's water remediation. We can't dither around searching for a fantasy team of engineers. We'll miss our golden opportunity. I'm not an unreasonable man. Take a look at this." He handed Henry the line graph Wade had prepared along with a written analysis.

"Not bad. Not great." Henry stubbed a butt into a jar lid.

Clete handed Henry the rest of the charts and written analyses the applicant had prepared. We should have paid that poor sucker for doing all this work, Clete thought. How was it that this highly intelligent, highly qualified Brit was blind to the fact that Clete was making his best offer. It seemed to be a trait, a flaw among near geniuses. They had technical skills, but no common sense. No feel for people. He could tell, he could just tell by the involuntary utterances coming from Henry that he was impressed with the applicant's work. Clete's patience ran out.

"Healy, you've burned your bridges in England. We can only afford one part-time employee. I suggest you play ball my way or no way."

"That's all there is for it then."

Shatz let the door slam behind him. He hadn't meant to come off like a tyrant at all.

CHAPTER 3

Parking lot protocol was Wade's first hint that Shatz Company valued and guarded the chain of command. A gas guzzler's bumpers overshot the yellow lines of the asphalt parking slot beside the main door in front of the one-story white brick building. Office professionals parked their electric cars in two rows on either side of the vintage Pontiac. Production and lab employees slued solar-powered pickup trucks and electric SUVs around the back.

The professionals slid pass cards through an electronic reader that logged employee identification numbers and released the main entrance door lock. Although his cowboy hat and black jeans clearly shouted that he was not a front-door employee, no one challenged him. He followed a man carrying a thin briefcase into the reception area.

Lucinda Ray looked up from her keyboard. "It's fine today, but from now on park out back and use the lab entrance." She lifted one shoulder delicately as if to say, sorry, that's the way it is.

"I don't have a car," Wade told her, knowing that that was not her point. He was disappointed that she hadn't commented about his clean-shaven jaw.

She stood and handed him a cup of coffee. "You'll be working for Henry Healy, Chief R & D Engineer. He's a strange bird but respected in his field. He's working on a special water remediation project. This is your pass card."

"Thanks." He swallowed the coffee quickly, bypassing his taste buds as much as possible. "And for the coffee." The black liquid had tasted like tar.

"I'll escort you to the lab," she said. "Follow me, OK?"

"OK." She was wearing a dress made of that new weave which from one angle appeared to be water-smooth, from another waffle-textured. How does the fabric feel from the inside? Like a second skin as the advertisers claimed?

"This is the sales and accounting area." She waved her fine-boned hand at office cubicles—cloned islands of black desks and gray chairs on a sea of blue carpet. Gray grit trailed from some of the cubicles over to the factory. One woman had brought in a barrel cactus, and only two desks were personalized with family pictures. In-baskets containing less paperwork than the out-baskets lay on the desks. Not a few desks were unoccupied. The office workers looked up, some nodded and returned to their work.

"That's the door to the production area," she said.

Wade peeped through the door as Lucinda held it ajar. He'd worked in factories before and knew exactly what was going on. People moved deliberately, doggin' it, stretching out jobs to make them last through next month's mortgage or the kids' orthodontics bill. She shut the door. She opened another door marked "Research and Development Laboratory Employees Only" and told him to go on in. She turned and headed back down the hall toward the reception area. With every step, Lucinda's thighs moved pleasingly against her slim skirt. She slowed and turned, her one foot pointed out like a ballerina's.

"You look different today," she said. She pursed her lips, rotated her shoulder and walked away.

Half a dozen lab employees, all men, flicked their eyes up and back down when he entered. He thought he should introduce himself, but no one seemed curious about who he was or why he was standing there in the large, chilly lab. He looked around. Dented file cabinets. Implement-jumbled workbenches. Bow-legged stools. Styrofoam cups with brown stains in the bottoms. Orange rags. Overflowing ashtrays. "NO SMOKING" signs. Wade was appalled.

A man blustered through the back door, and burst out, "Are you being served?" Gnawed pencils and pens lay like fallen timber on one desk in the lab. The man set his satchel and thermos on that desk.

"I'm new," Wade said. "I'm to report to Henry Healy."

"Bloody hell. The gaffer hired you." He lit a cigarette and sucked gratefully. "Sweep the floor and tidy up, then."

"I'm a data analyst." Not a janitor.

"Sorry, old boy, I'm fresh out of data at the moment. Someone finished graphing it for me the other day." Henry flicked his ash at the lab technicians. The one wearing heavy-framed glassed winked. "You see those blokes? When they complete the phase they're working on, we'll run tests, collect data and then, and not until then, I'll give you data to analyze."

"Do you mind if I nose around a little to get a handle on the project?"

"I'm not bothered. Please yourself."

Wade approached the young man who had winked, or had that been an optical illusion caused by the translucent windows reflecting on his glasses?

"I'm Lowell," the man said. "Grade 6 technician. Henry pulled the same stunt with me."

"Yeah?"

"I can tell you everything you don't want to know about OSHA regs and that you can purchase unobtanium from the same vendor that sells left-handed smoke shifters. That's what Henry had me doing before he'd set me loose on a real project."

"What is the real project?"

Lowell pushed his glasses tight against his nose. "Well, you can see we're working on filters. A few years back two scientists coupled ceramic membranes with a bioreactor to filter waste water from an ice-cream factory." Lowell spoke at length, animatedly about the scientists' findings. Wade's spirit was buoyed by the flocculations, permeations and sedimentations, and he latched onto the fact that treated water was called liquor. Man, if that guy Henry and his techs were working on a system that was going to help solve the water problem, then Henry could smoke as many cigarettes as he wanted as far as Wade was concerned.

"In a nutshell, that's where the technology stands today," Lowell concluded.

Lowell hadn't answered Wade's question to his satisfaction. "What are you working on?" Wade asked. "Specifically."

"We're designing a water remediation system that's more economical, durable, bigger and simpler than what's currently out there."

"What's special about this project?"

"We're developing a new class of polymeric membranes to filter water. The ones used now for industrial effluent and, on a limited basis, for public drinking water are affected by chemical contaminants. Pops degrade the filtering apparatus."

"Pops?"

"Sounds innocuous. Like an old man with a pipe." Lowell allowed a one-sided grin and turned to his workbench and resumed working on an electronic schematic. "Persistent organic pollutants: POPs. Pesticides mainly," he explained.

"Well," Wade said, "I'll get out of your hair and let you get back to work."

"Talk to ya later."

As Wade swept a pile of debris over to a cardboard box sitting beneath the trio of fire extinguishers, he replayed Lowell's words in his mind. He didn't believe in fate, but this was definitely a stroke of luck landing a job with a company striving to help solve the water problem. Definitely. Empty oilcans, flattened packs of Benson & Hedges and rags swathed in cobwebs and factory detritus lay in the box. Also in the box, Wade found a large rag to use to wipe the shelves. He shook a cloud of dust off the rag. He held the rag up by its shoulders. Heavy blue cotton coveralls. His size. S. The name Thane Gabler was embroidered in white on the front pocket beside Shatz Company's green and white triangular logo.

"Are any of you guys Thane Gabler?" Wade asked.

"He hasn't reported to work for…" Lowell pushed his bottom lip out. "Since last spring," he said finally.

Another technician piped up. "He used up his five weeks vacation and then he took sick leave. I think he's retired or dead or something."

Wade rolled the coveralls into a ball. After laundering them, he might wear them for however long he worked at Shatz Co. That way his few clothes wouldn't get grody.

Clothbound lab notebooks lay on the bottom of the box. He dusted the notebooks; they were numbered and dated. The inside cover of the first one had a quote written in old-fashioned fountain pen ink: "I maintain that the cosmic religious feeling is the strongest and noblest motive for scientific research. Albert Einstein, *Ideas and Opinions* (1954)." Something like this shouldn't be pitched, he thought. He stacked the notebooks on a shelf, tossed the oil cans and empty cig packs back into the box, dumped in the pile of dust and junk he'd swept off the floor and carried the box out back to the garbage bin.

It was bright and clear out. No clouds animated the sky. A brisk breeze parted his hair, acted like an astringent on his skin. He breathed deeply to flush out the dust and secondhand smoke he'd inhaled in the lab. He sat under a maple tree and listened to its leaves whisper the susurrative language of corn stalks and women's stockings. He clasped his fists above his head jubilantly and yelled, "Eeeeeeeyah!"

The wind shifted, bending the undersides of the dry maple leaves up. He went back to the lab before anybody got hard feelings about him taking too long of a break. He wanted to be a part of the solution in whatever way he could. Big. Small. Whatever.

Inside the lab Wade peered over the shoulders of an immense man plinking at a keyboard. A blue wizard's hat with "Futurist" written in silver glitter sat on his monitor. A 3-D model of the globe shifted shape on the screen. Blue water drops bobbed and faded. The man spun around, his braid flying.

"By 2025," he told Wade, "we'll be consuming 100 percent of

available fresh water supplies. That's the old prediction. Factor in current population growth rates, current global warming rates..." His fingers danced over the keys. "Unless we mutate mighty fast, my crystal ball says we are doomed, my friend." He turned around and extended his hand.

Wade shook the man's mitt and they introduced themselves. How did those sausage fingers fit on the keyboard? The name Mouse was embroidered on the extra-large blue coveralls.

"How long does our species have?" Wade asked.

Mouse twisted his braid with his thick fingers. "If we don't discover or invent a source of fresh water soon, you won't want to be the banker who's waiting to collect on thirty-year mortgages."

Wade recognized the severity of the water crisis more than most people did, and he thought Mouse's prognosis that people would be dying due to contaminated and/or insufficient water within thirty years was slightly off. The death of the species was going to happen sooner. In fact, the end had already begun with increased cancer rates.

"People will have a hard time believing that, you know," Wade said.

"And why should they believe me?" Mouse opened a drawer and pulled out a tri-folded photocopied brochure. He handed it to Wade. "Ever seen one of these?"

"'Actions add up for drinking water. Give drinking water a hand,'" Wade read. The brochure listed ways to conserve and protect water. "No, can't say that I've ever seen this particular brochure, but I've seen similar ones."

"Let's say," Mouse began, "a family's house is on fire. If you were the government agency responsible for fire safety would you lay a little pile of fire prevention brochures with tips like 'Don't play with matches' on your office counter in response to a conflagration in progress?"

"Uh, no. I'd make sure everyone already had the brochure with information to prevent fires breaking out in the first place, and if a fire did break out, I'd dispatch firefighters."

"I'll vote for you," Mouse said. "These water use brochures laid around in county extension offices and state health departments for years. If citizens wanted one, they had to go to the office and notice it lying there, brush the dust off and take one. And look at these tips: 'Know how to turn off an automatic lawn sprinkler system in case of rain.' Sprinklers should have been banned! And this: 'Reduce the amount of lawn chemicals and garden toxins you use. Select the least toxic product to do the job.' Least toxic? Least toxic!" His voice catapulted, pretty much the same way Wade's voice had when he'd had his last conversation with Kim. Mouse went on, "Nice lawn, neighbor. Too bad about junior's birth defects."

Mouse shook his head without pity. Quietly he said, "Insidious, silent, odorless poisons have been contaminating water supplies for decades. Everyone began drinking bottled water. They accepted it unquestioningly. Nobody, that is, nobody anyone'd listen to stepped up to the plate and demanded to know, Why do we need bottled water? What's happened to the reservoirs? Who was minding the store when they dumped herbicides, pesticides and industrial waste into our water? Who's 'they'? They is us. And it's too late." Mouse bounced in his chair agitatedly. "People didn't see it coming."

A sickening spasm gripped Wade's stomach. He saw, in his mind's eye, the blue images of his computer screen that winter years ago in his bedroom. Then the red-orange. And then the screaming. People would have seen it coming if they'd been given accurate information. "What about the project you guys are working on?"

"A Band-Aid in my opinion." Mouse draped a dust cover over his computer. "Eleven-thirty. Lunch break."

Wade was surprised at the alacrity with which Mouse re-channeled his passions from the extinction of the human race to feeding his face. He supposed everyone had different ways to keep from going insane. He followed the big man to the company canteen.

Vending machines lined the cafeteria's left-hand wall. A sink, paper towel roll and soap dispenser were on the adjacent wall. A "Please Conserve Our Water" poster was taped above the sink. Someone had scribbled "Just add water" in the margin of the sign and had drawn an arrow to the spigot. Wade twisted both water faucets. Nothing. He washed his hands with waterless-hand cleaner. (Just like brochure Tip 19 said to.) An office employee paced in, punched coffee machine buttons, chewed on the Java Break Tablet that tumbled down the chute and left without acknowledging the production workers seated at the two ranks of trestle tables. Mouse and the other lab employees sat by the vending machines. Henry sat by himself in the far right hand corner at a table beneath an "A clean workplace is a safe workplace" poster. Wade sat at the end of a table with a group of factory workers. Let's see what their take on the place is, he thought.

"Who they gotchya workin' for?" The man's southern accent slipped through his beard like gumbo.

Wade bit into his apple. "I'm in the lab." Had pride informed his tone of voice? "Part-time," he added.

A young man with a diamond-studded nostril sneered. "Always happens when there's a lay-off. Management goes and hires part-timers. We got two kinds of employees here: ones that've been laid-off and ones that will be laid-off." His voice sounded as if it were squeezed through a pipe.

"Hang in there," Wade advised.

"Said the man at the gallows."

Everyone chuckled.

The canteen door opened. Lucinda Ray smiled brightly when she saw Wade, only to falter when others at the table ogled her out of habit. Part of him responded physically, instantly when she walked past. In defense he detached.

"It's not his fault." The bearded man pointed a stub finger at Wade. "He needs a job like anybody else. It's ass-backwards management. They fire a lotta workers an' hire part-timers cheap. We're all part-timers."

The Stud Nose's diamond sparkled. "You think things are bad now? How about when Shatz opened up his dump as a tourist attraction? No shit," he said for Wade's benefit.

Everyone gave Wade sidelong glances when Lucinda walked toward their table again on her way to the door. Without moving her lips or slowing her stride, she said, "You shaved off your beard."

Someone whistled lowly. Should he have replied nonchalantly, *Why, yes I did, this morning in fact.* Wade convinced himself she'd said something else to somebody else. He wasn't alone in watching her leave the canteen.

"A tourist attraction," Stud Nose said. "Back in Ninety-eight—"

"Ninety-seven," a woman corrected him. Harassed purple hair shivered when she chewed peanut butter crackers. "You weren't hired till Ninety-eight, so you don't know, but go on. It doesn't matter."

"Back whenever," he slid his dark eyes to the woman, "Shatz opened up his garbage dump as a tourist attraction."

"This was all before he got outta trash, if you will, and into recycling systems." The bearded man from down South wobbled his head, ridiculing the prissy duet *recycling systems*.

"Like I was telling you," Stud Nose said, "Shatz convinced the town's holy-poly to give him a permit to open up the dump for public tours." The workers sitting at the table chimed in, between mouths full of lunch, to tell Wade all about Shatz's trashy enterprise.

Slick four-color pamphlets extolling the dump had been placed in tourist information offices and stocked in racks at local Chambers of Commerce offices and libraries. A trailer was rigged up as a visitors' center to sell tickets, loan umbrellas (to deflect seagull droppings), sell T-shirts and key rings fashioned from garbage preserved in epoxy. The concept was so macabre, people said Shatz had been bitten by a rabid rat, but tourists traveled from as far as New York City to trod the perimeter of the 50-acre icon to consumer waste. The multi-colored refuse mountain was especially popular with a sect of youths who pierced their cheeks with metal rings from which hung feathers and bone fragments. Fort Trust's conservative, nervous town council claimed the dump was unhygienic and threatened to close the site. Shatz countered that restaurants, hotels, gas stations and countless local businesses reaped trash cash. Shatz's pleas to the town council were unsuccessful. However, during the year the dump was a tourist attraction, Shatz had inadvertently indoctrinated a million visitors in the benefits of recycling and, as if it were all planned, Shatz Company won its first recycling system contract in 1999.

Wade shook his head appreciatively, saying, "Who says you can't make chicken salad out of chicken shit?"

Premeditated laughter rippled around the table. He knew by their reaction that he'd said the right thing and they'd accepted him.

"The dump's been reclaimed," the woman with purple hair said. "They grow soybean plants on it now."

"We've hauled trash. Exhibited trash. Recycled trash," the bearded man said. "What's next? Eat trash, I guess." He laughed at his joke. "Gettin' anywhere on that Aquamira?" he asked Wade.

Wade started to say, "Yeah, I'd say—"

Stud Nose snarled. "Henry's blowin' a gasket asking me to machine this and lathe that to a tolerance of plus or minus one gazillionth. What's up his ass?"

"Shatz is," someone said.

"Ask him." Wade gestured with his apple core toward Henry who was swabbing tea off this chin.

"Oi! 'Enery the Eighth!" The woman cackled. "What's goin' on with that there Aquamira?"

Henry smiled enigmatically, folded his lunch bag, tucked it into his ink-freckled breast pocket and left the company canteen. Wade followed soon after. He looked forward to meeting Clete Shatz, undoubtedly an entrepreneurial, maverick sort of guy.

After lunch Henry and three of the techs had squeezed into Henry's car to make a run to Harrisburg for a special part. Mouse,

Lowell and another tech had business to take care of in other parts of the building. Wade sat at the computer and began entering information that Henry had scribbled on scraps of paper to enter into the project planning and management software program. There were fields for costs, tasks, subtasks, sub-subtasks, personnel hours, raw materials and other variables that go into creating a new product before the production cycle is initiated. Once all the variables were entered, the software would perform automatic calculations and voila! the master chart would appear on the screen with the major tasks appearing on the vertical margin and dates of completion presented horizontally along the top. Unmindful of the time passing, Wade continued entering numbers.

A man with gray hair combed back to form a solid skullcap, with hands stealing in and out of his custom-tailored pockets, entered the lab. "Why isn't Henry Healy in the garage?" The man in a suit referred to the research and development lab as a garage, a holdover, Wade supposed, from the days when garbage trucks had parked in the building.

Wade stood and rubbed his back. He'd sat too long and had to piss, he suddenly realized. "Henry drove to MEMS-Tech to get a part," he told the visitor. Wade presumed from the man's sense of entitlement that he worked here.

The man walked between Henry's cluttered desk and the table holding the Aquamira. He eyed the chart on the computer screen. "You making progress?" he asked, brushing something off his pinstriped sleeve.

"Have a look at the master chart. See for yourself." Wade borrowed a metal file from Lowell's station at the workbench. He wiped the file on his sleeve. A tiny comet of stainless steel glittered on blue flannel. He pointed the file at the title on the screen: "Aquamira Project Master Plan - Shatz Company - 2005."

Visibly agitated, the visitor whipped his tie, tucked it back inside his jacket and said, "Just tell me."

Wade moved the cursor to tasks and subtasks in the left-hand column. With the crosshatched file he found March 2006 in the row of dates. The cursor and the file traveled until they met at a thick red line. Wade tapped the glass, his cuticle and knuckles stained with industrious lines. "It'll be ready for the prototype field test next spring."

The man's buffed nail hovered close to Wade's. He thrust his chin toward the factory on the other side of the door. "The first production model Aquamira can be built right after the successful field test."

It sounded like a statement rather than a question, so Wade didn't respond. A forklift farting rich propane fumes trundled past the open door.

"I'm asking you a question." He pounded his chest as if coaxing a burp.

"Yeah, production model," Wade said. "See for yourself."

"I don't want to see for myself. I want you to answer my goddamned question."

"The answer's right here." Again cursor and file met on the master chart and Wade interpreted its meaning for the man, who the entire time, didn't take his eyes off Wade, as if he were reading his face.

"Who prepared this chart?"

"Henry gave me the numbers. I entered them and the program did all the work after that."

The visitor left, his heel strikes dying on the blue carpet on the other side of the office door.

Wade went to the men's room. Probably a suit from sales, he thought. Amazing how sales guys could turn their charm on and off. Wade understood the man's anxiety and irritation with their slow progress. Executives were expected to be impatient: impatience fueled them to scale the rungs of the ladder. That man's imperial manner of questioning at first seemed to be his way of reassuring himself he was the one who asked the goddamned questions around here, and by God he got answers. But after a certain point, the tactic became excessive. Counterproductive. Wade thought of another possible explanation for the man's brusque, domineering behavior: he was illiterate.

He'd met other guys who couldn't read. They'd carry folded newspapers under their arms and during work breaks, flip through the pages at a studious pace. Or they'd stand in front of a bulletin board and say, "Whaddaya think of that?" and listen raptly to the answer to learn what the posting was about. In grocery stores they bought packages with illustrations of food on them and were disappointed to discover the Ritz cracker box didn't contain a wedge of cheddar cheese too. They usually had excellent memories and caretaker girlfriends or wives who read road signs, interpreted barbecue grill assembly instructions and filled out job applications.

How'd that suit keep his job? Wade washed his hands with waterless cleanser and returned to the lab. Henry and the three techs who had accompanied him on a part run had returned. Henry was drinking tea and admiring smoke sculptures he was erecting in the air.

The door leading from the offices to the lab opened. The atmosphere changed. Heavy weather or a flash flood was imminent. The techs slapped on bland masks, averted their eyes from each other, glumly concentrated on grinding edges, drilling holes, soldering seams on the prototype. The same arrogant suit that had come into the lab just a little while ago and had asked him a bunch of questions had re-entered. The man reviewed the lab with martial formality, all the while patting his open palm with a piece of rolled up paper like a baton. Wade gathered the papers Henry had given him with numbers scribbled on them and slipped them into a folder.

Mouse, Lowell and the other technician entered the back door behind their own raucous voices. When Mouse saw the man, he stopped talking. They all stopped talking and eased themselves to their stations. Mouse winched himself into his seat at his computer next to Wade and said, out of the side of his mouth, "Shatz is taking a walkabout."

"That's Shatz?" Wade whispered. He'd pictured someone younger, someone with charisma, someone literate.

"Put your flak jackets on," Lowell said. He pushed his glasses against the bridge of his nose and filed a stainless steel flange.

Clete Shatz hovered near Henry's ear. "Noses to the proverbial grindstone," he nearly purred, seeming pleased. Henry turned his head aside and blew a stream of insolence.

Lowell mumbled to Wade, "You think you've met dickweeds before? This guy is king dickweed."

"Rhodes!" Shatz jangled pocket change. He shot his wrist out from his cuff and checked the time. "Rhodes!" he shouted again.

Wade Rhodes, still unused to being addressed as Wade or Rhodes, realized when all eyes had rolled toward him that Shatz was summoning him. "I'm Rhodes."

"Show me that chart you were working on."

A management school dropout, Wade surmised. His stomach rolled oily-loose like it did when he had to deal with petty-minded authorities who wielded the power to deny you entry to Canada or to confiscate your (bogus) driver's license. His mind's skittery clawed feet scrambled for an exit. He cast about. The techs dropped their eyes. I haven't done anything wrong, he reminded himself. Slowly, to show Shatz his managerial style didn't incite swift obedience, he guided the cursor to the icons on the computer screen to bring up "Aquamira Project Master Plan - Shatz Company - 2005."

Suddenly uninterested, Shatz gazed off over Wade's head. Henry chugged smoke. The techs pretended to be absorbed in their sundry tasks.

As before, Shatz asked Wade to read out the Aquamira prototype field test date.

As before, Wade told him March 2006.

Stirring an eddy of cologne, Shatz laid his hand on Wade's shoulder. He spoke, his eyes glued on Wade. No looking up, away, to the side to exhume ideas from his mind. The uninterrupted eye contact unnerved Wade. Shatz unrolled the paper he'd been patting in his palm. "Please," he said, tapping the paper chart, "tell everyone the field test date according to *this* chart."

Wade recognized the tasks, subtasks, dates, all tea stained and handwritten in Henry Healy's tight, yet precise lettering as if he'd used an alphabet stencil.

Shatz's voice dropped. "Tell everyone the field test date according to this chart."

"January 2007," Wade said miserably.

Henry's stool fell over as he shot up and lunged for the chart. "How did you find that?"

Shatz straight-armed him, slamming him into the desk. Henry's reaction and choice of words had revealed too much. There was nothing Wade could have said or done that would have changed the outcome, yet he resented being used like this. The thundering of an air-hammer from the factory usurped all conversation for a moment, then the techs worked silently, waiting, waiting, for king dickweed to go ape shit.

Shatz squeezed the color out of his lips. "If you don't get fired with *enthusiasm*, you'll get *fired* with enthusiasm," he said to Henry.

Henry fumbled with his lighter.

"How long," Shatz wanted to know, "did you think you could hide it from me that the Aquamira is a year behind schedule?"

"Nine months," Henry said uselessly. "Not a year."

Shatz turned his attention to the techs and let his eyes rest on each one momentarily. Mouse met his gaze. The others did not. Then Shatz's eyes locked on Wade's. "Massage the numbers, Rhodes," Shatz said, "massage the real numbers and find some shortcuts. Get us back on course."

"I'm a data analyst." He'd almost said, only a data analyst.

Shatz slapped Wade's shoulder with force sufficient to have knocked down a weaker person. Lowell and the other techs held their breaths on the dull clap. Mouse started from his seat, but Wade signaled him to sit tight. Wade had seen the slap coming and let the force of it pass through him. Shatz wiped his hands on a handkerchief.

Was it the haircut, the imperial manner, the wary eyes that reminded Wade of his former boss at Statonics where he'd cranked out false numbers for the EPA? The oily looseness in his stomach solidified into an emotion just shy of hate. It demanded attention, commandeered expression. "Who are you?" Wade carefully put the stress on "Who." It had the effect of tearing a soldier's epaulets off his shoulders in front of the troops, especially because everyone knew he knew who this man was.

Shatz halted, showed his profile. Cords strained against his white collar. "Shatz. CEO and owner."

Mouse chewed on his braid and mumbled, "Shatz. CEO and horse's ass."

And once again, Wade marveled at how the laws of the jungle favored the creatures most inept at dealing with people, and let them rise to the top. Maybe bastardism was required for obtaining success in a capitalist system. He didn't think so, really.

CHAPTER 4

Clete swung around the block one more time searching for a parking spot. He hadn't been able to postpone it any longer. Thane Gabler, the senior R & D engineer under Henry hadn't reported to work for eight months and his health was deteriorating daily, according to Ginny Gabler. He'd done the most merciful thing for Thane. Retirement. He'd have preferred to lay him off without a pension and retiree health benefits, but his employee relations skills weren't *that* weak.

Cold drizzle streaked the windshield. Not a stinking one of the parking spaces in the restaurant's lot were large enough for his Pontiac. Clete finally settled for a parking spot at the Wal-Mart and walked-ran about one hundred yards to the Oasis Restaurant and Bar. He loathed speaking at functions like this, but Lucinda had persuaded him at the last minute to stop by the Oasis and say a few words at the informal gathering.

"Show the people your caring side," Lucinda had said. "I have more important problems occupying my mind," he'd protested. Such as deciding what to do about Henry. "Thane means a lot to them," Lucinda had countered. "If you let him go without saying anything, morale will sink lower than it is." He compromised and said he might show up after the chicken cordon bleu had been served. He opened the double doors to the function room and was dumbstruck. Roughly more than three hundred people—current, retired and recently laid-off employees had turned out to give Thane Gabler a rousing send-off. Furthermore, he was dumbstruck that Thane could still get around, but there he was, sitting with his wife, drinking Scotches on the rocks that his friends were happily lining up on the white tablecloth. Ginny Gabler smiled stiffly.

Clete ordered a martini and carried it with him to the podium and began speaking. "Thane Gabler and I go back a long way. Gabe was a different breed." He glanced up but didn't let his eyes rest on any individual long enough to throw him off kilter. A movement in the audience caught his attention. Lucinda was pounding her chest as if a chicken bone were caught in her throat, and she was mouthing words to him. He looked down at his own chest and saw his fist pounding vainly at his heartburn. Clete gripped the podium with both hands and began telling his favorite story about the time Thane Gabler had tried to inspire the technicians to dare to break free from tedious, plodding empirical methodology. To quit thinking through sieves. He'd posted signs in the lab and lavatory announcing a Rube Goldberg Contest. The winner who'd created the most useless, most complicated gizmo out of found materials won a $22.35 gift certificate. (The money was from the coffee fund.)

Lowell had built a device with microchips and heat sensors that warned an absent-minded ninny his or her coffee or tea was too hot to drink. Another technician built an automatic page-turner designed for the infirm to use while lying in bed reading a book, or for cooks with sticky fingers to use while preparing a dish. The page-turner was deemed too useful for the contest and disqualified and eventually patented. Mouse's entry, a computer program called Jizzmo', predicted the total number of times each technician will have had masturbated to the end of his natural life. Including gallons secreted. Jizzmo' was disqualified because it was a software program, not a gizmo, but Thane reneged, created a new category for computer programs and Mouse's entry won half the coffee money.

Thane's own Goldbergian contraption spanned half the lab. At one end was a simple on/off toggle switch. The switch activated a series of levers, bells, pulleys, gears, balls in channels, plastic chicken heads, hammers and a bicycle chain which ultimately activated the middle finger of a rubber glove filled with epoxy to flick the lab light switch at the other end. To turn the lab lights off, you flipped the contraption's toggle on. To turn the lab lights on, you flipped the toggle off. By popular vote, Thane won the remaining half of the coffee money. Thane's underlying objective, to force the technicians to recognize that science didn't always require a five-speed, oscillating, solar-powered swatter to squash a fly, caught on with some of the technicians and engineers. Many lab rats, though, like Henry, couldn't buck years of training and education.

The upraised, smiling faces below him lent Clete confidence to continue speaking. "I'll never forget our lunch breaks. Thane packed a brown paper bag." Clete went on, gesturing naturally with his hands to indicate a lunch bag. "He'd get so hungry working in the lab, that he'd start in on his lunch as early as eight a.m. By noon, he'd have it all drunk." One person laughed.

"Thane knows I'm pulling his leg, don't you Thane?" Ginny Gabler gave Clete a watery smile. "I know you'll be missed, Thane. Who's going to tell those stories you tell that are like steers—a point here, a point there, and a load of bull between."

"We're tired of bullshit, Shatz!" The audience turned around as one to see who had heckled the CEO. Someone in the back, in the shadows. "We want the straight skinny. Will we have jobs tomorrow?" The murmuring grew argumentative.

"I have two kids to support and a car payment and rent." Yelled a woman from warehousing. Kate? Katelyn?

The emergency exit was only a few steps to his left. Clete straightened his tie and searched for a friendly face, a refuge, to restore his confidence. Lucinda nodded tentatively. He said, "We're going through a normal cycle, people. This is normal. An unavoidable condition of business. Some of our material recycling systems are reaching the end of their life cycles. Competition is fierce. But unlike the companies your neighbors worked for, we won't get caught with our pants down."

"Give it to us straight!"

"I can't divulge too much at this point in time." Someone booed. A siren wailed outside, giving him a moment to pause and collect his thoughts. "Fortunately, I realized we'd put all our eggs in one basket with our material recycling systems and I thought far enough ahead to hire Henry Healy and his team. We're working on a revolutionary project in the lab. Henry and his team of highly trained technicians are developing a product that you folks will be building. I need you to promise to be patient. Research and development is our future. I'm not at liberty to comment about the specifics." Mentioning Henry made his mouth dry and his pits wet.

"Can you give us a hint? It's the Aquamira?"

"I'd like to tell you about the project," Clete said carefully, "but it's too sensitive. Our competitors have ears. I promise I'll tell you when the time is right. It won't be long."

The voice from the back shouted, "Smoke and mirrors. Can you promise us jobs?"

"If we all work smarter *and* harder." Clete's pager beeped. A few people had left their seats and were approaching the podium. He waved a dismissive hand at them and ducked out the side door. Driving rain pelted him. He stepped back inside.

"Shatz here," he said into the phone.

"Your janitor called me." His wife's voice. "He said the lab's on fire."

People talked, clinked ice in their drinks, sang "For he's a jolly good fellow. . . ."

"What? Speak up!"

"F-I-R-E. Fuck. You can't spell. Where are you? A party?"

"Why'd he call you? A fire? How bad?" He thumped his chest.

"I don't know." She hung up.

Mindless of the hard, stinging rain he ran to his car.

Wade was sitting at the Oasis bar relaxing into his second Grolsh. A TV on mute glowed in the corner. Cops 'n' robbers. A handwritten sign posted at the cash register said: "We Serve REAL alcohol! No suppositories or tablets." A string of banners strung above the liqueurs and spirits shivered as a man with his stubble tucked in his upturned collar staggered in. A frigid wind followed him, eddied around the stools. "Must be some do on the other side," the man said. Wade nodded companionably.

The bartender auto-smiled and slapped a packet of chips and a Bud on the counter for the man.

"Hi, Wade."

Anxiety alloyed with joy swept over him at the sound of her voice.

"Hey, Wade." It was Mouse. "I didn't see you in there."

"Where?" Wade asked as Lucinda and Mouse sat on barstools on either side of him. After they ordered their drinks Mouse said, "Thane's retirement gig." He jabbed his sausage thumb at the side door he and Lucinda had come through.

Wade stood and threw dollar bills on the bar. "I thought he was…I'd like to meet him."

"He and Ginny went home," Lucinda said.

Wade sat down and took a long quaff.

"Your boss is not quite the charismatic leader," Mouse said.

Wade turned to look at Lucinda.

She rolled her shoulder and blinked deliberately. "He's a misunderstood man."

Mouse snorted in his draught beer and told Lucinda about Shatz using Wade to embarrass Henry about the Aquamira being way behind schedule. Wade got into the spirit of trashing Shatz and exaggerated the CEOs swagger into a goosestep, his patting his palm with the rolled up chart to smacking his palm with a three-quarter inch rubber hose. Mouse and Wade were having a good time, anyhow.

Lucinda twirled the stem of her wineglass between her thumb and fingers, studying the lemon rind twisting on its axis of icy white wine. "He's under tremendous pressure," she said softly. "He's insecure down deep."

"He has a down deep?" Wade asked.

Mouse sputtered laughingly.

Wade tried to imitate a Scottish accent and said, "It's a life form, Jim, but not as we know it."

Mouse pounded the bar. The man in the coat grinned idiotically.

"What?" Lucinda asked, clearly unamused.

"Scotty from 'Star Trek,'" Wade said. He'd forgotten she was too young to remember the show. To her Cassius Clay, the Vietnam War and Watergate were obsolete concepts, not people and events that'd impinged upon her biography. The man in the coat demanded that the bartender change the channel to the Ravens - Steelers game.

Lucinda ordered another wine spritzer and put Wade's black cowboy hat on at a jaunty angle. She cocked her head coyly. "I'm cooking a small bird for Thanksgiving. Can you come?" Too quickly she leaned forward and included Mouse in the invitation. "You too."

Mouse held both his big mitts up. "I'm previously engaged. Catch you tomorrow." He paid his tab and loped out. The banners over the bar shivered.

"Can you?" Lucinda's shadowed face rose near his shoulder.

He smiled into his beer. You can start off liking someone, and the liking slips into intimacy, and the intimacy slips into love. A fondness, a liking, he could allow that. With fondness there were no ego battles, no strivings for power, no anxieties about sex, no laying your heart out where it could get mauled. What would making love to her be like? The question stirred a tender spot near his heart. He tipped his mug and watched wavy televised football tackles through the thick glass. "Thanks, but I think I'll lie low on my day off and relax a bit."

She rolled her eyes at the bartender. "Relax a bit? You'll have to do better than that. Try, I'm driving to Florida to see my great-great-grandma or I'm volunteering at the soup kitchen. You can relax while you're eating dinner." She smiled ironically at him.

"You've seen my application. You know what I'm like. I don't stay in one place long. I'd…Someone'll only end up getting hurt."

"Careful, Walk-Around-Joe," she said coolly, "you'll get a hernia."

What the hell…? The bartender lifted his shoulders and pulled the corners of his mouth down. He had no idea what she was talking about either. She was the only woman who reminded Wade of every woman, and who reminded him of no other woman but herself.

"Lugging that ego around," she told him. "You're cocksure about how this plays out: I get a crush on you. You play me along me for the hot sex. You leave. I get hurt. Weep. Weep. Boo-hoo. End of story." She gave him a sleepy look. "The male ego amazes me."

"You're twisting what I said." The muscles between his brows knotted up. He rubbed his forehead vigorously. In desperation, he confessed, "I'm a perfect son of a bitch. End of story."

Lucinda raised her glass to her lips and accidentally swallowed the lemon twist with a mouthful of wine. She began choking. She recovered before Wade had a chance to pat her back or hug her forcefully. She said, "Maybe I like getting hurt. Maybe I'll think you're a dipshit after I get to know you. Maybe you'll leave and I won't care. Maybe you won't want to leave. Who are you protecting? Me or you?"

The tender ache near his heart threatened to swell and close his throat. He eyed the door. "I've got to go." When he lifted his hat off her head, wisps of blond hair lifted with it, making her look a little wild, a little reckless.

Cold rain stung his face.

She shouted over the rain pounding her car roof, "Get in. I'll drive you home."

"Yeah, you're right."

"I am?"

"Don't want my male ego to get wet," he said. "It'll shrink."

Inside her car she said, "The rain's turning to ice."

She drove slowly, keeping her distance from cars in front. Every now and then she tapped the brakes to check the road condition. Wade opened his window and reached around the front to flick ice off the windshield wiper. "Pull over. I'll get the ice off your side."

The car released its grip on the road and skated sideways into the next lane. The driver of an on-coming car honked and swerved. His headlights lit the interior of Lucinda's car. They spun around one hundred and eighty degrees and lurched to a stop against the opposite curb. The other driver regained control of his car and drove past, the wheels splashing water on her car.

"We're fine. I'm fine. You're fine. I'm fine." Lucinda massaged her hands in a self-calming gesture. "It's my fault. I turned the wheel too hard. If anybody'd been hurt, I'd feel guilty. I'm afraid to drive now. My hands are shaking. Look." She held out her hands. They quivered like frightened birds.

"We'll sit here for a bit. We're not in anybody's way." He held her cold hands. Where were her gloves? Her hands were so small. Within the snug car her aroma of perfumed skin, and nervous sweat affected him. He let go of her hands, tuned in a radio station. The DJ announced an instrumental called "Tunnel of Mystery." He knew next to nothing about contemporary music, yet it seemed as if this were the only music that ever needed to be written and listened to, the only music that could have been played here and now and fit the mood. The oboe, bass and high notes serpentined. Rain lashing against the windows became integral to the theme.

When the song faded out she said, "I was organizing my files this morning and found your application mixed in with other papers. I'd forgotten to give it to Mr. Funk. I hope it doesn't cause any complications for you: I gave it to him today."

"What for?"

"He's our security officer. He initiates background checks on everyone involved with the Aquamira. What's wrong?"

The possibility that his past would be investigated hadn't occurred to him. None of his other employers checked his background. If they mentioned background checks, he split. "Did you see his report yet?"

"In addition to the fact that you lied about traveling with your father the photographer, which I figured out myself, what else will I learn?"

"The usual. Worked here. Worked there." His voice tremored.

"Why did you lie?"

"You don't know guilt until someone...." He couldn't say it. "...because of something you did."

Yellow flashing lights approached them. A truck spreading salt on the slick road. The car's interior took on an orange glow. Salt pinged the car. They watched the truck lumber past. He studied Lucinda's profile. He tried not to blink or the tears standing in his eyes would squeeze loose. Borne of thoughts of his parents, his wife, his fiancée, his buddies at the old job who were all locked away, frozen behind an impenetrable door, his tears often threatened to flow when he drank a lot of beer and let his mind follow its natural course, as it was now. Freezing rain thrashed morosely against the car. He felt entombed, partitioned from life, a man impersonating a person. He wiped his eyes inconspicuously. Her profile intrigued him. Those planes and curves assembled themselves into a different face than the one you'd expect when you looked at her from the front. A passing car lit the fuzz on her upper lip.

After a long while Lucinda said, "I don't think a painter could capture this beauty, the way the signs and street lights are reflected on the puddles. It's like the colored lights are leaking on a black ocean. It's magical. I've always loved rain at night." She looked at him and tried to cover her embarrassment with a tenuous smile. "I talk too much sometimes." She leaned over and hugged him, pressing his head to her shoulder.

Rain drummed the car, washed the ice away.

Clete wiped Maalox residue off his lips with his handkerchief and held the handkerchief over his nose against the acrid fumes. A brownish haze filled the lab. Rivulets of black water flowed toward the floor drains, clogged with ashes and charred chunks. Extinguisher foam lay in drifts on the desk, file cabinet and worktable. Everything was covered with black, greasy soot. Dripping water plicked and plocked, sounding like the woods when rainwater drips off leaves after a downpour. It didn't require the fire department's crew leader's experience to ascertain where the fire had started: The bottom metal rim was the only remaining part of the trash barrel. The fire had originated in the barrel, consumed it, leaped to Henry's desk where it burned papers, folders, brochures and then traveled along a paper trail to the worktable where its ravenous heat melted computer housings, warped file cabinets and destroyed the Aquamira under construction. The fireman explained that the fire suppressant sprinkler system was clogged with sediment. Few of the nozzles had flowed freely.

Clete felt entirely alone. Who, but he, cared? Who, but he, was going to straighten this all out? His employees were going to be inconvenienced by the fire for a day or two, but who among them really cared? Not a single stinking soul. It would be easier if he didn't care. Sell the company. Give Darla her divorce. Cut off his affair. Get a complete physical. Rent a condo on the Carolina beach. Go to bed at night with concerns no more critical than how crowded the greens will be tomorrow.

A man carrying a fire extinguisher walked up to him. "When I saw the sprinklers didn't come on," the janitor said. "I used this here stinguisher. I think I picked the right one. 'Dry and chemical fires.' Then alla sudden the sprinklers come on and this gunk come out of em." The janitor pointed to muck lying beneath one of the ceiling sprinklers.

"Didn't you smell the smoke?"

"I was at the other end of the building, accounting. I smelt it when I went in the hall to get my cart. I ran over here as soon as I smelt it. The sprinklers didn't come on at—"

"I know!" Clete pressed a button on his mobile phone.

"Healys'." The voice was muzzy, as if Henry'd been asleep.

"There's been a fire. The lab burned. Come in here now and start cleaning up."

"It's raining buckets."

"I don't care if it is raining 'boo-kits,'" Clete said. "Call your salaried men and tell them to come in here and clean up." Salaried technicians were paid the same no matter how many hours a week they put in. He heard Moira's voice in the background. She was asking Henry, *What's wrong* and *Tell him you'll go in tomorrow, first thing in the morning*. Henry wasn't asking how the fire had started or how much damage had occurred. "We can't afford a setback, Henry. Do you know what I told everybody at Thane's retirement party?"

"Thane's retiring?"

"For Christ's sake, Healy! I told them your project was the promise for the future. They are counting on you. I'm counting on you. The Aquamira is our future. Am I the only one around this stinking place with a sense of urgency?" He looked at the sodden, charred papers, warped metal and melted plastic. "It's not that bad."

Henry groaned and said something to his wife.

Clete stood in the middle of the lab. Although he hadn't touched anything, his hands were soiled. Floating soot had settled on him. His handkerchief was gray. Mouse and Lowell came to the lab. Shock registered on their faces. At a loss for what to do, Mouse chewed on his braid. Lowell draped shop rags on the banister outside in the rain and then used the wet rags to wipe soot off the Aquamira piece by piece as he disassembled the remains.

"My crystal ball!" Mouse ran to his computer and turned it on. A message appeared on the screen. He moaned.

"What? What's the problem?" Clete asked.

Mouse read the message flashing on the screen: "'Fatal shutdown. 0000XXX00.' It's fried."

Lowell pawed through soggy, charred reports. "FuckingAFuckingAFuckingA."

"What started it?" Clete asked.

Lowell inhaled an imaginary cigarette and flicked the smoldering butt into the charred rim of the trash barrel.

Clete's hands balled into fists. He pounded his chest trying to knock down bile burning at the back of his throat.

The back lab door crashed open against the cinderblock wall. Henry blustered in, flapping his umbrella open and closed to shake rainwater off it. He didn't look at anyone, but said to his Brogans, "Bloody mess, izzen tit?"

Fuck him and his fucking British accent. Clete jammed his fists into his pants pockets. Threads ripped like tiny machine guns. "What's your assessment, Henry? How bad of a setback is this?"

Henry toured the lab. He conferred with Mouse and Lowell and picked through the remains of his notes and folders. He stood for a long time in front of the disassembled Aquamira, poking the blackened, warped parts with his Dunhill pen. He stared up at the windows and said, "It's difficult to say."

"Take a wild-assed guess!"

Henry scratched numbers and words on an envelope from his pocket while muttering, "Tidy up, reassemble the Aquamira, that's after we replace damaged parts. Run the tests again, log the results, work out the new bugs, run new tests. I'd say, eh, perhaps, sixteen months?" He handed the envelope to Clete.

Clete wadded up the envelope, threw it down. "I ask you, as the man who owns this company, as the man who is your boss, is it sixteen months according to the faked schedule or the actual schedule?"

Henry, looking none too distraught, lit a Benson & Hedges. Lighter flame glinted in his eyes. Black water splashed on Clete's pants cuffs when he strode over to Henry. He snatched the cigarette out of Henry's mouth before the man had an opportunity to enjoy the first drag. Henry groped for the cigarette, missed. He inspected his fingernails.

"Wasn't Henry the Eighth the one they beheaded?" Clete asked.

"Actually, I believe that would be King Charles." Henry turned his back on Clete. Henry's shoulders jiggled. He sniffled, rubbed his eyes, dragged his shirtsleeve across his beak. Stinking hell, he was crying.

"He's losing it," Clete heard Mouse say. Clete offered his gray handkerchief in an outstretched hand to Henry.

Face in hands, his back still toward Clete, Henry said, "You Americans think history started when the pilgrims landed at Plymouth Rock." He turned around. Thin lips peeled back revealed snaggled teeth.

Clete balled his handkerchief in his fist.

"King Charles the First." A gulp hitched in Henry's throat. "King Charles the First dissolved Parliament in 1629. He ruled alone, not unaware of the dissention growing all about him. A Civil War developed between the Royalists and the Parliamentarians. The Parliamentarians won, which with or without the advantage of historical hindsight, was right and proper. The British never did and never will tolerate dictators. The King was executed in 1649."

Mouse, Lowell and Henry watched him, faces curious, open. His move. *Fire Healy's ass! Right now. In front of the technicians.* He turned his back on the tech rats and examined the Aquamira skeleton. None of the applicants and none of the technicians were remotely qualified for Henry's job as chief R & D engineer. The lab rats performed the tasks they were assigned. Performed them well and thoroughly. A somewhat introverted group, they nit-picked problems, relished the sub-problems they found during their search for solutions, side-tracked each other with incidental discoveries. Henry fit right in. He never rode their backs, never accused them of over-engineering.

Henry could never dream up anything as lighthearted and hyperbolic as a Rube Goldberg Contest. No, Clete thought, but he was one of the best water remediation engineers around. If he fired Henry, no one, no one any good, that is, would work for a company with the cash flow problems Shatz Company was suffering, for the salary and perks he could afford to pay. Henry was bright. Bright and thorough. His thoroughness was an asset and a liability. Henry, humming monotonically, dried a document over his lighter flame.

"Get this mess cleaned up by Monday morning." Clete flung his handkerchief to the floor. It plummeted, a soiled dove. Fighting a gag reflex, he fled the lab.

CHAPTER 5

For three days, Clete fought the desperate urge to get in his car and drive away from his problems. His Pontiac was a microcosm of the world as it should be. Push a button, warm air blew. Push another button, music filled the plush space. If he didn't care for the music, he could tune in a suitable station. With subtle pressure on the accelerator, he could make the car surge ahead and pass slow vehicles. The world didn't work that way. An enemy was pushing the buttons, pumping the brakes. Absently, he rolled a golf ball between his palms and stared at the grilles on his office window.

"Mr. Ingle wants to have a word with you," came Lucinda's voice over the desk intercom.

Odds that the head of accounting was going to bring good news were about the same as the odds that the Aquamira would begin its production run in his lifetime. He slugged down Maalox. "Send him in," Clete replied as even-tempered as possible.

No one called Fred Ingle by his first name. His reserved manner and tweedy suits imposed a barrier against first-name comradery. He carried a ream of papers under his arm and thunked them on the conference table behind the sofa. "These are this month's year-to-date figures," Ingle said, spreading paper like a tablecloth over the long mahogany table.

Clete's legs felt heavy—a sensation he'd begun noticing more and more lately and trying to ignore. He pressed his hands against his glass-topped desk to help raise his weight without stressing his knee joints excessively. Christ, he thought, I'm only fifty-six. How rotten will I feel when I hit sixty, seventy? He walked around his desk, past the sofa and took his customary seat at the head of the conference table. He pretended to study the spreadsheets and asked, "What's in the tea leaves?" He knew Ingle equated joviality with irreverence, but hell, running your own business was supposed to be fun, wasn't it?

Not one for small talk, Ingle circled a number on a spreadsheet and said something about "unanticipated hits" in his usual gloomy timbre. "The last lay-off didn't ameliorate the negative cash situation. It gave us a brief reprieve, but as I'd informed you at the time, the effect was nominal." Ingle licked his lips carefully.

"OK," Clete said slowly. Ingle was leading up to something and it was going to stink. "And?"

"That in and of itself was an insufficient measure. The sales department is projecting soft prospects for income in the foreseeable future and we haven't met our sales forecasts for the past year."

This kind of talk rankled Clete. "The sales department is supposed to *sell*, not forecast."

"And our warranty work this last quarter spiked." Ingle pointed to the chart. He must have perfected his hangdog expression in college.

"Any good news to report, Ingle?"

"No."

"What about accounts receivable? We sold two material recycling systems this quarter."

"Like bailing out the Titanic with a thimble."

Clete groaned. "This company's mine. From the ground up. I willed the company into existence and I will it to prosper and grow."

Ingle made humming noises in his throat.

Beyond the grilled window, electric cars slid by almost noiselessly. The silence seemed eerie, something Clete couldn't get used to. Ingle cut all checks late. "Payable in 30 days," Ingle had told Clete, "actually means 90 days. Companies wait 90 days. Standard practice." Clete had argued that delaying payments distorted the true picture, not to mention the time and aggravation wasted fending off angry vendors and creditors. If Shatz Co. owed money, they should pay it. Then he learned that Shatz Co. imposed late fees on customers who didn't honor their 30-day payment policy. Over the long haul, delaying payments wasn't going to get them ahead. Harassing customers for timely payments eroded goodwill and hurt Shatz Company's chances for repeat business.

"I thought," Clete said, "you bean counters knew how to finagle things, knew your way around the banks and laws so entrepreneurs like me don't have to worry about soft markets and sales forecasts."

Ingle licked his lips. "We need to find a couple mill per quarter to tide us over until the Aquamira reaches the market and we realize return on investment. Even that prospect seems iffy. Henry is months behind schedule and over-budget and the fire—"

Clete rubbed his eyes hard enough to make stars dance in the blackness. "All my assets go home every night."

"I don't get your meaning, Clete."

No, you wouldn't. "My employees, unfortunately, are the only hope I have. I'm sucked dry. What liquid assets I have, I've already poured into Shatz Company." The sky outside the grilled windows had a dead skim-milk quality to it. An airplane flew unseen above the strata. "Darla's filed for a divorce," he told Ingle.

"Hmm." Together they considered this, and suddenly Ingle said, "You're obsessing about ice cubes when the ship is on a collision course with an iceberg!"

"Shit. Let me think for a minute." He leaned against the window grilles and stared at that blank sky. What did other companies do? Could Shatz Co. qualify for a government bailout like Chrysler did back in the Eighties? Lay-off more people like IBM did in the Nineties? Lower his prices? Raise his prices? Apply for another business loan? When he suggested each idea, Ingle said, "Nix. Nix. Nix," and explained why the ideas were unfeasible. Clete had the profound sense the accountant was holding something back. It was the way he licked his lips carefully and flipped from spreadsheet page to spreadsheet page, pointing at the dismal numbers.

"You think of something!" Clete waved his hands in the air and fell back into his chair.

"I've been telling you since I walked in the door."

Ingle aligned the spreadsheets into a tidy stack and made departing noises in his throat. "The projection I just gave you, assumes that you lay off another thirty percent."

"We're already undermanned."

"Cut research and development."

"How the fuck you bean counters expect me to make money if I don't have an R & D shop to design tomorrow's products?" Damn, it felt good to yell. Yelling at the people who pissed him off might alleviate heartburn. Darla had told him how many times that he kept his emotions too bottle up.

"I know what you're thinking," Ingle said, one eyebrow lifting knowingly.

"You do, do you?"

"Yes. My staff is trimmed back to the bone. It's myself and two clerks."

"This company is not run by accountants. I run this company. I will not lay off more people." He sat up in his chair and folded his hands on the table. He arranged his features into what felt like confidence, a leader's face. *I am strong enough. I am smart enough. I can do this,* he told himself. Clete stroked his tie; the silkiness assured him. "What's the bottom line? Please, don't flower it with fancy words you learned at Columbia."

"Wharton," he corrected Clete. "By this time next year, if not sooner, Shatz Company will be insolvent. Will fold. Bankruptcy."

When Clete spun around in his chair he cracked his kneecap on the table leg. "Bankruptcy! Why did you wait until now to tell me! We've weathered rough times before. What's changed?"

"The bank is calling in the loan."

"What?" Clete was incredulous. He'd golfed with the loan officer plenty of times and let her win, goddamn it.

"The bank is call—"

"I heard you. Why? Laying off ten percent of the workforce was a cost-saving action, the kind of thing those bankers eat up."

"Our insurance company will not pay for damage and losses incurred during the fire," Ingle said.

"Why the fuck not?"

"The cause of the fire was a burning cigarette in a non-smoking area."

"How do they know that?"

Ingle said nothing. It was obvious how they knew. If the insurance company's fire forensics team had been wearing blindfolds the day they visited the lab and had missed the blatant evidence, then the lab rats would have drawn a cause-and-effect diagram for the insurance company.

"The loan officer put it this way," Ingle said, "the loan was intended for capital expenses, not to replace assets destroyed by the fire."

"Every company goes through highs and lows. I'm going to set up a meeting with the bank president."

"What will you say to him?"

He didn't know. Clete clamped his hand on the spreadsheets. "The Titanic had lifeboats. Find us a lifeboat."

"Far too few," Ingle said balefully, "as you undoubtedly know."

Ingle left the office and shut the door as if it were made of spun glass. Clete threw his bottle of Maalox at the door. Chalky medicine snailed down the door.

The next morning, Clete told Lucinda he had an appointment off-site. And he did. With himself. He pulled out of the company parking lot and headed back home. A stout woman carrying a jug full of water away from a government tank staggered off the corner onto Point Street. He hit the brakes. "Jerk. Watch where you're going." He waved her by.

The scene rolling past depressed him. Realtors' signs had faded after several seasons of slow sales. Even businesses in the business of no-business—outplacement centers, temporary employment agencies, job skills retraining centers—had outlived their usefulness. He lowered the heat in his car. Abandoned buildings gave way to Tudor and Spanish mission-style homes. He guided the Pontiac past the wooden sign with the name of the housing development he lived in carved on it and coasted on down his S-curved driveway. The garage door opened automatically. A ray of optimism lightened his black mood. As he saw it, the problem he was faced with was basic. And the solution was basic. He needed more time and more money. Time was money. He needed money. Money.

A refurbished Victorian bar he'd retrofitted to house mementos and his entertainment system dominated the east wall of his den. The chestnut wood had sprung to life under his hand when he'd rubbed tung oil into carved fruit and floral garlands and chubby angels. Clete pulled a putter out of his golf bag and adjusted his stance on a patch of artificial grass affixed to the carpet on the den floor. Every bean counter he'd ever hired exaggerated. That's their nature. Accountants don't manufacture anything, so they foretell doom and gloom so company owners had a reason to pay attention to them. The golf ball stopped short of the cup.

Among the golf tees, towels, caps and commemorative plaques sat pictures of his children. The blurry one of his son from his first marriage had been snapped in Cambodia where he thwacked Bibles. His son from his second marriage posed with a poetry magazine editor nobody'd ever heard of. In another, Clete and his daughter Janice stood behind Darla. The photographer had manhandled them, arranging their bodies in a way that brought to mind a poster family for spinal problems. Shoulders canted inward, chins up, heads tilted. His one hand lay on Darla's shoulder, the other on Janice's. He put all but one of the family photos facedown in a drawer. The photo showed Janice reaching over a fence to touch a rabbit in a petting zoo. Her eyes peered with an admixture of pleading and confusion at the photographer. She'd been eighteen then. Clete was the photographer.

She'd never smart-mouthed him. Never struggled through rebellious phases like his sons had. Never buttered him up and then asked for the car keys. Never came home drunk after curfew. Never dropped out of Syracuse to spread the gospel. When she disobeyed him, it wasn't a volitional act of commission or omission. She simply didn't know better. Darla never did learn to feel at ease around their daughter Janice. Clete knew she'd tried pretending she didn't notice Janice gripping her over-loaded fork in her fist like a starved prisoner. Clouds of soap dried on her dirty neck.

Darla hadn't agonized over the decision. Cut and dried. Janice would live among mental peers. Staff would plan activities for them. She would learn marketable skills. Janice was stifled at home with them. Afraid she'd say something wrong, do something wrong. Provoke parental opprobrium.

It was his job, his duty to disagree with Darla and fight for Janice. Even if Darla was right. Especially because Darla was right. But after years of firm reminders, (Janice, say thank you. Janice, not so much jelly. Janice, don't pet the bunny too hard. Janice, you left the shower running. Janice, use a tissue to do that.), he'd given up trying to change her. He'd given up believing she was capable of change. When he and his wife had told Janice she was going to live in a special home with other people like her, she'd asked if it was a college dorm. No. Not quite. Am I getting married? she'd asked, in her flat-footed way. No, honey.

Somewhere deep inside, did Janice experience joy? Love? Or was she sluggish emotionally too? He'd lie awake watching shadows on the wall, trying to convince himself his daughter was happy, in her own dull, lethargic way. And sometimes he thought mercifully, perversely: She's too retarded to know she isn't happy. The thought wrung his heart. Clete blew his nose on his monogrammed handkerchief. You're not supposed to love one child more than you love the others.

He ran his finger through a film of dust that Alita, the housekeeper had missed. It felt like sawdust rather than the usual house dust. He pressed the entertainment system's remote control. Electronic sounds blasted out of the speakers set in the refurbished Victorian bar where bottles of absinthe had stood one day. Damn!

Alita had changed the station. She was getting ballsy now that Darla was gone.

He went to the kitchen, opened the fridge. Two beers, a bottle of flat tonic, mustard, mayo, a small jar of olives and a deck of lunchmeat. He grabbed a box of crackers from the cupboard. He laughed. At least he'd lose weight without Darla around. He returned to the den and surfed channels while waiting, for what, he didn't know. He fiddled with the volume, but couldn't adjust it to suit him. It was either too low to hear or so loud it echoed off the cathedral ceiling. He watched the news with the sound muted.

The newscaster's expression flipped from chipper to solemn. The picture cut to a raggedy line of people passing buckets of water from hand to hand. The camera panned to the man, a shaven-headed fellow with a potbelly, at the head of the line. He was bailing water out of a swimming pool.

Jesus. Nobody had pools these days. Not pools full of water, that is.

The camera cut to a teenaged girl at the end of the line. She dumped the water onto the street.

Clete turned the sound up and caught the tail end of the voiced-over report.

"Philadelphia Mayor Jordan Wallace allegedly told one of our sources that the water in the pool is collected rainwater. He's said to be meeting with his advisors as we speak."

Police weren't arresting the trespassers. They seemed to be monitoring the situation rather than trying to break up the mob.

"Chief of Police Thomas Golden urges citizens to remain calm until the results of an investigation are made public, but it appears the citizens of the City of Brotherly Love are short on patience."

The picture of the brigade emptying the mayor's swimming pool was replaced by a myriad of scenes shot around the city showing rioters breaking storefront windows and turning cars over.

"Water riots," Clete said. That's not news.

He brushed crumbs off his cashmere sweater into a houseplant and sauntered to his closet to change into a lighter sweater. His suits were arranged by color: fawn, navy, charcoal gray. Shirts, shoes, sweaters and ties were organized in color-coordinated order. She'd taken her best clothes and shoes with her, left a few older suits and gowns behind. Soiled clothes overflowed the laundry basket.

Letting laundry accumulate didn't, over the long haul, conserve water. He dumped the large bundle into the washing machine and turned the dial to small load. Letting laundry pile up reminded him of the walnut game the company accountant played with bills.

He shambled to the den and propped one hand on the antique bar. The wood sunk under his hand. When he pressed, his finger poked through and sawdust puffed out. He pushed and probed the shelves supporting the entertainment system. He swore he could hear termites gnawing. No telling how much damage they'd caused already.

All this navel gazing. Nothing comes of it but heartburn. Heartburn, he had. It was money that he needed. Sometimes bright ideas came when he quit stewing over them and just played golf.

After he'd cleaned grass and mud off his golf clubs and shoes, Clete lugged his bag to his car. He threw his score card in the trunk. Stinking score. Too cold to play to his handicap. He kept chicken winging on the swing. The greens were brittle and lumpy. After shooting an abysmal fifty-four on the front nine, he switched to winter rules. According to winter rules, as long as the ball drops on the fare way, the golfer is permitted to move the ball to his advantage before swinging. He scored forty-six on the back nine and wondered why he'd made it unnecessarily difficult for himself on the front.

No bright ideas had come on the front nine or the back. He checked his watch and decided to drop in at the Apex Golf and Country Club clubhouse to put out feelers. Network, as they used to say.

A wagon train of topiary yews circled the club, a Federal-style two-story rectangle of liver-colored bricks, formerly a wealthy farmer's home. Folded down the center, the structure's two halves would have been identical. Only the discreet five-by-seven inch brass plate screwed into the brick beside the solid white door upset the symmetry. "Apex Club. Members Only," said the engraved lettering.

Clete pronounced his name into the speaker of the voice recognition system. He heard the reassuring snick as the door unlocked. Checking his reflection in the foyer mirror, he checked for residue at the corners of his mouth and stretched his neck with a thrust of his jaw. The linen draped banquet room was empty. Voices charged with cocktails trickled in from the lounge. A poker foursome hunched at the green baize. The immaculate birch logs on the fireplace grate were for ornamentation only. Clete walked past a trophy cabinet, nodded crisply at Senator Krumrine and Scott Billet and ordered a drink from the bar.

"Green olive as usual, Mr. Shatz?"

"As usual." Here was order. Here was hierarchy.

He'd studied the contents in the Chippendale trophy cabinet numerous times while waiting for vodka martinis. Most of the awards were framed certificates or photographs documenting the club members' good deeds. A glossy Senator Krumrine shook hands with the U.S. President at the National Water Resource Management Conference held a few months ago. Clete had been in the club lounge when the senator placed the photo in the cabinet. Drinks and sycophancy flowed that day. No citations with C. Shatz in bold, sweeping serifs rested behind the polished glass doors.

"Your drink, Mr. Shatz." The handsome bartender smiled fawningly.

Clete sank into the leather chair to the right of the oxblood couch. Leather creaked against itself. From this position he could see out the picture window. Though summer had passed, Cinzano umbrellas still shaded the wrought-iron patio tables. Occasionally golf balls had sailed into the patio. He could monitor who entered from the foyer and listen in on Senator Krumrine and Scott Billet's conversation and perhaps join in.

Krumrine reigned from the middle of the couch, his arms extended across the back, one ankle propped on his knee. He turned away from Billet and toward Shatz. The senator's head, as round and shiny as a wheel of cheese, was pitted with late afternoon shadows. Krumrine rattled ice in his highball crystal. "That brouhaha in Philly is spreading a stink like shit flowing from a hill-top outhouse," Krumrine said, referring to the mayor whose constituents had drained his illegal swimming pool free of charge.

Clete contemplated his red-eyed olive and tried to arrange his face into a countenance that struck a balance between mild interest and hunger for whatever tidbit Krumrine might toss from the inner-sanctum. The senator rose and strode across the blood-red oriental carpet to the bar.

Clete cut a look to Scott Billet and asked, "How did the mayor pull that off?" Billet, the Pennsylvania governor's top aide and number one confidante had graduated magna cum laude from Temple. He was six feet eight inches of trim, toned muscle topped with well-cut, thick brown hair framing a face that swiveled women's and men's heads. In spite of all that, he had an enviable easygoing manner.

"The mayor was in cahoots with the water authority and fiddled the requisitions to increase his household allowable allocation and," Billet leaned forward, elbows on thighs, "he embezzled water tax monies to pay for his re-election campaign. They say the only person not involved in the scam is the street cleaner and he's under suspicion too. You didn't hear it from me."

Clete maintained an impassive expression.

Scott Billet added, "Madam President is p.o.'d. She's putting the squeeze on the governor and Senator Krumrine."

"What kind of squeeze?"

"She wants my boss and the good senator to—"

"Quit suckin' up. Krumrine can't hear you," Clete said.

"To set the pace, create the benchmark for the rest of the nation. She wants them to lead the way so a revolutionary device can be invented to 'eliminate,' that's her word I think, the water problem." Billet sipped white wine when Krumrine rejoined them.

"President Flores is pushing for a solution," Senator Krumrine said, "and Pennsylvania will deliver it! Every problem's an opportunity, Shatz."

"When life hands you a lemon, make lemonade!" Billet said. Billet's mistake, Shatz knew, was catching Krumrine's infectious, false high spirits. You couldn't trust Krumrine any further than you could throw Billet.

"You need water for lemonade. Yes, we got no water." Krumrine laughed, making the chandelier's waxy reflection slid up and down his forehead.

Shatz gulped his olive and took three steps toward the bar, but when he was in Krumrine's line of fire, he pivoted. Mocking Krumrine's tone of voice, he said, "What we got is polluted water."

"And not enough of it," Krumrine said.

Clete didn't even pretend to laugh at that worn out joke.

"You're right, Shatz. Any bozo in a garage can knock together a conveyor belt with sensors on it and call it a recycling system. Isn't that what you call them, materiel recycling systems?"

He envisioned strangling that arrogant gleam out of Krumrine's eyes.

"Material, I believe," Billet said, "is the more appropriate term. Materi-el pertains to weapons and equipment as opposed to personnel."

Clete ordered a fresh martini and eased into the chair so it wouldn't squeak. He heard the tail of one of Krumrine's favorite idioms: "I wouldn't piss on him if he was on fire!" and convinced himself the senator hadn't been talking about him.

Billet smiled wanly and tried to get the conversation on an even keel. "The Japanese have developed advanced membrane technology. They successfully reclaim wastewater from apartment buildings. It's remarkable. These membranes filter out human excreta."

"I believe," Krumrine said, "kaka is the more appropriate term."

Billet smiled graciously and went on. "The Japanese combine the membrane filter with biological treatment. Still, they have problems, too. Bacterial flora thrive on the membranes. Pollutants degrade the membrane's effectivity. The membrane designed to filter the water becomes a new source of pollutants."

Clete would have to remember all this and ask Henry what he knew about it.

Billet turned to Krumrine and asked, "Is Madam President aware of silica sponges?"

"Billet, don't you think President Flores is aware of the state-of-the-art water remediation technologies? She has a crack team of advisors."

Clete knew about silica sponges. Lucinda had seen to that. He said, "Tests show that the sponges only absorb certain contaminants. Some remain. On top of that, the sponges are prohibitively expensive to manufacture and maintain for treating significant volumes of water."

They looked at him as if he'd just spoken Martian-ese.

"How do you know that?" Krumrine asked.

"I read it in a trade magazine or a technical journal. What does the president have in mind?"

"One-stop shopping," Krumrine said. "Current water remediation technologies have short-comings and disadvantages, not to mention high costs. She's looking for a method that is economical and can remove all pollutants from mass quantities of water quickly. She wants a quantum leap. Heaven knows we won't survive without a solution." Krumrine searched inwardly for something. He appeared to be genuinely distressed about the water crises. He shuddered, donned his public mask and slapped Clete's knee. "What say you, Einstein?"

Clete Shatz's jacket felt too boxy in the padded shoulders. The Aquamira could be that quantum leap, but it was gestating too slowly on Henry Healy's scorched workbench. If only he could light a fire under Healy's butt. The man had the skills, the technical insights, dogged scientific methodology, the inspiration, but he was incapable of making those creative leaps that had spawned miraculous inventions like virtual sight for the blind, smart materials that repaired themselves, or birth control injections for men.

Tomorrow he'd ask Lucinda to ramp up the blind ads in the papers and on the Net for Henry's replacement so no one would know what company was recruiting an engineer with water remediation experience. A reddish-brown blur on top of the wooden fence surrounding the patio outside caught his attention. "A fox," Clete told them. "I haven't seen a fox since my brother and I used to hunt them for fur."

Krumrine twisted around to look out the window the instant the fox jumped onto the brick patio and trotted to the ivy bed. The fox picked something up in its mouth and peered at the window. Its sides bellowed with small rapid breaths. The three men watched the fox sniff the air, leap up onto the pit barbecue cover and slip over the fence.

An unidentifiable rumbling, querulous and familiar, grew louder. Glass exploded and flew onto the leather couch. Clete instinctively raised his hands to protect his face. The men playing poker looked up. Krumrine leaped up and shook shards of broken glass off his head and shoulders.

"Wild golf ball," Billet said.

"It's a rock," Clete told them. He walked to where the thrown rock had landed on the carpet and picked it up. He handed it to Billet.

A horde of shaven-headed teens flowed into the patio and rammed wooden stakes through the jagged window glass. "People for water. Water for people. People for water. Water for people," they chanted. They knocked over patio tables and ripped out the ivy plants, exposing dirt and a bright idea that only Clete could see.

His mind whirred. He ran out the front door. Four ruffians surged toward him. He raised his hands and shouted, "I'm not a politician. I'm a good guy." He pointed toward the brick clubhouse. As the four ran to the front porch, the ruffian wearing a ski mask winged a stone at Clete. It fell impotently at his feet. He hopped into his car, turned the key and spun out of the parking lot.

Gut instincts were worth their weight in gold. He'd done right by not telling outsiders, especially Krumrine, about the Aquamira project. Clete pulled onto the road, the place where he navigated the tricky surface of tactics and strategies. Taking advantage of a business opportunity was not an unethical act. It's admirable. It's why businesses exist. Fabricating, the word popped to mind, fabricating a scenario that was going to load the deck in favor of Shatz Company troubled him.

Was it his fault people had their weaknesses, their vulnerabilities, their ambitions? Hell, winter rules were invented for situations like his. Only idiots play it as it lies. He'd tell Krumrine about the Aquamira if, no, no, no. *When* the time was right. The end would unquestionably justify the means. He glanced at the speedometer and eased up on the gas. He hadn't realized how fast he was traveling.

It just didn't seem possible. He couldn't believe how the idea had come to him. It was a hole in one. To have an idea all laid out, pre-made as detailed as the project master plan with its tasks and deadlines was. It was almost more than he could bear to think about. And all of it because he had convinced himself that he could will his vision into existence. He could impose his will on others. The glitch was that his grand plan depended on Henry. Christ. Why hadn't he thought of this plan sooner? Plump raindrops splattered the windshield. The wipers smeared a double fan of fine mud across the glass. Clete pulled over and cruised along the shoulder of the road. He opened the window and waved at a van driver to overtake him, go on around.

Henry had estimated that the Aquamira field test would take place sixteen months from now. Ingle had projected that Shatz Company was going to fall into bankruptcy within a year or less. Somehow, some way Henry or his replacement had to get the Aquamira finished before, way before the company went bankrupt. And, owing to Clete's bright idea, when that happened, he was going to be a rich, rich disgustingly rich man. His daughter could live in the fucking Taj Mahal if that was what she wanted and she could drink all the pure water she wanted. Future generations would tell stories about the old days when babies became brain-damaged and millions of citizens fell ill because of contaminated water. They would speak worshipfully about the man who solved the world's water crisis.

Filled with an unaccustomed excitement and energy, he pulled onto the road and drove, he drove.

With a grating stutter of metal against concrete, Henry pushed his bow-legged stool away from the new workbench the production workers had knocked together for him. With his ample rear end, he pushed the bar on the door leading to the production area and twirled clumsily to stop the door from crushing the engineering drawing he was carrying. Wade knew Henry was going to cajole Stud Nose again to make an investment casting all the while dismissing the machinist's suggestion that using standard dimensions could save one-hundred twenty dollars, on just that one part. When Henry latched onto an idea, though, he wouldn't let go. He'd rather engineer it to death, cling onto a stone while watching the life raft float by. The lab technicians laughed at Henry's hand-wringing high drama.

"I wonder if that was his job in the want ads?" Mouse said.

Wade had seen the ad too and wondered how hiring a new chief engineer was going to affect his job. More than anything, he wanted to help Henry, but what could he do? He was only a data analyst. He massaged his knotted brow muscles.

"Do you know of any other local companies that'd need someone with water-remediation expertise?" Lowell asked.

"Nuh-uh. If there is one, I'm going to spiff up my resume." Mouse busied himself at his keyboard.

Henry returned, dropped the blueprint on the floor where it curled into itself. He threw a butt on the floor. The smoldering butt rolled into an expansion joint. Wade stomped it dead. Henry knelt awkwardly in front of his file cabinet and tugged on a drawer. Tufts of his gray hair flopped with each jerk on the drawer handle.

The technicians sneered at each other. They had agreed among themselves that Henry had purposely started the fire to buy time.

So much for teamwork, Wade thought to himself. A cancer had infected morale in the lab, a cancer that prevented progress. He strolled over to Henry and stood beside him. Together they scowled at the recalcitrant drawer. "Let me try," he said finally.

"Bugger off! What I'm doing now is beyond your realm of experience." Henry stepped back and kicked the file cabinet. It didn't budge.

"Yeah, I guess opening a drawer is rather esoteric technical science." His sarcasm disappointed him.

"Have a go, clever clogs." Henry stepped aside and lit a cigarette.

Wade knelt and pressed the drawer handle in with firm, even pressure. Maintaining inward pressure, he pulled down, felt an infinitesimal letting go of a metal catch and gently opened the drawer. It was so incredibly easy. He felt embarrassed for the man.

Henry slumped.

Feeble light from the lab windows enervated Wade. The lab clock, wearing a toupee of dust, indicated four-thirty. Half an hour to punch-out time. He'd finished entering data Mouse had given him. To kill time, Wade perused Thane Gabler's lab books, the ones he'd unearthed from the box of oil cans and cigarette packs on his first day in the lab. He'd managed to re-rescue the lab notebooks from the garbage bin after the fire. The retired research engineer's printing was neat, squared and plumbed as true as a row of apartment blocks. Every few pages of the printed community of problem, hypothesis, experiment, predicted result, observed result, and conclusion was interspersed with cursive passages. The cursive sections said things such as "Everything vibrates at its own unique rate and mode. The difference between a hydrogen atom and a carbon atom is its varying rate and mode of vibration. Somehow light, heat, magnetism, electricity and chemical makeup are results of vibrations. Quest: Can an instrument be designed and built to alter vibrations at the atomic level? And thereby transform molecules?"

Were statements like those physics laws or chemistry axioms or the maundering of an aging dotard whose hard drive had crashed after working on one project far too long? If the notation on the inner leaf of the first notebook was accurate, Thane Gabler had puzzled over the vibration conundrum, in addition to his regular assigned projects at Shatz Company, for at least sixteen years, his handwriting becoming more and more wavery in the final two volumes of his lab notes.

"What was Thane Gabler trying to prove?" Wade asked Henry.

Henry sighed raspily and pushed himself away from the workbench – the workbench where he gnashed his teeth, dog-eared suppliers' catalog pages and smoked meters and meters of tobacco for a living. "Who gives a toss?"

"You don't know what Gabler's project was."

Henry held cigarette smoke in his lungs as if saving it for later enjoyment. "In the odd moments, he was messing about with vibration rates at the atomic level. If you'd read his notes, you'd know that. Give me your timecard. I'm ready to flit." With lighting behind him, Henry's hair appeared to be molting.

"The Aquamira you've been working on is behind schedule. You're spinning your wheels with polymeric filters and Shatz has been breathing down your neck. How do you plan to deliver, Henry?"

"Deliver?" His close-lipped smile died instantly. "Right, then. I am supposed to involve you in the project. Participative management and all that. How do you propose to build the Aquamira to recycle and purify water, meeting all written specifications?" His eyes crossed slightly, concentrating on the ash at the tip of his addiction. "From a data analyst's point of view, that is."

The technicians made no pretense of appearing not to be eavesdropping.

"Charcoal. Have you thought of charcoal? Use silver treated charcoal filters." He'd read up on it at the library. "Charcoal is a renewable resource."

Henry flicked an ash at Wade's boot. "Charcoal filters are used for domestic purposes and limited commercial purposes," he allowed, "and you're proposing: build the same type of filtration system on a larger scale to service industries and municipalities, and Bob's your uncle!"

Wade felt a set-up coming, but he let Henry continue. He held Thane Gabler's lab book lightly in his hands.

"First," Healy stabbed a smoke cloud with his cigarette, "the amount of silver treated charcoal required to filter the prescribed gallons per minute for the Aquamira would fill this lab a hundred times over. Second, silver is prohibitively expensive. Not to mention the government's carbon tax on charcoal." Henry trotted out more statistics and documentation supporting his position. Evidently he'd investigated the same idea. Otherwise, how could he have known the downside of using silver treated charcoal filters?

"But we won't be burning charcoal as a fuel," Wade countered. "Its use in the Aquamira should be tax exempt."

"The tax is unilateral, regardless of end use." Henry tucked his shirt in and verbally, petulantly outlined the scientific treatise he had written for Republican lobbyists opposing the carbon tax bill proposed by Democrats and subsequently signed into law by the former president of the United States. "And lastly," the cigarette stab again, "in case you haven't heard, charcoal comes from trees, trees come from forests. The Global Climate Commission reported that increased deforestation accelerates the acceptable projected global warming rate. Plus, processing charcoal pollutes the air and water." A discourse on the relationship of charcoal production to the economics of ecology ensued.

"You probably have ruled out reverse osmosis water filters too," Wade said.

"RO filters are slow, slow, slow. Secondly, they remove needed minerals as well. Therefore, because water without minerals is insalubrious to the body, especially the liver, one needs to augment mineral intake from another source. My research led me to obtain a pressed carbon block filter which is not slow, nor does it filter out minerals, but soon it actually adds to the rotten egg odor associated with sulfur."

Wade mentioned desalination.

"Crikey! Desalination doesn't remove the type of pollutants that are harming us." Henry searched for and found a document titled "Transcript: Water Supply & Wastewater Treatment Summit." "It's right here, look. 'The members concur that large-scale desalination of ocean water is economically unfeasible.'"

Wade remembered that particular summit. It was broadcast repeatedly on television and photos were splashed across the papers and the internet because representatives from Mexico and France had exchanged blows, igniting a multi-national fracas.

"Last year," Henry said, "I attended the Water Environment Federation conference in Alexandria, Virginia and I'll wager you don't know that…"

The technicians punched out. Wade tuned in and out as his supervisor prattled on: "Nine-hundred-thousand gallons to grow an acre of corn…consume 300 gallons a day…closed-loop system reuses cleaned processing water…extraction or separation…two-thirds frozen in ice glaciers…Safe Drinking Water Act and the Clean Water Act…." Henry, forgetting that Wade was on his side, was enjoying the full flush of his filibuster. Finally, his lecture concluded, Henry grabbed the lab book out of Wade's hands and hurled it into the trash barrel. "Thane Gabler didn't know bugger all. And you don't know eff all!" He collected his thermos and satchel, his smashed Benson & Hedges pack, their timecards and he flounced through the doorway to the offices with more verve than usual.

Wade sat on Henry's stool and stirred the butts and ashes with a pencil. His cells sure would welcome a nicotine jag after years of abstinence. He mulled over Henry's oration, not the facts and data and rebuttals, but the emotional amplitudes that informed them. The rant about why charcoal filters were not viable was fraught with frustration disguised as disdain for a greenhorn suggestion.

The clock ticked. The overhead lights hummed tirelessly. He

retrieved the lab book from a mound of sodden tea bags in the trash barrel. Henry had become especially discomposed when he'd spoken of Thane Gabler. Something was there. Some sliver of insight waiting to be extracted. He opened the book and read a trickle of Thane's curving writing at random. "If matter is energy in vibration it follows that all elements vibrate. One element revs to the next higher level to become another element et cetera with all 107 elements. Quest: Can vibrations be increased and decreased by man to create different elements? What would the process be called? Creation? Retro-creation?"

What made vibration rates change naturally? Did it occur over time or instantaneously? If change happened instantaneously, your underwear would turn into salami, your salami into Fruit of the Looms without warning. Did vibration rates change when the universe was born or did they change constantly and that's what accounted for erosion, rust, decay, aging, fermentation, mold, eggs, sperm, babies, wisdom? Thane's jottings had a religious reverberation to them. Even the fluid script Thane had used imbued his notes with sanctity. Retro-creation, however, hinted at blasphemy. Heresy. Wade closed his eyes and breathed deeply. Tried to be in the now.

Henry was a stubborn, withholding, by-the-book, hug-the-shores-of-tested-postulates engineer. His habits were ingrained, like his addition to nicotine. His animosity toward his former colleague, Thane Gabler, was more than base jealousy, it was a conventional mind's frightened response to a superior mind's explorations of taboo terrain. There be dragons. Thane Gabler had been doing what was natural, extending humanity's reach, attempting to tug on God's beard. It must have frightened Henry.

Wade's beliefs had evolved over the years, expanding and contracting under the pressures of experience. A belief in a personified God, vengeful or merciful, was not among them.

This time he's driving a VW bug on a four-lane highway. His is the only vehicle on the road for as far as he can see and he can see for miles ahead where the ribbon of road cuts through green meadows. Invariably a tractor-trailer, klaxon blaring, gears grinding, diesel clouds spouting, bears down on him. He stands on the V-dub's accelerator. The steering wheel shimmies, tires wobble. He can't drive any faster. Suddenly he's on an exit ramp. It ends at a cliff edge. The sound of the truck growling at his tail loosens his stomach.

That dream. That damn dream. Wade sat up in the cot, pressed his back against the cold iron bedrail, and crossed his arms over his chest. His palpitating heartbeat resumed its normal rate. His eyes gathered light, his mind assembled memories, telling him where he was. One room with a bath. Unexpected orange walls, now brownish in the dawn light. Single window facing west. Gambrel roof forcing the ceiling into claustrophobic angles. A light fixture resembling a frosted glass mammary with metal nipple was affixed to the flat area of the gambrel ceiling. He was in the garage apartment he rented on a weekly basis.

The apartment smelled vaguely of oil from the cars parked below on the ground floor garage. Letting tattered remnants of his dream evaporate, he postponed dream analysis for another time and slid under the cot covers. Spread about his apartment the lab books, strange birds unable to fly, had dried. Ink had bled in the margins. They'd gotten soaked during the fire. He angled one so the light illuminated the pages.

And again he read the passages written in Spenserian penmanship with a fountain pen. They were more interesting than the formal lab experiment write-ups and they sounded more mystical or metaphysical than scientific. "Man is a concentrated form of energy," and "Technology well-designed and executed is nothing short of magic." True. Wade imagined how primitive cultures might react to Concordes, CD-ROMs, Cheeze Whiz. Next he read "Quest: Can I transform Henry Healy into a pillar of salt?" He laughed, empathizing with an old man he'd never get a chance to meet.

He ambled to the kitchen area and washed off soot his hands had picked up from the books. He opened a tin of mackerel with his Swiss army knife and dribbled habanero sauce on the fish. He resumed reading. "We know that atoms are composed of electrons and ions, et cetera, which revolve around each other in rapid motion. This manifests a rate and mode of vibration. All matter vibrates. All matter, that is; all atoms have unique rates and modes of vibration. This unique rate can be detected, measured, and simulated." Next were some calculations and what looked to be the vibration rates and modes for hydrogen and oxygen.

From what Wade could ascertain, Thane "had all but uncorked the genie's bottle." That, too, had been written in cursive style. He'd designed a system that modeled atomic vibration rates and modes of all the elements on the periodic chart. He had, after several years' of trial and error, transformed some of the "slower" atoms into next slower atom, if you believed an elaborate chart he had drawn which listed elements in descending order of vibration rates. A separate overlay chart depicted vibration modes. Thane had written, "He who understands the principle of vibration understands the Mind of God. If I am the one, the life force will give me the means to continue. If not, a greater wisdom is at work." The final notation said, "The Beach Boys were right. Good, good, good, good vibrations!" Thane Gabler stopped reporting to work a week after that optimistic entry.

Thane's preoccupation with the idea of transforming other substances into water captivated Wade. He felt a sense of brotherhood with the man whom the lab technicians had described as "a genius," "a little nutty." For thousands of years, scientists had experimented with alchemy hoping to change lead and other base elements into gold. Thane had paddled upstream against convention. An anti-alchemist, he'd attempted to transform elements into water. Wade amended that last thought. In the present state of the world, water was becoming as precious as gold. He paced barefoot across the short white floor space between the window and the counter. Why hadn't anyone followed up on Thane's project after he'd retired? Did Henry or Shatz know how close their colleague had been to possibly solving the water problem? And where was the system Thane had built? Where was Thane? Was he still alive?

Was he still working on his vibration device? Was he as impractical as Shatz had said, a quack as Henry had said? Were Thane Gabler's lab books science fiction?

He bundled his soiled clothes into a plastic bag, locked the apartment door and stepped cautiously down the wooden steps from the tiny second-story landing to the driveway. That one rotten step, third from the top, supported the landlady's weight but probably wouldn't support his.

"Hello, Wade!" The landlady held out her sinewy arms as if welcoming a swaddled baby. "That's not laundry is it? It'll cost a fortune at the laundry mat what with the water rates."

"Yeah, it's my laundry." He squinted through her flossy hair at the morning sun.

She tucked her chin determinedly into her neck and took the bag from him. "Oh, there's hardly much in here. A full load is more water-responsible. I'll do your clothes with Len's darkies tonight when the rates are lower." Len, her tinker husband.

"Thank you, Mrs. DiMartino. Thank you."

"I dug up the glads and the geraniums are hanging in the garage, but have you ever seen mums like this?" She stooped to touch the objects of her pride—chrysanthemums as creamy and round as cafeteria saucers.

"No, never."

"Football chris-ee-an-thums." She grunted and reached up to take his hand so he could help her stand up.

"I'd like to stay for a month," Wade said. "Is that possible?"

Her eyes widened. "Oh, dear. I thought you said one week. Something happen?"

Yeah, something happened. Lucinda's breath on his ear? The possibility of Henry being replaced? The intriguing prospect of seeing the Aquamira come to life? Simple road weariness? All the above.

"Pay me by Monday." She walked away on the sides of her feet as if her corns hurt, and into the back of her house. Two figures—

Mr. and Mrs.—moved behind the kitchen curtains. Salt of the earth.

Although it was cool, the sky was clear, air crisp, shadows sharp, colors intense in the morning sun. He'd met a woman who interpreted dreams. Where was that? The apple orchard in Washington. Standing by the cider press, she'd told him that his recurring dream indicated his subconscious was trying to tell him to rethink his route. *Although you might never crash or drive off the cliff, you need to slow down and integrate.* He'd argued that some events were unintegratable. She'd counseled him to live in the moment.

Wade tried real hard to live in the moment. Now. Walking on the sidewalk. Now. In Fort Trust. Now. On the third planet from the sun. Now. He chortled. When he lived in the moment he always found himself spinning in a mental hamster wheel. Without the past or the future to flee to, his mind resorted to thinking about itself thinking about itself thinking. The self-reflexive loop reminded him of a cartoon he'd seen depicting a cartographer drawing a map that showed the cartographer drawing a map and that showed the cartographer drawing a map....

A building with 1991 carved in the cornerstone cast a blocky shadow across the sidewalk. They probably called The Fort Trust Public Library architecture *fin de siecle* style. The best part about the new millennium was not having to hear pundits say *fin de siecle* for the next few decades. He entered the library, a safe harbor, and researched technical concepts mentioned in the lab notebooks. The more he understood the more questions he had. He was in way over his head.

He stood and rubbed the ache out of his back. He found a paperback copy of *Shibumi* abandoned, wings splayed on the table as if the reader had left hastily. He began reading the page where the previous reader had left off. As foreplay, the protagonist and his Oriental mistress stroked each other's naked body with razors. The light strokes tickled like a breath or a feather. One wanton giggle or aroused gasp, and blood petals would bloom on excited flesh. The lovers employed different techniques to distract themselves from the razor's exquisite danger and titillation. Self-control simultaneously reined in and whetted their lust. Their desire simmered, boiled, gathered force, and grew uncontainable.

Wade stood and located the men's room. With economical strokes, he relieved his sexual tensions.

CHAPTER 6

Thanksgiving Day broke bright, filling the garage apartment window with hope. Wade dressed quickly, and stepping outside onto the small redwood landing, reached upward, wiggling his fingers at the cornflower sky streaked with jet vapor trails. The savory aroma of roast turkey escaped Mrs. DiMartino's kitchen. She made fussy movements at the sink between the curtains. He hoped his landlady wouldn't see him, rush out, hands smelling of onions, and ask him again to join her clan, "twenty-two at last count," for Thanksgiving lunch. He'd promised her he would drop by later in the day when there weren't so many relatives around.

His rent was paid to the end of the month and then it'd be time to shove off, catch up with the migrating geese, and stay ahead of the nightmare truck bearing down on his tail. But these were not ordinary circumstances. Last night he'd fooled with the idea of hanging around a while longer and locating Thane Gabler, if he's still alive. And if the old man were willing and coherent, revive his project.

He walked down the driveway, past the library and to the pond. His boots crunched dry grass as he approached the bench he had sat on when he'd first arrived in Fort Trust. The gingko trees had since shed their yellow goosefoot foliage. The pond had shrunk, depositing rings of dried muck. Seated on the weatherworn bench, Wade kicked his legs out. The sun warmed his inclined face. The town almost felt like home. He followed some threads that needed tied up.

That damn dream. The one telling him he needed to integrate, the one where he's driving a V-dub came again last night.

The accelerator didn't work. A Mack truck bore down on him. Klaxon ripping the world apart. The road ended at a cliff edge.

Normally he didn't put much stock in dreams, blew them off as scrambled images. But this one was too vivid and persistent. It was difficult to believe the Techni-Color images, Dolby sounds, diesel smells, dread and adrenaline were meaningless.

Wade loosened his duffel coat. He rested the back of his head on the hard bench back and watched a polar bear scud across the sky. That dream interpreter had told him he needed to integrate. He'd known then and he knew now what it was. He couldn't kid himself any longer. Telling someone, like Lucinda perhaps, what had happened wouldn't relieve his ache, his guilt. It would make it worse, bring it closer to the surface. He needed to do something significant to atone for her death, to give it meaning, not that anything he could do could make up for it. He wanted to do something worthwhile. Something good for humanity. Running from his guilt, from his role in it wasn't the answer. Staying in one town this long was risky, though. Oh, hell, if the goons who'd bombed his car were still after him, then so be it. Maybe that was a form of divine retribution. Or as Thane had written, let the "life force" speak. In what he knew was childish superstitious Queen-of-Hearts illogic, he made a deal. If Thane's phone number were listed and he contacted him, he'd stay in Fort Trust. If not, he'd leave town before a Mack truck, real or dreamed, nailed him.

He walked to a corner phone booth and rifled the phone book pages. His stomach tightened as if expecting a belly-punch. The life force had collaborated with AT&T, but had failed to put coins in his pocket.

"I's afraid you weren't coming." Mrs. DiMartino wiped her hands on a towel tucked into the elastic waistband of her pants. She took his hand and led him to a stool at the breakfast nook. The kitchen smelled wonderful.

"May I use your phone?" Wade asked. "It's a local call."

"You go right ahead while I fix up a doggy bag for you."

Wade punched in Gabler, Thane's number. Listening to the dial tone, he surveyed the room. The landlady's kitchen was warm, almost tropical. The countertops nearly sagged under the weight of casserole dishes containing scraps the DiMartino clan had left. There were the remains of green beans, creamed corn, dinner rolls, potatoes au gratin, mashed potatoes, turkey, dry and from-the-bird stuffing, gravy, sliced ham, mashed sweet potatoes topped with miniature marshmallows, pickled cucumbers and cauliflower, can-shaped cranberry sauce, pumpkin pie, coconut angel's food cake and applesauce. She must have used up a week's worth of water tokens to cook up this feast.

Len DiMartino was dozing in the living room in front of a wide-screen football game. Even so, his grip on the beer can looked pretty tight. Wade's parents had probably prayed over their turkey for the safe return of their missing son. He was ready to hang up.

"Hello?" Mrs. Gabler he assumed.

"My name is Wade. I'd like to speak to Thane Gabler. He used to work at Shatz Company."

"What's your name?"

"Wade Rhodes. He doesn't know me but I'd like to speak to him about...about his work."

"Mr. Gabler retired. He's pretty confused these days." She sighed: a willing martyr. "I don't think it's a good idea for him to get worked up over anything else today."

"No, ma'am. I won't upset him. Would it be OK if I visited him?" He heard muffled voices. She must have cupped her hand over the receiver to talk to someone. In front of him at the breakfast nook, Mrs. DiMartino apportioned dollops of leftovers into recycled butter tubs. She smiled cheerily.

"What do you want to talk about?" The man's voice was as careworn as Wade's flannel shirt.

"Mr. Gabler?" Wade pressed his left hand against his ear to block out the sound of Mrs. DiMartino's ripping a sheet of aluminum foil.

"Now don't get worked up, Thane." Apparently the Gablers had two phones.

"Mr. Gabler, my name's Wade Rhodes."

"Are you the man Lu was telling me about?"

That Lucinda had talked about him knocked him off balance. Wade heard Thane tell his wife, "We must have got cut off. "

"I'm here," Wade said. "I'm working at Shatz Company and I came across your notebooks. I'd like to talk to you about your vibration hypothesis. Not on the phone. In person."

"Thane won't be much help to you," Mrs. Gabler warned. "He gets confused."

"Fiddle sticks!" Thane Gabler said. "She accused me of peeing in her potted palm."

Maybe Henry and Shatz had been right: Thane Gabler was short a few quarts of oil.

"Now, Thane." Mrs. Gabler's wheedling tone seemed to egg her husband on.

"I'm innocent. Sooty peed in your potted palm."

"Sooty was put down last April, sweetheart." Her voice became firm. "It was thoughtful of you to call, but please, don't call again. He's not well. He's tired."

"I think this is pretty important, Mrs. Gabler," Wade said. "I just want to meet him one time."

Len DiMartino awoke in the living room and began cheering, "Go! Go! Go!"

"I'm not tired," Thane protested. "Do you have our address?"

"Thane, sweetheart—"

Thane interrupted his wife. "Come by the house tomorrow. Anytime. I'm home all the live long day."

Len hollered, "Touch down!" jumped up, flapped his knees and dribbled beer down his chest.

Mrs. Gabler said, "I suppose it'll be all right if you visit for a few—"

Thane hung up.

"—Minutes."

Mrs. DiMartino handed him a plastic bag bulging with containers. "I hope you like dark meat. That's all that's left. It's wrapped in foil. Unwrap it before you pop it in the microwave," and on she went, giving instructions for reheating numerous food items that he'd probably eat cold. He wondered if he'd understand the technical aspects he hoped Thane was going to explain to him. He wondered if perhaps Thane were too addlepated or infirm to complete the good vibrations project.

"Can you remember all that?" she asked.

"Thanks, now I won't have to eat dust bunnies."

Mrs. DiMartino grimaced.

He poked in the bag. "Where's the stewed tomatoes?"

She looked stricken.

"That's a joke." He tried to hand her a wad of twenties.

She jerked her hand back as if scalded. "I don't want your money!"

"It's for the rent."

She pocketed the money. "It's good having a man we can trust living in the apartment. Len thinks having a lodger up there discourages burglars. He'd just as soon shoot anyone who tries to mess with his vintage cars." A delightful idea obviously occurred to her, and she asked, "You wanna call your folks?"

"You are my folks."

Mrs. Gabler, a handsome woman wearing a frosting of platinum curls, only allowed Wade in as far as the foyer of their white Georgian-style home. She made her husband vow not to buy cigarettes or whiskey. She made Wade promise not to let Thane drive. Would be a pleasure. The old man's neglected Porsche needed a shake out cruise. Wade backed the car out the driveway very carefully.

Driving the black car, it turned out, was not a pleasure. Initially the car felt like that taut, spastic wrestler with the spring-loaded joints he'd lost against in the district finals his junior year. The kid weighed in at the top of the weight class, thanks to self-induced constipation. Wade, a small teenager, barely qualified.

Mr. Gabler had Wade drive them into a seedier section of town and park the car in front of a pawnshop next door to a pool hall. With a peculiar forward list, springing from his toes to compensate for locked-up knees, Thane Gabler teetered into the gloomy pool hall. The left wall contained the bar, eight swivel-stools, and the barmaid whose skin had been cured with cigarette smoke and alcohol. Just past the bar were vending machines and a jukebox. Booths lined the right wall. The booths and tables were crudely carpentered from plywood that had been varnished dark brown. Beyond the four booths was a small dance floor and six pool tables; beyond them, the restrooms. The lights over the tables were not turned on.

The woman behind the bar said, "Hiya, Gabe, long time no see." Her voice told you she'd worked in Kokus' Pool Hall or a similar hangout for a long time. She set up a shot of Glenfiddich.

"The warden says I can't buy whiskey," Thane said, diving for the shot glass.

"You aren't buying it. It's on the house," the bartender rasped.

"She didn't say anything about drinking it," Thane pointed out. After drinking a shot, he said, "Let me guess." He turned his bulbous head fringed with white hair toward Wade. "Shatz still has a ramrod up his ass. 'Enery is hardly working. Lucinda's the brains of the organization and Ingle is *capo di tutti capo* in the accounting department." His warm gritty voice was like grounds floating in sweet coffee.

"Things haven't changed, Mr. Gabler." Wade was liking him a whole lot already. He'd hoped the old man would invite him to call him Thane or Gabe, but he didn't. As Wade's eyes adjusted to the dim light, the chocolate age spots on the man's pate became more noticeable. No signs of confusion or a predilection for pissing in palm pots, yet. On the opposite side of Kokus' Pool Hall front window, a woman opened a red umbrella.

"How long have you lived in Fort Trust?" Thane asked. His eyes lingered on the cigarette machine.

"Since October."

"What's your plan?"

"I thought I'd work a few months. Collect more dough and hit the road."

"You often on the go?"

"Usually."

"Go to that machine and buy a pack of Marlboros. Smokeless. No. Regular."

"I think I remember a promise you made." Wade regretted saying it, but felt he had to stay off the warden's shit list.

Thane's spatulate fingers slid a hunk of turquoise up and down his bolo tie. "I'm three-quarters of a century old. You think the threat of cancer scares me?" Rich laughter originated from deep within his compact barrel-shaped chest. "My wife, she scares me." He dragged on the contraband with appetite and dreamily blew ephemeral clouds. He held the pack toward Wade. "I promised not to buy cigarettes. You bought them. Smoke?"

"No, thanks. What happened with your experiments to transform elements into water with vibrations?"

"That project was a widow-maker. I worked on it between my normal projects and at night way past Scotch o'clock."

"I've read your lab books several times. I think I understand the principle you were testing, but I'm not a scientist, Mr. Gabler. From what I gather, you transformed some elements into other slower elements. I think you were on the brink of discovering how to change other atoms into H_2O."

Thane's interest wandered to a pool table where a shaven teenager wearing a Genuine Miscreant T-shirt racked the balls. Another teenager with one blond dreadlock depending from an otherwise bald head cracked the cue ball into the others. The eight ball spun into the right corner pocket. "Shitfuck!" He put coins into a jukebox. Caustic music, a cacophony kids called fragsounds, blared from the speakers. It bothered Wade that he hadn't seen the kids come in.

"Everything vibrates. Terrible vice," Thane said, crushing his cigarette into an ashtray. "Henry wouldn't touch my work. Shatz thought I'd gone around the bend. He didn't believe my lab reports. Or didn't understand them." Thane slurped his drink. "Ahhh. Maybe it's just as well. Magic is evil if trifled with by the corrupt." He lifted his right hand off his glass long enough to pat Wade's knee. Arthritis had drawn his knotty hand into a permanent C.

Wade stiffened, bolstering himself to convince Thane Gabler he wasn't corrupt, he'd never trifle with vibrations as a means towards evil ends. He reassessed his position: Thane didn't know him from beans. It was not only right, but also prudent for him to sound Wade out first. A process as revolutionary as transforming elements into water should be treated as sacrosanct, he agreed. But not withheld from society.

Someone fed the jukebox again. The bartender sang along with an oldie Roy Orbison ballad. Thane eyeballed his empty shot glass. "Pretty song. I can't stand those fagsounds the kids listen to nowadays."

"It's vital that your experiment be completed, Mr. Gabler," Wade said. "You recognize that, don't you?"

"I'm an old man. You're thinking, what does he care about the future? He'll be dead within five years or five minutes. He doesn't care that in a few years fresh water will be as rare as—"

"If you want to know what I'm thinking, ask me, Mr. Gabler."

"Good, good. A little fire in the belly. Fact is I'm too old for the rigors of work. Have been for a while. Shatz let me stay on as long as he could. My project..." His eyes searched inwardly. He ran the turquoise slowly up and down the string around his neck. "Someone else will discover it. The great inventions of all time were being worked on and discovered simultaneously by men and women in many parts of the world. I call it parallel development. Maybe I stole that term. Anyway, historians only bother crediting one person, usually a fellow countryman, with discovering or inventing something. I'll bet my bottom water token somebody's beavering away in a lab in California or Egypt or France. Any day now you'll read about it in the papers: Eureka! Water Crisis Solved! I'm not foolish enough to think I'm the only man on the planet pursuing this line of experimentation."

Wade ordered a Rolling Rock for himself and another Glenfiddich, quietly telling the bartender to water it down. With a sidelong glance at Thane, she rubbed her thumb and first two fingers together. W*ater costs extra.* Wade nodded. He tried to think how to reach the old guy. Sometimes the best offense is feigned apathy. "How long have you lived in Fort Trust?" he asked Thane.

"All my life. Nothing's changed. Everything's changed." Thane clamped his lips around his second cigarette. The bartender lit it for him. "Let's move to a booth."

When they'd settled in, Thane said, "I'll tell you one thing."

Wade flattened a sheet of paper on the varnished plywood table. He was ready to scribble notes about how to transform salami and underwear into potable water.

"When you drink nowadays," Thane began, "are your hangovers worse than they were when you were young?"

"Yeah. I thought it was a natural consequence of aging."

"It's the unnatural consequence of contaminants. Toxins cause the symptoms we associate with hangovers. I drink only old Scotch and old wine. Less contaminants were present in the water back then."

The bartender brought a Rolling Rock and a weakened Scotch.

"The good thing about water is it's a universal solvent." He sipped his watered-down Scotch and scowled at it. "The bad thing is it's a universal solvent."

Wade commented that that was one of the paradoxes life liked to deal you.

"This burg used to be a thriving community," Thane Gabler said in a voice that led Wade to believe this was going to be a saga. He stuffed his paper and pencil in his pocket.

"A back porch community but a pleasant one nonetheless, mostly. The largest food processing plant on the East Coast used to be located near Lesher's farm. Do you know Lesher's farm? But the water rates were astronomical. As a result the company relocated. We shot ourselves in the foot with that one. Unemployment spiraled. Other companies followed suit and relocated to sites more hospitable to business." He paused to watch Genuine Miscreant attempt a tricky bank shot without aid of the sissy stick. He sunk a solid. Side pocket.

Thane nodded appreciatively and continued his story that Wade had thought the old man had lost track of. "So the development subcommittee hatched this bright idea to create a Civil War memorial to qualify for State economic development funds and tourist dollars. Before that time the town was called Trust, not Fort Trust. The so-called Fort," he stretched the F-word cynically, "was Lesher's front yard." Thane's cloudy eyes surveyed the smoky pool hall. "There was a battle. I'm not denying that's a fact. Have you seen the place?"

"Once." Wade concentrated on making three interlocking wet rings on the table with the condensation dripping off his beer mug. The old Ballentine beer logo. He'd hitched a ride to Lesher's Farm after several of the workers around the company canteen tables had insisted, "You gotta see Lesher's Farm." It was tacky. The farmhouse was an unremarkable, albeit sturdy limestone structure. The gift shop was larger than the multi-media display area where he'd read convoluted accounts of a battle between Lesher and a splinter group of Union soldiers. Once a year a group of dedicated Civil War buffs re-enacted the skirmish that had occurred on Lesher's Farm in 1863. Two more wet rings. The Olympics logo.

"Then you know the party line," Thane said, his high forehead crinkling. "My great-great-granddaddy told me the true story. I'm not the only one who knows it. Most people do." He loosened his bolo and settled deeper into the sprung upholstered bench. "Under cover of night Sterling Lesher was selling goods—flour and cornmeal—to the Confederates."

Wade drained his suds and hoped the saga was drawing to a close. Mrs. Gabler would be getting antsy by now and he had started to get the feel of the Porsche right before he parked it in front of the pawnshop. The car wasn't temperamental. It was responsive. Manhandling and coercion weren't necessary to get the vehicle to fulfill his mind's desire. A relaxed hold on the steering wheel, an insouciant push on the gearshift, light feet on the pedals were sufficient. He was itching to drive the car again.

"One night, a group of men shot at Lesher. Lesher didn't scare. He shot back. In the end Lesher killed twenty Unions soldiers. Doesn't that seem suspect to you? One man, oh, and one collie dog wiped out twenty Union soldiers who'd set out on an ambush mission allegedly to hijack Lesher's provisions cart?"

"Yeah."

"How can that be?"

Before Wade could formulate any plausible theories, Thane gripped his shot glass and said, "Six of the Union soldiers were actually Confederates. They'd bamboozled their fellow-soldiers into thinking they were going to stop Lesher from smuggling goods to the South when in actuality the turncoats used the ruse as an opportunity to kill Union supporters and make it look like Lesher did it." He trembled at the audacity of it.

Between the froth and the backwash, Wade was learning too much about Fort Trust and nothing about Thane's abandoned project.

"Do you see my point?" Thane asked.

Yeah, your mental circuits have shorted out. "Point? No, sir. I don't."

"This town's forefathers were traitors, con artists, fraudsters, shysters, pettifoggers." He was enjoying himself. "Benedict Arnolds, Quislings, wolves in sheep skins. Everything's changed. Nothing's changed. These people today are the fruits of that rootstock. Think upon it." He waved his glass.

Despair overtook him. There was no out, no solution to the water crisis. May as well prepare to meet Jesus like that red sign at the edge of town exhorted. "One for the road?" Wade asked.

"I know what you're after." He wagged a craggy finger at Wade. "You want to finish my experiment and present it to the world so nobody will have to worry about obtaining fresh drinking water again."

"That's right, sir."

"First I have to know why you're bent on pursuing this, apart from the obvious reasons. Look what they did with atomic energy."

"My motivations are purely—"

He held up his crooked palm. "Don't answer. You'd only lie. I'll discover your reason by and by." Thane got a glass of water from the bartender. When she left, Thane asked, "What will happen to this water if we let the glass sit on the table for a while and no one drinks from it?"

"The water will evaporate."

"We call it evaporation. Do you know what's happening at the molecular level?"

"Sort of."

Thane smiled as if to say, Then I won't insult your intelligence by rambling on.

"No," Wade admitted. "Not really."

"Because the molecules are electrically charged, they tend to hang together. We call that molecular attraction. The molecules whiz around at high velocities. Some of the molecules close to the surface whiz right out of the glass. The electrical charge is not strong enough to rein them in. Have you ever seen a molecule of water jump out of a glass?"

Wade was feeling more foolish by the minute. "No," he said.

"Do you believe in evaporation?"

"Believe in it? Sure."

"We accept the theory of evaporation. Science is inferential. Explanations of so-called reality are deduced from evidence. Evaporation is a theory to explain reality."

"What are you saying? That your experiment can't become reality?"

"No-o-o-o. I'm saying science is a sanctioned form of fantasy. I'm saying if you accept the premise that science is fantasy, reality won't slow you down or put blinders on you." He drank the water and smiled.

Wade liked the sound of that. Don't let reality slow you down. He settled up with the bartender.

"Bring Gabe in more often, will ya," she said.

"He will," Thane replied. He held onto Wade's elbow and headed toward the front door in that peculiar bouncing gait of his.

On the drive back to the Gabler's house the Porsche purred, obeyed his thought-commands. At the Gabler residence, as Mrs. Gabler was shutting the front door, Thane said, "Would you do me a favor?"

"You name it."

"See if the gray metal cabinet is still in the lab."

"Sure thing."

Wade headed toward town. The temperature was dropping. He burrowed his hands into his coat pockets and found the pack of Marlboros Thane must have slipped in there. He doffed his black hat and let cold mist caress his face. He was still undecided about the old man's sanity. He could go either way.

CHAPTER 7

Mouse was sitting glassy-eyed in front of a computer borrowed from a former sales rep. Lowell and the other technicians were attending a meeting with a prospective vendor. The factory was quiet because the majority of production employees had been laid off.

"Where's the key to the metal cabinet?" Wade asked Henry again, but louder this time.

Engrossed with his calculator, Henry ignored Wade.

Wade straightened a paperclip. With a practiced touch, he probed the cabinet lock. The double doors opened to a morgue of factory castoffs: oil-stained work gloves, a spent acetylene torch, a metric socket set, coils of narrow-gage copper wire, and brochures from the days when people paid admission to gawk at Clete Shatz's dump. On the bottom shelf sat a black plastic box the size of a four-slice toaster. Everything was covered with a filmy soot from the fire. He recognized Thane Gabler's system from the sketches in his lab notebooks. It consisted of a keypad, a small screen and a black casing with vents so the inner workings wouldn't overheat. His pulse gathered in his chest. Simply plugging the device in and hitting the right key was a naïve wish, but he also hoped that getting the system operational wasn't going to be impossible. He saw Henry stealing glances at him over his burning cigarette.

Wade set the system on the worktable and paged through Thane's notebooks until he found the drawing that resembled the components he'd found in the cabinet. The toaster-like component in front of him contained the system's hardware or brain. The entire system, when completed, also included a liquid substance intake tube, a membrane to filter out gross matter, a "bladder" or chamber where the filtered liquid would be transformed into potable water and neutralized, and an egress tube from which H_2O and salvation would flow. A rough sketch in the margin of one of the pages showed the entire system being transported on wheels to a group of little cheering stick people. The word "Portability" was double-underlined. Thane's prototype bladder of heavy-gauge flexible synthetic rubber had a 935-gallon liquid measure of capacity. (In theory, capacity was limited by the size of the bladder only.) Within the bladder, according to the design, was an inner "skin." This skin was a protective layer of energy between the bladder and the substance undergoing transformation. If not for the skin, the system would transmogrify itself into water. Wade removed six screws and lifted off the black casing. The hardware inside appeared exactly as Thane had represented them in his drawings, but Wade was as helpless as a carpenter in a hospital operating theater.

"Henry, come here and look at this," Wade said. "What's this neutralizing function supposed to neutralize?"

"I don't have time." He turned his back and picked up the phone.

Wade grabbed the receiver from Henry's nicotine-stained fingers. His teeth clicked shut.

"Henry, Henry, Henry," Wade said wearily. He almost laid his hand on his supervisor's sloped shoulder but remembered how Henry had shrunk back when he'd touched him before. "You were going to call your wife Moira. I know she's not well. Cancer."

"That's personal." Henry blew a smokescreen between them.

"People who are trying to keep something private don't talk about it everyday at two p.m. on the lab phone when others are within earshot."

"Fair enough."

"I think what might be happening," he lobbed his words softly so Henry could catch them, "is you're trying to ensure your wife can get the best treatment possible. So you're doing what comes natural, what seems logical to you." Wade paused and glanced overtly at the partially assembled Aquamira behind Henry.

Henry started to twist around to follow Wade's line of sight, but he flicked his ash instead. "I don't see how this is your worry."

"You are dogging it."

Mouse looked up from his computer screen, cracked his meaty knuckles and left the lab.

"I'm doing nothing of the sort," Henry said.

"You're afraid when you complete the Aquamira that Clete will lay you off, so you're trying to make this Aquamira job last as long as you can. That way your wife can continue to submit company health benefit claims to pay for her treatments. Either that," Wade took a breath, "or you haven't the foggiest clue about how to purify water."

"Benefits don't pay for the whole thing." Henry's quibble told Wade he was on the mark.

"I know it's expensive. I know you want to do everything you can for Moira, but...." "But" wiped out the foundation he'd laid, so he backed up and tried again. "You want to do everything you can for Moira, and I wonder if you'd be willing to hear another opinion about how to do that? How to help her?"

"What are you on about?"

"Remember when the file drawer was stuck and someone kicked it to force it open and that didn't work. And we learned that by pushing it in and gently pulling we could get it open?" Wade wasn't surprised that Henry didn't quibble about his diplomatic use of *someone kicked, we learned*. Henry had kicked. Henry had learned, in spite of himself. "That was an illustration," Wade went on patiently, "that sometimes going contrary to conventional wisdom unlocks a problem. It's like swimming upstream. It's a struggle, but you get to the fresh water that way."

A rushing shadow smashed into one of the rectangular windows, knocking it loose from the frame. Brown feathers flurried onto the worktable. Henry jumped up, upending his stool. Wade ran toward the bird, but stopped when he recognized the species.

The red-tailed hawk thrashed its wings, shedding small feathers among loose nuts and bolts on the table. With its razor sharp beak and lethal talons, the bird was designed to shred flesh, crush the life out of furry creatures. Even in its dazed condition, the raptor was capable of slicing a man's face, breaking a man's bones.

"Blimey. It must have mistaken the window for sky." Henry picked up the snow shovel from the corner by the exit door and wielded it like a cricket bat.

"Don't, Henry. Hold your horses a minute."

The hawk blinked. A drop of blood fell from a nare on its beak. It bobbed its head forward, fell sideways then flapped its wings madly, scattering more nuts and bolts to the concrete floor.

Wade found a cardboard box, clapped it upside-down over the bird and began pulling the box to the edge of the table. He crouched and carefully tucked the box flap over the opening of the box so that as he pulled it over the edge of the table the hawk had a floor to stand on. He felt the raptor scrabble and flutter inside the box. The hawk's screeches hurt Wade's ears. When he got to the half-way point, he didn't know how to close the second flap without the bird falling out first.

Henry threw his butt on the floor and slid a piece of sheet metal under the box. He held the sheet metal tight to the bottom of the cardboard box creating a floor for the bird to stand on. But standing wasn't what the bird's instincts were urging it to do. It hurled its body against the sides of the box. Although it weighed only five to six pounds, the shifting power careening inside the box made carrying it difficult. Holding the box between them, the two men sidled to the door. Wade pushed the release bar with his elbow and wedged the door open with his boot. Three talons slashed through cardboard and through the ham of Wade's right hand.

"Henry, if he scratches you, hold tight. Don't let go!"

Henry screamed, "I'm bloody bleedin.'" He let go of the box.

The box cantilevered. Wade held the sheet metal floor and the box himself until Henry decided he hadn't been mortally wounded. The men took mincing steps until Wade could push the door fully open with his hip. Henry followed closely, holding the metal floor against the bottom of the box. Once outside Wade lifted the box from the sheet metal platform.

The red-tailed hawk cocked its head and took flight. It roosted in the maple tree for a second, screeched and then flew over the building.

Panting, Henry sat on the back steps. His hands lay palms up on his thighs, fingers clutching at air. Droplets of blood beaded a scratch on his left thumb. "Why didn't we catch the bird with our hands?"

"Because it wouldn't have been 'we.' It would have been me."

"You can't pick a bird up with your hands?"

"It was a hawk."

Henry shrugged and sucked the blood off his thumb. He trudged into the lab.

Wade tossed the box toward the trash bin. As the box spun in the air, three long gashes in the cardboard, stained with his blood flashed in his consciousness. He looked down at his hand and saw three deep cuts. His jeans were sticky with blood.

Inside, he wrapped a shop rag around his hand and pulled the knot tight with his left hand and teeth. "If we can get the Aquamira operational," Wade said, "you won't have to worry about job security here. Or anywhere. Headhunters will trample each other to recruit the man who made the Aquamira work. Shatz will pay primo bucks to keep you. Shatz Company will thrive on Aquamira production contracts, and by that time you'll be designing the next generation Aquamira."

"You think I haven't thought of that? It's like the coal filter idea. I've examined every possible option. I've even thought of a scheme to import moon surface water for drinking purposes! I'm not a moron. I'm far too busy to summarize this with you. I'm trying to recover our losses. In case you failed to notice, we had a fire, Wade."

Wade let the comment pass. Henry occupied himself with smoothing out a cigarette.

"I honestly do not believe there is a solution," Henry continued, calmer. "If there was, another inventor would have thought of it by now. His filter or vibrator or what have you would be on the market."

"Help me get Thane's system running. It's the only option we have," Wade said, chagrined with his pleading tone. "'Good, good, good, good vibrations,'" he sang in a high tremolo voice.

Henry's beaky face creased with a wide smile. "If going contrary to convention solves problems, then going contrary to your convention means Thane's system won't solve the problem. I'm merely reversing your reverse logic, you understand." His cigarette tilted up rakishly.

"Henry, my man, staying here is contrary to everything I'm about."

Henry's chin poached with umbrage. He plowed his fingers through his feathery hair. "Errr, bugger! I've got nothing to lose. Clete trotted a woman through here yesterday. He thinks I don't know she applied for my job. Show me the schematics for Thane's thingy. Perhaps I can make something of them." He offered his hand.

"Perhaps we can," Wade said. He used his uninjured left hand to shake hands with Henry.

The air felt pregnant with rain or snow. He screwed his hat down tighter and continued heading toward the suburb the Gablers lived in, about an hour down the road by foot—an enjoyable hour walking along the berm next to the bittersweet brambles and locust trees, breathing the crisp air, losing his thoughts in the solitude. He, the techs and Henry had put their heads together and re-assembled part of the system according to Thane Gabler's drawings and instructions. They'd had no trouble with the hardware, it was, after all, late Nineties technology, but they'd hit a snag with the software programs. It was more than a snag. It was the Great Wall of China.

"Can I take you somewhere?" came a woman's voice through

the opened passenger window of the car that had sneaked up to a stop beside him.

Women rarely picked up hitchhikers. Wade bent to look into the car and saw Lucinda wearing a flowing black velvet jacket with soft-looking pants and boots. He wanted to reach over and stroke her, feel her body's warmth through the plushy fabric. "What are you doing here?" he asked.

"Paranoid?"

He let that slide.

"Get in," she said. "I'll take you where you're going."

"I'll catch another ride. You go on wherever you were going."

"Maybe I'm going where you're going."

Wade held up one of Thane Gabler's notebooks. "I'm going to Mr. Gabler's house."

"What a coincidence," she said. She leaned over and opened the door.

He got in her car and interlaced his fingers on the notebook in his lap.

"I know where he lives." She pulled into traffic without signaling. "His wife used to host the best parties. Professionally catered. Handsome waiters in tuxes. Canapés, sushi, champagne."

"Yeah?" Wade pressed the button to close the window. The finality of the glass plate plunging into its snug rubber molding made him feel ill at ease.

"If I were overly-sensitive," she said, "I'd think you were uneasy being with me."

"No, no," he said too hastily. "I've got my mind on other stuff."

She gave him a sidelong look and veered off the road.

"Watch it." When she straightened the car out, he said, "Thane and I are going to discuss his project. It got deep-sixed when he left the company. I think there's something to it. And so does Henry. Maybe."

Lucinda stopped abruptly at a four-way stop sign. She waved the other cars through the intersection and leveled her nail-head pupils on him. "Any significant progress?"

Wade explained the gist of Thane's water purification system to Lucinda.

"I remember it. I typed correspondence and researched scientific journals for him. I also kept Mr. Shatz informed about it. Thane wasn't working on fusion. That's where you divide atoms. And he wasn't working on fission. That's where you unite the nuclei of atoms. Both of those processes create energy."

"Wow! You know a lot—"

"Here we go again: You know a lot for a secretary."

"I never said that. You said it. Henry and I are stymied. We reconditioned the keyboard, screen and the hardware, but we don't know what to do next. What's your understanding of what Thane was trying to do?"

"Here's how I explained it to Clete. With fusion and fission, you alter the atoms and create energy. Thane was doing the opposite, trying to alter the energy of atoms with vibrations to create different atoms. Make water." She threw him a wry smile. "Clete didn't have any confidence in Thane's project. Called it Thane's hobby-project. He wouldn't give Thane a budget for it. Not a 'stinking dime.'"

He wiped his right hand, oozing dark blood from the hawk's fury, on his thigh, and selected a passage in the notebook burgeoning with block letter notations. He read a cursive sentence: "'Anyone who can change the vibrations of elements at the atomic level will perform magic.'"

"Nobody listened to him. I felt sorry for him. He was a genius in a company of nay sayers and illiterates," she said, eyes scouring the roadside signs. "I'm starving. Mind if we stop at Green Dragon?"

He checked the dashboard clock. "No. Yeah, that's OK."

"I'd once read that the Chinese don't have a word for chopsticks, but that seems impossible." She asked the waiter to remove their cutlery and bring two pairs of chopsticks. She got up from the booth and followed the waiter to the service counter where she spoke to an elderly Chinese woman. The waiter laid down paper placemats printed with Chinese astrology signs. Lucinda ordered stir-fried scallops and cashews. Wade ordered lemon chicken.

"Give me your hand," she said.

He did.

She wiped his wounds with a wet cloth and applied cream she must have borrowed from the woman behind the counter. Lucinda worked slowly, lightly like a mother tending to a child, or a seamstress doing close stitch work. Her fingers, cool at first, warmed. The tightly wound gauze made him feel secure. Their meals came. His turned out to be too sweet, like lemon lollipops. He wished he had his flask of habanero, but it was on the counter in the garage apartment.

"What Chinese animal are you?" Lucinda asked him.

"Monkey. 'If you are a monkey'" he read from the placemat, "'you're chivalrous, sociable,' so on and so forth and, 'You are self-preoccupied with an elastic conscience,' Why's 'elastic conscience' under the negative characteristics and not the positive ones? Isn't an elastic conscience the trait of a survivor, one who adapts?"

"No," she said, pinching a cashew between her chopsticks. "Someone with an elastic conscience is predisposed to commit crimes, petty or grand larceny. Their elastic consciences stretch, in a manner of speaking, to accommodate moral fat. I'm a dragon, believe me. I know whereof I speak." She was kidding of course.

"An elastic conscience is a tool, a capacity, a skill. The endeavors that you apply the tool to determine if people are good or corrupt." He wasn't kidding.

"You're reacting as if you believe this nonsense."

"Well, I am sociable and chivalrous." He twirled a pretend moustache.

"And incredibly modest." Lucinda folded the placemat with the astrological traits on it and wedged it under her plate.

"Now," he said, "you'll never know the rest of my negative traits."

"Nothing like finding out through firsthand experience."

They both laughed.

After a few beats she said, "Clete's a monkey too."

More customers came into the Green Dragon and the plate glass window became steamy around the edges. Beyond, farmers' fields and woodlands had been scraped away and housing developments had been erected. Clouds rubbed against blue mountain backs. He'd enjoyed their badinage and had absently eaten the last morsel of lemony-sweet chicken.

"Monkey man," she said, as they approached Thane's house, "I don't feel as if I know you. Things like what you do when you're not at work. Your family. Your you-fill-in-the-blanks."

"Another time."

"I'm holding you to that, Wade." Lucinda pulled into Thane's driveway. The old man tottered out of the house, grimaces wrestling with grins as his temperamental knees protested each step. "Oh, boy. He's ready to go."

"I'll say."

She opened the window, as it looked like Thane Gabler was going to kiss the glass.

Thane leaned in and planted a kiss on her cheek. "Lu! Are you coming along?"

"No, she dropped me off." Wade walked around to the driver's side and steadied Thane's elbow with a firm grip.

Thane chewed on air. His eyes were aswarm with confusion. He jerked his elbow from Wade's steadying hand and hobbled around the car, pressing his knotty hand on the white hood and fender for support. He dropped heavily in the passenger seat.

"Wait. Get up! You're sitting on your lab book." He helped Thane out of the car. "I'll get in the back seat."

Thane sat in the front again.

"Look. It's snowing a little." Lucinda sounded excited.

Best not to drive the Porsche in the snow anyhow, Wade thought. Small trade for Lucinda's continued accompaniment. Her presence really cheered Thane up.

"Molson, shotta Glenfiddich and one wine spritzer," Wade told the bartender. "None of those pills or suppositories."

"The only thing people can stick up their patooties in here is their shitty attitudes," the bartender said tiredly, as if she'd said it a hundred times a day. She wrinkled her nose while she mixed Lucinda's spritzer.

The three of them settled into a booth and talked about inconsequential things until their drinks came. Thane made a show of throwing back his Scotch and ordered a second before the glass hit the varnished plywood table. He slid his turquoise stone up and down his bolo. "Lucinda, your boyfriend here assumes I'm a crotchety old geezer. He thinks I don't care about water because I'm going to kick the bucket any minute. You tell him, tell him about the microbes."

Lucinda began explaining how Thane and Clete Shatz had inquired into developing microbes to eat impurities in water. Thane interrupted and relived every setback and advance they'd made in their quest for a bioengineer who could develop what they were asking for. In the end they'd aborted the project. "It would have taken twenty-five years to breed and train microbes to eat the type of pollutants in our water we were targeting. Too damn long. Where's my Marlboros?"

Wade flipped the pack and a sterling silver lighter he'd bought over to him.

The flame spit, guttered and flared. "What are you two sitting in here for?" Thane said. "You should be off somewhere whispering sweet nothings."

That caught Wade off guard. He'd been wondering why he hadn't thought of the microbe concept himself. "Henry and I got the hardware running on your atom vibrator."

Lucinda rolled her eyes.

"But we can't get the software program running. It's frustrating as hell."

"Good, good. Frustration is a healthy emotion." Thane nodded and rubbed his balding crown with the hand holding a long scimitar ash. A man wearing an olive drab camouflage hat entered the bar. Hat still on, he ordered a Schlitz pill and ate it dry. He slotted quarters into the pool table. The balls grumbled into place.

"It's like getting the engine of a car running but not the transmission," Wade said. "It's worse because I know how to fix transmissions." On the old gas-fueled cars, anyhow.

"You want me to tell you how to get the program running," Thane said matter of factly.

Wade got out a pencil and paper to write notes on. Maybe Lucinda could help him take notes if Thane talked too fast.

Lucinda sang along with a jukebox oldie. "Kah-ray-zee. I'm crazy for lah-ah-vin you."

"OK," Wade said, pencil poised over the paper. "Shoot."

Thane rutched in the seat and finally extricated himself from the booth. He held out his arm, which Lucinda took, and he led her to the dance floor. Wade slumped into the seat. "Shoot," he said to no one.

The only two on the floor, they danced, chattering like kids at a high school sock hop. Another song came on. An oldie from the Fifties. Apparently, Thane's arthritis resisted his attempts at articulating his arms and legs so he settled for resting his head on Lucinda's velvet chest and shuffling his feet occasionally. Seeing them close and touching hit Wade like a pleasant odor from the past. He couldn't bear it, the memories washing up, the listless eyes of the Schlitz pill-popper, the bleakness of the bar, the broody weather outside Kokus' Pool Hall street-front window.

When Thane and Lucinda returned, a patina of perspiration moistened her forehead. Thane's age spots appeared in dark relief against his ashen skin. His lips looked purplish.

"He taught me the cha-cha," Lucinda said breathlessly.

"I understand there's a few irregularities," Thane said, "about your past. The story about Wade Rhodes begins where another man's story dead-ends."

Wade banged his empty mug on the table.

Lucinda's smile curdled. "Funk gave me your background report to file," she said.

"Did Clete Shatz read it?"

"Funk probably briefed him."

"I didn't do anything illegal."

"Me thinks he doth protest too much!" Thane said. "Let's swap. You tell us who you are and after that, I'll consider telling you how to run the software program."

"That's ridiculous. My past doesn't have anything to do with the future of water."

"Have it your way. Another dance, m'lady?"

Lucinda reached across the table. "Rusty."

Hearing his name made his stomach somersault.

"Rusty, Thane's request is reasonable. He doesn't want to turn his project over to just anybody. We don't know who you are." She tucked her hair behind her ears in an almost violent gesture. "The mafia's got its fingers in everything."

"If I was in the mafia, do you think I'd be wasting my time in this sorry-ass town?" He'd apologize later, maybe.

She cast her eyes downward. "We know your old address in Boise and that you were a data analyst for the government."

"Why did you change your name?" Thane asked.

"Why would you believe anything I tell you? It might all be lies." He couldn't meet their questioning eyes. "Statonics wasn't a government agency. They were contracted by the EPA to compile and graph data they gave us."

Thane rubbed his eyes. "Look at me. My vision is impaired. My joints ache. Dancing with a pretty girl nearly gives me a heart attack. I couldn't finish the project because my health wasn't up to it. Now you waltz in poking your nose in something I'd given up on and you want it handed to you on a silver platter so you can get your face on the TV. How do I know you're not going to complete the project, with my help, and then hold it for ransom? It belongs to the world, but I can't give it to them. Not single-handedly. Assuming that it will even work."

Rusty knew what Thane and Lucinda were asking of him. A trade. If he told them his story, and they judged him to be a trustworthy Boy Scout kinda guy, why, then Thane would consider helping him complete the system that theoretically could convert substances into potable water.

How far back should he begin? At the last day of his last happiness, or before that? How will it sound, his story? How will it feel? Will that ache near his heart rupture like a blister? He was going to have to listen to himself and see if he could endure it. Or be a broken man for the remainder of his life. He ordered another round and after the drinks came, said, "Can I bum a cigarette from you?" He lit it and inhaled deeply twice. A dizzy rush. He began: "Funk's investigation shows Rusty Sinclair was a data analyst for Statonics. Does the report explain why Rusty went underground?" It felt odd, speaking of himself as if he were another man. In many ways he was.

Lucinda seemed to be suppressing a burp or worse.

"Does it?" he asked again, sullenly.

"The report," she began reluctantly, "says Rusty Sinclair changed Statonics' proprietary statistics equations without proper authorization. When this was discovered by upper-management you tried to destroy the evidence by burning the floppy discs, but the fire got out of control and your car burned up. You ran away rather than face certain termination from Statonics and a possible jail sentence as a result of charges filed by Statonics and the EPA."

"I'm a 22-carat slime ball, aren't I," Rusty said. The skewed report shouldn't have surprised him, yet it did. He vacillated between letting them think that was the true story and spilling it all. Neither option set well. He felt inordinately tired. Maybe he'd drunk more beers than he realized, or couldn't handle alcohol the way he used to. He wanted to ask her if the report mentioned a body found in the car, but instead he ordered another beer and set Lucinda and Thane straight on some of the salient points.

Rusty told Thane and Lucinda briefly about his job. He told them about the time he'd discovered the company he'd worked at had been submitting erroneous data to the EPA for at least three years running and that he'd advised his supervisor that he was going to the EPA and blow the whistle. He told them his girlfriend Kim knew about the fraudulent reports. He told them a hacker had wiped out his revised data derived by using the correct formula. That was enough autobiography. His beer mug was empty.

"The bogus report went to the EPA? You didn't stop it?" Lucinda asked.

"Yeah it went. I couldn't stop it. Didn't you listen? I couldn't stop it."

"You left a whole life behind because of that?" Lucinda seemed stupefied.

"That's not the entire story." Thane said. His coffee-grounds voice was so knowing, so soothing.

No it wasn't the entire story. Rusty felt the man's weighty gaze reach inside him and gently touch a spot. And fly back out. His limbs were torpid with beer. The three sat silent in the booth for a while, letting the sound of the bartender's setting glasses on the shelf take the place of conversation. The man at the pool table had left without their noticing it.

"Take me home," Thane said. He handed Rusty a small bag from the Pharm$_x$ drugstore with a password and log-on commands written on it in crumbling block letters.

CHAPTER 8

Clete Shatz crawled out of their king-sized Louis XVI bed. Sitting on the edge of the bed he absently massaged his chest. He loathed the white and gilt curlicue bedroom suite he'd bought for Darla in Seventy-two as a wedding gift. *Third time's a charm,* she'd quipped of her status as Mrs. C. Shatz Revision No. 3. *Three strikes and yer out,* he thought. In this bed she'd interspersed bedroom tutorials (Don't be afraid to get rough with me down there. Higher. Yes. Right there.) and with business maxims (Play to win). He'd learned a lot and was still learning.

The phone on his wife's vanity rang. After the beep, Darla's voice snapped out of the speaker: "Call me right away. It's important." He didn't recognize the number she left. He committed it to memory.

In those early days, he'd worn a brown J.C. Penny polyester suit saturated with nervous sweat. Shatz Co. was in a slump in the early Seventies, too. Convinced finally that image was everything, he borrowed six hundred thousand bucks from his third bride's father. With the money, he bought a tailored suit, five silk ties and second-hand equipment from a company that'd filed Chapter 11. Not one week had passed since then during which Darla let her family's generosity remain unremarked.

As he walked from the master bedroom to the master bath, the phone rang again. The machine taped Darla's message: "I know you're there, Clete. Call me. It's urgent!" He was going to call her after his meeting at the Apex clubhouse.

Clete jutted his chin at the bathroom mirror and shaved silver whiskers off his jaw. Fuck her and her money. The lab rats had progressed with the Aquamira by leaps and bounds. It was a miracle. A goddamned miracle. He spoke into his voice-activated mini-recorder. "Emphasize win/win possibilities with Krumrine. Remember President Flores is pissed and hungry for an answer to the water problem. Don't tip my hand. Note: Put kibosh on Aquamira after field test if Krumrine bites the bait. Stall Darla."

Standing under the higher of the two his 'n' hers shower nozzles, Clete lathered his arms with the natural sponge and olive oil soap Darla had bought on their vacation in Istanbul last spring. She loved haggling with the tobacco-faced Turks as much as they loved pocketing her lira. He turned on the hers nozzle and let scalding water runnel down his narrow chest and belly. These damn water-saving, low-flow showerheads just didn't feel as good as regular ones. If he could change that, he'd feel justified to a lifetime's pass to heaven. Too soon he felt guilty about taking a simple shower. He got out.

His housekeeper, a petite woman with a multi-hued mane, wearing leopard print leggings, a gold halter, and vermilion toenails entered the steamy bathroom. "Morning, Clete."

He intoned into his recorder, "Note: Hire new housecleaner. This one walks in on man of the house naked."

Alita snapped his thigh with a towel. "Don't flatter yourself, I'm not naked yet. Want your clothes laid out?"

"Coffee too."

"Inna minute. What kind of day is it? Meet and greet the commoners or press the flesh with your own bourgeois ilk or kiss a politician's ass?"

"I should fire your ass."

"You love my ass."

"Breakfast meeting at Apex. Dark suit. White shirt. Conservative tie."

He followed Alita as she padded into his walk-in closet, curling her toes into the furry carpet. The cedar aroma faded as his nostrils became accustomed to the woody redolence. He watched her trail her hot-tipped fingers over the fabrics—cashmere, camel hair, mohair, fine wool. No brown polyester.

"They feel like air, like bath water on my fingers," she said. The phone rang for the third time. Darla had begun speaking before the beep. "...Pregnant. You'd best call me now, you useless sack of shit!" She hung up. With what he thought was a remarkably calm demeanor, Clete explained to Alita, "Couldn't be my doings. We haven't slept together for months." He ripped the plastic dry-cleaner bag off of one of Darla's designer dresses and handed it to Alita. "Here, try this one on."

She peeled off her leggings and halter and skinnied into the dress. "This material feels like nothing. I feel naked."

Lowering her to the carpet, he lifted the sheer fabric and tongued her until Darla's scent was overpowered by Alita's.

Clete twisted a smile into the full-length mirror. The Italian suit hid his gut and built up his shoulders. Amazing what a good tailor can do. Standing next to him, Alita slapped his padded shoulders into place. He kissed her roughly, open-mouthed, clamping his hands on her firm naked butt under the dress.

She tucked a red kerchief in his breast pocket. "Go get 'em, soldier," she said mockingly.

"I knew you detested your uniform, Alita," Darla's voice was ice water, "but you've carried it to extremes."

Mistaking the figure of his wife in the corner of his eye for an h-mail projection, he barked, "Switch that bitch to text mode!" Clete pushed Alita away. Her multi-dyed mane flared about her shoulders as she spun to regain her balance.

"She's in h-mode. H for human," Alita quipped. Arms akimbo, the housecleaner regarded Darla, then gathered her own costume and strutted out of the bedroom. "Your rags aren't my style," Alita trumpeted from the hall.

Darla drew her eyelids down, letting them quiver with an emotion he didn't care to think about. She'd recently dyed her hair coal black and wore severe bangs. Clete heard himself groan. The gastric acid ember burning in his esophagus glowed hot. His legs, heavy iron posts, were welded to the floor. What could he say? *Fuck her*, he said to himself in an effort to buck himself up. "I was planning to call you back later this morning."

"You are depraved, Clete."

He withered. "What do you want?"

"Our daughter is pregnant."

"Janice? How could that happen?"

Darla wiggled her hand at their unmade bed, implying *The usual way, you dope.* Had Darla always been this cold and practical? Or had she perfected the art of heartlessness while he'd been working late at the office? Her funhouse mirror image came back to him. They'd both slipped away from their offices and met at the county fair. Nobody they knew—coworkers, neighbors, their spouses—attended the fair on workday mornings. The warped mirror had elongated her teeth and nails, truncated her torso. It was a hideous reflection.

"What about the staff people in the home?" he asked. "Don't they keep an eye on residents? Isn't there a policy against…Who did it? Someone took advantage of her! She didn't know what was happening to her!"

"We had a long talk. She knew. She wants to keep it."

In movies and documentaries, women who'd had abortions spoke in terms of regret and loss, of unsatisfied curiosity. Who would the child have become? Some of the women were haunted years afterwards and sought counseling. Even if they'd had other children, they spoke of voids. Of course Janice would have her baby. They could help her raise it. Maybe it would be normal. "Is the father mentally disabled?" Clete asked.

"Don't be asinine. They're not getting married! She's only seven weeks pregnant. The thing, it's not a person, is this small." She pressed her thumbnail into the second joint of her little finger.

"Not a person in the eyes of the law, you mean."

"Clete, she's a child herself. She can't take care of a baby and neither can we. Not now." She picked up an atomizer from her vanity and dropped it in her purse. "I've scheduled an appointment with Dr. Weller for an outpatient procedure."

"You've got it all under control," he said. "What do you want from me?"

"There's a small hitch," Darla said. "I'm due for deposition in Atlanta the day she's to see Dr. Weller."

Christ. He'd have to accompany her at the abortion clinic. Poor Janice. Her trust. Her imploring eyes. Could she ever understand why? Could she ever forgive him?

"Darla, I—" His voice cracked off like a dry branch.

"I love her too. That will never change." She tossed another perfume bottle into her bag and left.

In the garage, sitting in his car, Clete tuned his car radio to the business news and sobbed.

Scott Billet was telling the Apex club members about a cartoon in the "Wall Street Journal" drawn by a well-known political satirist. "It shows the president crying crocodile tears in a desert. Little people are running around beneath her catching her tears in cups to drink."

"He'll be audited by the IRS," Senator Krumrine said.

Clete rolled his after-breakfast cigar ash to a point in a cloisonné ashtray. Time to pick up the golf ball and move it closer to the pin. "Speaking of 'The Wall Street Journal', did you read the article about the Japan Ministry of Trade providing seven-hundred million US dollars to industry for research and development?" He assumed the newspapers had covered the story he'd heard on the radio.

"No, I haven't been to the library yet." Krumrine's euphemism for the toilet.

"I must have missed it. I have a yen to know more about it." Billet's idea of a joke.

Clete pointed his cigar pedantically, caught himself and sat back, trying to relax. The leather chair protested. "Our government can do the same," Clete said. "Let me lay out a scenario for you,"

"Short version," Krumrine commanded.

"A progressive senator convinces his esteemed colleagues under the dome in Harrisburg to set up a multi-million dollar grant program for the design and development of a water recycling and purification system. Womb to tomb. Maybe they pool state funds with the greenies, the feds, EPA, other interest groups.... A company applies for the grant, wins it and develops the world's first large-scale, economical water purification system." Setting his cigar in the tray, Clete checked Billet's reaction. Billet was listening attentively, leaning forward. Krumrine picked lint off his sleeve, but his eyes were bright. "Then the senator and the governor of that state receive presidential commendations, ambassadorships maybe. Their constituents worship them. They're heroes. Everybody wins."

"Touching fairytale. What's your stake in it?" Krumrine asked, his round head rotating like a tank turret toward Clete.

"The future's at stake. Our kids need water and their kids and their kids' kids need drinking water."

"You're still assembling material recycling systems, aren't you?" Billet asked.

"Right, Shatz Company's niche is material recycling and handling systems. Lately," Clete brushed his hands in a gesture of dismay, "we've become a stinking boutique company. One of these. Two of those. Plus the warranty work. It's busting me."

"Plus the fire," Krumrine said.

"My company doesn't manufacture water recycling and purification systems. We're sticking to our knitting."

Billet said, "I like it. Ohio is doing the same thing, a grant, except they're researching methods to extract water from plant matter. The grant covers ten years of research."

"Ten fuckin' years!" Krumrine slapped the leather sofa. "What's so novel about a grant? There's already grants galore, but still no solution to the water crisis."

"Write a one-year grant." Clete wished he hadn't said that. Too eager. Almost hit the ball into the rough.

"That's impossible. Nobody can design and build a water remediation system in twelve months. Womb to tomb," Billet said.

Krumrine nodded in agreement, eyes scanning the far wall as if watching something engrossing.

I'll do it in less than a year, Clete thought. His scalp prickled. *The timing is critical,* he reminded himself. *Hit the ball on the fat side of the swing and follow through.* He had nine months to go until the Aquamira would be field-tested, according to Henry Healy's revised master plan. Billet and Krumrine were eyeing the bait, so he back peddled to appear disinterested. "One year is extremely aggressive. Too optimistic. It's a bitch managing fund disbursement. Plus someone highly technical would have to verify the grantee's progress reports. Even so, after all that effort and money you still might come up dry."

Scott Billet snuffed his smile when he saw Krumrine frown.

"It's impossible to make Perrier from sludge." Clete waved his cigar.

"What do you know about the companies currently working on water recycling and purification projects?" Krumrine asked the question for which Lucinda had prepped Clete.

Clete orally reeled out a roster of Fortune 500 companies and hopeful basement Thomas Edisons who were striving to pull off a miracle of Biblical proportions. So far none of their systems exceeded current water remediation systems' capabilities, which everybody knew were inadequate.

"Throwing more money around won't solve the problem," Krumrine said.

Clete was searching for a voice that wouldn't sound over-rehearsed when Billet cut in.

"Throwing money around *is* the problem. A little here to this university. A little there to that research center. The shotgun approach is ineffective. Shatz is suggesting a grant program large enough to change lives. The grand kahoona! You remember Kennedy? I read that he told the nation we'd have a man on the moon, and you know what? Everybody wanted to believe him.

They believed and it happened. It happened! With money. Money and brains. It happened!"

"The Russians beat us with Sputnik," Krumrine said caustically. "That was the impetus, not patriotism. We couldn't stomach being out-maneuvered by the Commies."

Billet forgot himself and mussed his hair. "You think if Iraq or China or, oh, hell, who's our enemy now? You think that if a foreign nation invents a water purification system they'll sell us the rights to it? Hell, no!" Eyes at the poker table peered over their newspapers. Billet lowered his volume but not his intensity. "Hell, no." He settled into himself. All blown out, embarrassed.

Krumrine's eyebrows climbed up his forehead. Clete watched a sparrow peck at a worm on the brick patio.

Evenly, Billet began again. "In the 1400s and 1500s the countries with the strongest armadas ruled the world. Later in the late 1800s and most of the 1900s steel ruled. He who made steel, ruled. Then it was information technology. Today it's water. If we're left behind we'll be on our friggin' knees paying out the whazoo to the water czar for a drink." Red angry blotches mottled his handsome features. Billet was making Clete's arguments for him, reeling Krumrine in, inch by inch.

From the corner of his eyes, Clete watched Senator Krumrine gazing at the display case of trophies and pictures of Apex members posing with foreign dignitaries and D.C. creatures on golf greens and in fashionable restaurants. Nerves singing, Clete pushed himself out of the leather chair. "Well, gentleman, I work for a living." He had swung and hit the sweet spot. Now, where was the ball going to land? He walked out of the lounge and the oriental carpet felt like clouds under his feet.

CHAPTER 9

The thermometer in Len DiMartino's garage indicated forty degrees, but Rusty didn't notice the chill. Contentment was oblivious to chills, to vague backaches, to sawdust tickling noses. Thane's system was no longer a figment of the old man's imagination. It was becoming manifest on the workbench in the cinderblock lab. Henry, the techs and Rusty worked as a team. They spliced wires, told jokes, drank Twinings tea and briefed Shatz daily. The cancer that had sapped the lab of morale and cooperation was in remission.

Rusty drilled inch-and-a-half openings in the front panels for three birdhouses while Len buffed imposing fenders on his red 1966 Oldsmobile Toronado. Len whistled a three-note continuous loop-tape tune until Rusty interjected, "Virgil Exner's designs broke the mold, wouldn't you say?"

The electric buffer wound down to a dizzy halt. The whistling stopped. "Who?"

"Virgil Exner. Designer of those lethal fins on the Chrysler C300. The first muscle car." He sanded a birdhouse opening, waiting for Len to buff on that.

"I'm sorry to be the one to inform you, Wade, but this here is an Olds not a Chrysler," Len finally said.

"Nineteen sixty-six, Olds Toronado, designed by Bill Mitchell. Also famous for the Corvette Stingray."

"Hey! Righto. Now I had a Stingray once."

Listening to Len reminisce about his cars—glass-packed mufflers, mag wheels and roll-bars—provided entertainment while Rusty painted the three birdhouses he'd made: one to look like

Lucinda's stucco cottage, another a replica of the DiMartino's home and the third, the Gabler's white Georgian-style home.

"Gapping sparkplugs is a bitch," Len said, holding the offending AC Delco between his greasy fingers.

"You have a matchbook?"

"I thought you didn't smoke. Elsewise we wouldn't have rented you the upstairs."

"I'll gap your plugs for you."

Len found a matchbook in a coffee can full of fuses, knobs, eyehooks, hinges, and shotgun shell casings.

Rusty wedged the matchbook cover into the sparkplug gap. Filed a few strokes. Worked the cover in again. Filed a few more strokes and laid in the cover once more.

He plucked a loose white hair off Len's 20W-50-stained sweatshirt and made a squeaking noise as he slid the hair between the plug and matchbook. "Voodoo mechanics," Rusty told him. "Try her out."

The Toronado purred. Len gave Rusty two oily thumbs up.

"The gaps have to be set precisely the width of one matchbook cover plus one hair of the person who drives the car," Rusty explained.

When the paint dried, he gave a birdhouse to Mrs. DiMartino and told her it was for the wrens that lived in the lilac bushes. She rolled on the outside edges of her slippered feet and sang, "Teakettle, teakettle, teakettle," in a joyful voice, mimicking the call of wrens.

"Yeah, that's what they sing," he said. Together they measured the prescribed height and he mounted the wren house on the utility pole at the bottom of DiMartino's yard.

And the following spring, fledgling wrens took up the cry.

"If Lucinda wouldn't have told me it was in his monthly report to Clete, I wouldn't have known Henry committed us to have the Aquamira prototype working by August," Rusty told Thane from the back seat of Lucinda's frigid car. He hated air-conditioning. Clammy. Invasive.

"What a schmuck," Lucinda said. "Less than three months away."

After Thane Gabler had given Rusty the log-on commands on an envelope Rusty and Henry had begun calibrating the water system's software program parameters to replicate the vibration modes and rates of hydrogen and oxygen. The tedious process, entailing a seemingly infinite series of steps, required testing and retesting before proceeding to the next incremental step. They worked alone, for the other lab employees had been laid off. Rusty especially missed Mouse and Lowell, but he understood that the techs' efforts were no longer necessary for the completion of the Aquamira. Eight cooks can't boil water faster than two can. Henry staunchly refused to call on Thane Gabler, although sometimes he called Mouse in on an hourly basis, sometimes they worked through lunch and dinner. Rusty did so gladly for it kept his thoughts off other things—women from the past, women from now. Seemed like the few times that he and Lucinda had been alone, he'd felt like crying. And it seemed as if she'd make it OK for him to unload on her. Which was not OK.

For respite from the tedious programming work, Henry and Rusty sought old-fashioned hands-on work and retrofitted Henry's defunct Aquamira frame to accept Thane's "black toaster," the component Rusty had found in the metal cabinet. Rusty conducted a funeral ceremony when they dismantled Henry's Aquamira and tossed it in the bin outside. Henry sniffed, but otherwise had kept his upper lip stiff.

Lucinda slowed the car and pulled off Point Street and into the parking lot. Shatz Company loomed before them. Insects flew in crazy orbits under the sultry security lights. She parked in Clete Shatz's reserved slot. She ran her employee card through the electronic card reader.

"Wait out here until I deactivate the alarm system." She went inside and a minute later she returned. "The coast is clear!"

Thane, gripping Rusty's elbow, followed Lucinda. She had changed clothes after work and was wearing shorts and a T-shirt.

Her damp feet made kissing noises as they lifted from the inner soles of her sandals. Her perfume hit middle notes similar to the fragrance of hyacinths. The three walked past the darkened offices toward the lab door. One word-processor's ghostly screen saver glowed. Lucinda sucked disapproving air between her teeth and turned it off. After consulting a small laminated card in her wallet, she pressed numbered buttons on a panel beside the lab door. When the panel light changed from red to green, she opened the door.

Shadows reassembled, as if caught in the act, into the familiar landmarks of file cabinets, workbench, table, stools, Henry's mess of pamphlets and cigarette stumps.

Rusty switched on the overhead lights. An electronic buzz enveloped them. He showed Thane Gabler how far he and Henry had come with the system until they'd hit another roadblock. Thane listened, his brain sorting, transcribing, filing, resorting as Rusty spoke in layman's terms about their foiled attempts to "get this baby hummin'."

"Are we on the right track?" Rusty asked hopefully. He smiled when Lucinda handed him and Thane vending machine cans of lemonade.

"Thanks, Lu." Thane's spatulate fingers fumbled with the can tab. Lucinda handed his lemonade to Rusty who handed his opened can to Thane. They drank, arched throats vulnerable.

"Yes," Thane said, "you're on the right track, but the way you're going about it, you won't get the program finished for a coon's age."

"I know. I figured that much out. Henry and Mouse both thought there'd be some sort of logical, mathematical progression and we could extrapolate once we figured out the first few steps, but...." He ran his hand through his hair. He'd noticed a few more silver filaments this morning in the shaving mirror and had wondered, *What's taking you so long?*

"That's what I was calculating in the car on the ride over," Thane said. "There is a progression which to the untrained eye appears to be random." The old man had built long equations, course by course, resembling inverted pyramids in his lab notebook. He held the pages of his lab book open for Rusty to see numbers and functions and operands, p and $^{10.}$ The equations may as well have been hieroglyphics carved in sandstone. Rusty knew algebra and calculus, but when it came to applied physics he had no clue what to do, how to proceed.

Remembering a conversation he'd had with Henry, Rusty asked, "How can we make sure the Aquamira doesn't eliminate minerals we need for our health?"

"We'll program it to leave the right proportion of essential minerals remaining," Thane said. "That's the plan. Or we can fortify the water with additives. As I read the numbers you enter them into the program where I tell you to. There's a long stretch of green between us and the eight ball. Lu, can you wait for us? Two hours is all I can take of this."

"I'll go polish paperclips or something."

The two men had worked, heads bowed over their task, for an hour when Lucinda interrupted.

"Have a chocolate donut?" she asked, offering them junk food.

"No," Thane said, "but I'll have one of those Styrofoam circles covered with brown wax that you're holding."

Both men absently chomped on donuts. In his peripheral vision, Rusty watched Lucinda perch on Henry's stool and prop her feet on his drift of papers. She licked her finger and rubbed saliva into a mosquito bite on her calf. "You know, Rusty," she said, "I've got to tell you, in my mind, I make up stories about you, why you really ran from the job at the EPA lab."

"Statonics," he reminded her. "Not the EPA."

"To be honest with you, none of my stories are flattering." She was fishing again.

"Rapist, serial killer, a freezer full of Häagen Daz and human heads. That kind of thing?" he asked.

She rolled her shoulder as an answer.

"Nothing that interesting." He rolled his knuckles into his aching lower back muscles. "Thane, Thane! Take a break, man."

Thane raised his head, emerging from a world of algorithms. He rubbed his eyes, smearing chocolate icing on his forehead.

"One time me and five other guys," Rusty began, "were out horsing around. In Seattle. We would buy as much beer and gas as we could afford, which was a lot at fifty cents for a quart of Olympia and ninety-nine cents a gallon of Esso. We all piled into Greek's Dodge R/T. He'd reupholstered the seats that day with green velvet stuff to match the paint job we'd given it. Racing stripes, the works. We all decided, no we didn't decide, the car gravitated toward Mt. Rainier. We couldn't see it. It was covered in clouds. Batshit tells me to open the glove compartment and get a piece of paper out of the worthless little first-aid kit in there."

Rusty'd flipped open the AAA kit and held a square of paper between his fingers. He knew what it was and tore off a patch for Batshit and the boys in the backseat. He laid his dot like a sacred wafer on his tongue and let the wind blow his mind away. The Dodge lifted her wheels and floated above the road on a mutually hallucinated cushion.

"We're flyin', man," someone said. "Yeah. No fuckin' lie."

He didn't know if the radio was on or off. Didn't matter. The stars hummed like a train whistle when it's a mile or two away. Each star reverberated with a different musical tone and each star tone was assigned a different color. The notes streamed down to the earth, sweeping the Norfolk pines that soughed in answer. Braids of color unraveled, fell from the sky like a woman's long tresses and blew in the car's open windows. Tickled the skin sliding off his face.

A voice from the back seat wended its way through psychedelic strings of star music. "I think I'm gonna puke."

Rusty twisted around in time to see his fellow tripper crank the window handle and spew his chilidog on the closed window. In slow motion. The boys laughed. They barked, holding their stomachs in ecstasy. They were unable to prevent the smell from making their laughter take solid form and melt all over their shirts, their jeans and the gagging green seats.

He'd told this story many times and relished the reaction it got him.

Thane's shoulders jiggled as he laughed quietly.

"Oh, gross!" Lucinda bent forward laughing, patting her chest. "I'm going to my desk." She threw her empty lemonade can in the trash and left the lab. A second later she returned. "That had nothing to do with why you've been living incognito all these years."

"Half-time entertainment," Rusty said.

The two men resumed working. "Enter three-point-four to the fifth—"

Wailing assaulted their eardrums, erased coherent thought, froze them.

"I forgot!" Lucinda's stark white face, eyes round, appeared at the office doorway. "I opened Clete's office door and set off the alarm!"

Rusty saved the work they'd done, exited the black toaster's program and shut the system down. Thane listed like a storm-driven galleon to the door. Rusty flipped off the lights and they ran out through the foyer and jumped into Lucinda's car.

Cold blue police lights flashed on the building.

"Cool it, Lucinda!" Rusty laid a hand on her arm. "We work here. We're not thieves. We have a right to be here. We'll tell them the truth."

A policeman's flashlight blinded them.

On the security monitor in his office, Clete Shatz and the security manager watched the recording of a policeman aiming his beam in Lucinda's face.

"She's as jumpy as a cat in a roomful of rocking chairs." Funk scratched his crotch. "Yes, sir, chief, I knew you'd get a kick outta this recording, so I brought it to you post haste. I already conferred with the police. It's your ballgame. Your call whether we file charges or not."

Clete looked askance. The iron window grilles dissected the sky, the trees and Point Street traffic into orderly segments.

Funk seemed to realize his mistake and reworded his statement. "Whether *you* file charges. We can sock them with trespassing, unauthorized use of company property, jeopardizing proprietary information and processes, admitting entrance to a non-employee...."

Give the dog a bone. "Good job, Funk. Set it for replay. I'll take another look."

Funk diddled importantly with buttons and controls. Poised to murmur security-related commentary, he pressed play and sat on the edge of Clete's desk to watch the video.

"You've done your job, Funk."

"Anything else I can do, you know where to find me. I have contacts. I can call up some favors."

"I'll remember that, Funk."

Funk backed out of the office, leaving the door ajar.

Security hounds: the sleaziest breed. Clete made a mental note to lay-off Funk. He opened a drawer and picked up his golf ball. No longer perfectly spherical–perhaps it never had been–the ball's hide reminded him of orange rind. "Wm. Gourlay 26" was stamped on the antique ball Darla had bought for him during one of her business junkets about seven years ago. "It's 150 years old," she'd told him. He liked the feel of it in his palm.

Perfect. He couldn't have set it up better if he had planned it. Now that he had dirt on Lucinda, Thane, and Wade Rhodes a.k.a. Rusty Sinclair, it'd be easier persuading them to follow his grand plan. On screen, Clete watched her white car pull into his reserved parking slot. Rusty and old Thane waited at the front door until Lucinda returned to let them in. Clete shook his head. The lab cameras recorded the trio in infrared until Rusty hit the light switch. Clete pressed the fast forward button and watched Thane, Rusty and Lucinda drink Chaplinesque lemonades. Thane jittered through some sort of calculations while Rusty seemed to be entering them into a program.

Clete propped his feet on his desk and rested his head against the chair's high back. He pressed the intercom button. "Lucinda. You there? Get in here." He was enjoying the tragicomedy on screen when Lucinda's knuckles rapped on his partially opened door.

He hit pause, waved her in, hit play.

They watched Lucinda nearly fly out of her sandals when she'd set off the alarm in Clete's office. They watched the three scurry from the lab. They watched the policeman suddenly look up from his notepad, run around the car to pull the old man out and stretch him prone on the parking lot.

Lucinda whimpered, muzzling her mouth with her hands.

The policeman radioed for an ambulance. More lights flashed on the white brick façade of Shatz Company. After the ambulance drove off with Thane, the policeman resumed questioning Lucinda and Rusty.

"Explain," Clete said.

Lucinda sat on the slate-colored sofa facing his desk. She crossed her legs, picked at the hem of her skirt and stood again.

"I'll tell you exactly what I told the policeman. We did nothing illegal." Sweat darkened the fabric at her armpits.

"Go on." He rolled the golf ball between his palms.

She told him everything she knew about what Thane and Wade, she called him Wade when speaking to Clete, were working on, which satisfied him immensely. Based on what she was telling him, it sounded as if the men might meet Henry's optimistic promise to have the Aquamira prototype running in three months. As Clete listened, though, he realized they weren't working on Henry's Aquamira. It amused Clete that Henry, that sly dog, had lead him to believe that they were working on the device Henry had invented, or to put it more accurately, had tried to invent. They were, in fact, resuscitating Thane Gabler's hobby project. *The old coot's still up and taking nourishment. And I don't have to pay his high-falutin' Ph.D. salary.*

Clete gathered from Lucinda's tale that Rusty was the wild

card who'd pushed the Aquamira project back on the rails. Clete had him in under his thumb in case the red-haired rogue contracted a sudden case of ethics at an inconvenient time, which he was susceptible to, based on his performance at Statonics where he'd worked until shucking his true identity and skipping out. He knew Rusty Sinclair was hiding from someone and why. Funk's further investigations had connected the dots. Clete sure as hell wasn't going to tell Rusty he was no longer under pursuit. The picture needed one more piece to frame Rusty in so tight he couldn't squeak. For that job, Clete was going to call on the services Henry the Eighth.

"That's why," Lucinda was saying, "Thane was in the lab with us. I mean, Henry was stuck on a problem and Mr. Gabler is the only one who could help." A strand of hair she'd constantly tucked behind her ear during the telling hung limp and greasy against her face. "Am I in trouble?"

He didn't answer. Approaching her from behind the imposing desk, he sat lightly on the arm of the sofa and gestured for her to sit down, please sit down. Looking down at her upturned face and watching her tongue dart in and out of her mouth like a mouse in the wrong hole, he asked. "How's your love life?"

"That's none of your business."

"You're interested in Wade Rhodes? In his welfare?"

She shook her head minutely. "Our relationship is professional."

"As far as you and I are concerned, this," he pointed to the monitor where the screen saver bubbled and boiled, "this never happened. If you tell anybody about this recording, I'd be forced to press charges against all of you. Kapish?"

"Kapish." She blotted the corners of her eyes and shut the door behind her.

CHAPTER 10

The last time he'd visited a hospital room was during his wife's final weeks. He'd pleaded with her to come home where she belonged. They could hire caregivers to assist them. She'd said no, that she didn't want him to have to look at her when all he wanted to do after crunching numbers for eight hours was to just zone out on nature shows about rainforests. Toward the end, they grew closer, more intimate, trusting and vulnerable. Impending death made it easier to love her they way he'd wanted to love her all along. Rusty turned his hat in his hands, round and round. He entered the room the receptionist at the counter had told him Mr. Thane Gabler was staying in. Hospitals everywhere smelled the same.

Mrs. Gabler's lips pursed when Rusty entered the hospital room. He felt maligned by her accusatory body language: *I told you not to bother my husband*, her jerky hands signaled. *Taking him to the lab brought this stroke on*, her sharp stride tapped out. Without preamble, she said, "They gave him Citicoline. The doctor says it reduces brain damage. He thinks they got him early enough." Eyes averted, she smoothed down her skirt front. He knew it was futile to try to mollify her or offer words that might sound apologetic. He watched her leave. The silent form on the bed next to Mr. Gabler's didn't seem to be breathing.

Rusty pulled up a chair and held Thane's cool, dry hand. The old man's knobby collarbones stretched his crepe skin. His lips were colorless. His fringe of white hair lay transparent against the pillow. Rusty felt helpless, and responsible for the man's condition. "I'm sorry," he said.

The old soul behind the cloudy blue eyes surfaced. Thane

said, "I told the warden working on my project gives me a reason to live. Otherwise that little stroke might have killed me. You bring my Marlboros?"

"No."

"What good are you?"

"None whatsoever."

In lieu of his turquoise stone, Thane worried the sheet with his gnarled hand, a sign that his mind was careening ahead of his words. "You ever ski, Rusty?"

Skiing was a foolish sport. Why participate in an activity where people bragged about broken bones, dragged plastered limbs around like war trophies? "Yeah, one time in Colorado."

"What was the first thing the instructor taught you?"

A nurse entered the room and drew the curtains around Thane's roommate's bed. They heard groaning and her cheery "That's the way. Good. That's the way. Good." The nurse beamed indiscriminately and soft-shoed out.

"The first thing they taught us was how to stop," Rusty said.

"Bingo!"

Bingo what? Rusty gnawed on the skiing gristle with part of his mind while using another part to string together anecdotal reports of how he and Henry were progressing with the Aquamira. He hoped Thane would be well enough to come and observe the prototype field test. Rusty's jaw snapped shut. He suddenly understood why Thane had asked about skiing lessons.

The old man hadn't yet told Rusty and Henry how to stop hurtling down the white slope, how to snowplow their skis to prevent themselves from crashing into the ski lodge's bay window. "All the energy that ever was or will be is here now." That statement was written near the front of Thane's final lab book, in a section about the problems entailed in neutralizing the energy. If the energy were not neutralized within the Aquamira, an explosion of neutron bomb proportions would occur when excess energy was expended as atomic vibration rates and modes were decreased to match that of hydrogen and oxygen. And conversely, explosions would also occur when energy was added as vibration rates and modes were increased to become hydrogen and oxygen. Unlike water, energy doesn't quietly evaporate. He envisioned the cataclysmic, chaotic fluctuations of energy surpluses and deficits as an infinity of popcorn popping and black holes sucking up the puffed kernels. This ridiculous analogy pointed out his ignorance to him. Suddenly, he recalled an entire notebook dedicated to the subject of "Neutralizing."

Rusty didn't know the technical jargon, yet he attempted to express his understanding of the cataclysm the Aquamira could create if it weren't properly programmed. "We need to program the system to neutralize the effects of energy surpluses and energy deficits."

"Bingo again." Thane's breathing was labored.

"Why didn't you tell me about this sooner?"

"I was afraid if you knew all the problems we had to solve, you'd give up before we got started."

"This coming from someone I practically had to beg to help me! I wouldn't have given up. I'm not giving up!"

After a thoughtful pause Thane said, "I admire your altruism."

"Altruism has nothing to do with me being here or working on your project. I consider you a friend."

"I consider you a friend too, but I'm not talking about friendship. You've spent endless hours working on a project that others disregarded. Your dedication to my 'black toaster' is extraordinary. Do you have kids?"

"None that I know of."

"Use me as your straightman, will you! It took me twenty years to learn about employee relations. I learned *I* couldn't motivate my staff. Motivation is personal. Each man has his private reasons urging him to conduct one more test, redesign the part one more time, report to work one more day."

"I understand what you're saying. Henry's motivation is his wife. Her health. Her ill health."

Thane closed his eyes.

"I've been there," Rusty said softly. "My wife, Nina. I haven't spoken her name for years. She had cancer, breast cancer." He jumped up from the chair. "Breast cancer, prostate cancer, girls getting their periods earlier, sperm counts dropping, boys' penis openings in the wrong place. Lifestyle diseases. Yeah, right! So we cut out fat and we cut out red meat. We ate more fruit and veggies. We took vitamins. Nada. Then the gurus blamed the diseases on negative thought-patterns. We were thinking ourselves sick. Sorry, guys, but that didn't explain why animals were suffering from similar diseases." The patient in the other bed moaned. Rusty lowered his voice and sat down again. "It's a crime. We dicked around documenting diseases while pretending we didn't know the source. Man-made contaminants in the environment. In the water."

"Nina never cried," he whispered. "The last time we talked she said I was a good husband." He didn't believe it. She said it only so he could live with himself afterward, he knew that. He turned on the TV. A sitcom about intergalactic teenagers. He searched around for water, a jug or thermos, but found none and walked over to the louvered window. A man and a woman on a bench in the courtyard five stories below were necking, heads gyrating. The couple rose and walked along the brick path, swinging their clasped hands between them. A boy wearing a black helmet skateboarded between the couple, breaking their grip. The old hurts twisted in on themselves.

"You see the pattern?" Rusty said, staring at the empty bench. "Disease attacking sexual organs. It's a Darwinian principle: A species stupid enough to poison itself deserves to die. We're perpetuating our own extinction event. After Nina died, my parents, my own parents said it was high time for me to let the past go, get on with my life. Some nights before I fall asleep, you know, when your mind quits thinking and ideas float in, I remember I forgot to think about Nina today."

"The ones who are supposed to love you don't know how,"

Thane said, eyes open again. "The ones who do know how to love you die."

"What do I do?" Rusty smashed the windowsill with his fist. "You can't give up now, Mr. Gabler. We're too close!"

Thane seemed to be holding an interior debate and then resolved it. His eyes became vacant, and fluttered shut. His breathing grew deep and even. What was he dreaming about?

The Victorian bar he'd refinished and retrofitted had come to mean more than simply a collection of shelves containing an entertainment system. The termites eating the rare chestnut wood were gnawing away at his confidence. The time to implement the next step of his grand plan had arrived. *Don't choke now*, he coached himself. He covered his face with his handkerchief and sprayed insecticide liberally. He hoped that would knock the termites back until he had time to hire an exterminator. It was time. Time to recruit Senator Krumrine, bring him into the fold. Where should they meet? The senator was accustomed to five-star hotels and swank hunting lodges, no doubt, but Clete couldn't throw that kind of money around. The Elf Motel down in Maryland off Route 94. Discreet. Cheap. Juicy prime ribs too. Favored by truckers and adulterers. No constituents lurking around.

Clete punched in the senator's home number. The neighbor kids' soccer ball bounced into his backyard and rolled onto the patio. A boy stood at the boundary between the two yards. Clete opened the French doors leading from the den to the patio, scooped up the ball and lobbed it to the boy. "Here you go."

"Thanks."

"You're welcome, John."

"I'm not John. I'm—"

Someone was on the line. He shut the doors. After telling the minion who'd answered the phone some bullshit story, he was put through to Krumrine.

"Senator Krumrine speaking."

"Clete here."

"Shatz? This is a rarity." He switched from unctuous to mocking. "To what do I owe the honor of this call?"

As he listened to the senator, he opened the French doors in order to air bug spray odors out the room. A gust smelling of snow swept oak leaves over the threshold. "I'm calling," Clete said, "to offer you a chance to become the most beloved, respected, famous senator in the history of the United States."

Krumrine's guffaw exploded in Clete's ear.

"I could have offered this opportunity to someone else, Senator, but you're the only man, um, qualified to—"

"Spill it."

"I can't discuss this matter on the phone."

"Do you have an insider's investment tip?"

"Meet me tomorrow afternoon at the Elf Motel—"

"The Elf! People will think we're homos."

"Nobody down there will recognize you, will they? Senator, are you still there?"

"The Cumberland Inn in West Virginia. Seven p.m." The line went dead.

Clete called Krumrine again, and was put through quicker this time because the house servant recognized his voice.

"When you get there," Clete said, "ask for Mr. Gourlay." He didn't want any record of a man named Clete Shatz being at the hotel. He poured a snifter of brandy and downed it, forgetting to savor the liquor's fruity, nutty complexities. He refilled his snifter three-quarters full and smelled the bouquet, let the liquor explode on his tongue and warm his throat. The soccer ball rolled into the yard again. He ran out shouting, "Hey, Johnny, I'll show you kids how to spike the ball. Watch how I do it." He tossed the ball up and hit it with his head. The ball sailed farther, much farther than he'd intended or even thought he was capable of, considering he'd never played soccer in his life. Three boys converged on the ball, vying with each other to kick it. Clete Shatz's prowess pleased him to no end.

The angles of the garage apartment's sloped ceiling pressed his anger into a hard lump he couldn't ignore. Rusty kicked the cot, ramming it against the wall. He'd misjudged Thane after all. The old man was quitting on him. Senile old booger. He'd refused to give him the formula to neutralize energy. Thane didn't give a hoot about the water crisis. It was all malarkey. All malarkey. Stringing me along. What a fool I've been believing you can turn salami and skivvies into water. What a fool. If the project were viable Thane never would have retired from Shatz Co. Or he would have continued working on it alone with the same passion as when he'd started on it back at MIT. He'd spent his whole career puttering with that black toaster. Never produced anything. He should have been fired. He hadn't even named his process like genuine scientists did: Newtonian physics, Brownian motion. Vibrations my ass. And then that crap about the molecular energy causing catastrophic explosions. What horse shit! If Mr. Gabler was any good he'd have been working in a sprawling lab for a giant company with its own fitness center, cafeterias and an administrative staff large enough to run a small nation. He'd have been pulling down an obscene salary. Henry'd even fallen for it. Well, shame on us. The passions of science yoked to the whims of a feeble brain.

He pulled the cot away from the wall and rubbed the black streak the iron bed rail had made. Henry was no fool. Foolish, but not a fool. He was a bona fide scientist. Conservative. Logical. Probably graduated from Oxford or Cambridge or one of the other reputable college for scientists in England. He believed in Thane's Aquamira, eventually. Yeah, Henry believed in it.

On second thought, Newton probably didn't name his work after himself. And you can bet Buckminister Fuller didn't coin the phrase Bucky Balls any more than Plato labeled sexless relationships Platonic. Future scientists or a clever journalist would be responsible for naming Thane Gabler's invention, and thereby immortalizing it. The Gablerian Formula. The Thanian Method. TG's Vibrator.

It's no good. Nothing worse than locking horns with yourself. He'd learned a long time ago that arguing with himself was unsatisfactory and fruitless. Rusty bounded down the cedar stairs and went into Len DiMartino's garage. Len wasn't there. Rusty turned on the lights and began adjusting the lens of the right headlamp on the gleaming Toronado. Righteous yammering voices continued debating in his head so he turned on Len's radio and caught the last riffs of a rant-song by Shedding Flesh before the news.

"In lieu of our usual news round-up we'll take you to WAXX, our affiliate station in New Jersey. Thirteen families, including infants and children, have chained themselves to the Rosstown water tower. They say they are protesting the government's lack of initiative in solving the water crisis." A child's wailing was heard in the background. "A state social welfare agent filed a lawsuit on behalf of the children of the protesting adults, alleging child abuse, but the judge ruled that the children are not being harmed. They are released to attend school, are fed and generally well—" He turned the radio off.

Thane liked to talk about how much the world had changed in his lifetime. "My life span," he'd say, "has included buggy whips and space shuttles." That seemed an exaggeration, but Rusty never challenged it. "Assume an average life span of 65 years. Line up 770 people on a timeline representing the last 50,000 years of human existence. The first six hundred of those people lived in caves, only the last 68 people could communicate over distances, only the last six saw a printed word, only the last two used electric motors. Almost everything we take for granted today was invented during the life of the 770th person. Me and my generation. You can't hide from technological progress."

Which got Rusty to thinking about innovations during his own lifetime: heart transplants, DNA fingerprinting, the Internet, one-inch thick wall-mounted television screens that were works of art when not in use, plants genetically altered to produce medicines.

Many scientists and visionaries who'd made groundbreaking discoveries were ridiculed, pilloried, reviled in their day. Rusty felt ashamed, for that's exactly what he'd been doing to Thane Gabler in his head. He tightened the screws holding the headlamp lens in the front bumper and remained crouching in front of the vintage muscle car as he followed a thought to the next junction. Let's say Mr. Gabler is on the right track. Give him the benefit of the doubt. He's too infirm to carry on. He falls asleep in the middle of sentences. Who could help them finish the Aquamira now? Who could pick up where Thane left off? A molecular physicist? A chemist? An alchemist? Where do you find guys like that?

He stood, arched his back and rolled his knuckles into the bottom of his spine. He turned out the garage lights, locked the walkthrough door and knocked on the aluminum door at the back of the house. In Mrs. DiMartino's kitchen, he telephoned Henry Healy's home.

"Wade? We're having tea now. Couldn't this matter wait until Monday?"

"No. We need to go to the lab tomorrow!"

"Whatever for?"

"To work on the Aquamira."

"Have you gone wonky? We don't know the energy neutralization formula." Henry took an audible sip of something. "Do we?"

"Yeah, we do. Meet me tomorrow at eight o'clock." He'd think of something by then. He went into the night, searching for draught beers. And inspiration.

CHAPTER 11

The Cumberland Inn, formerly a coal baron's mansion, had that hushed quality of places where money was not mentioned but elegantly evident. Sitting on a brocade davenport beneath hand-hewn beams and candelabras fashioned from deer antlers, he rehearsed how he'd lay out the plan to Krumrine. The senator would demand guarantees of success and confidentiality as conditions of participation. Clete checked his watch. It was seven p.m.

Krumrine stood before him and said, "Now what is it you wanted to talk about, Clete?"

He didn't know how the senator had entered the spacious lobby without his seeing him. "My name," he said, "is Mr. Gourlay."

"Mr. Gourlay, then." His round face took on a blandness that almost covered the curiosity playing under the surface of his oily skin.

"Come to my room, the Mountain Laurel Suite, and join me for dinner." Clete glided across the carpet to the wide staircase and thought that his words had had a quaint sound to them. He'd spoken the way he supposed Mr. Gourlay might have, back in the Nineteenth century. It boosted his confidence having Krumrine following his footsteps like a spaniel puppy. He opened the door to a large room on the second floor decorated with rich maroons and greens and golds. He handed the senator the room service menu. No dollar signs on the menu. "Everything comes highly recommended," Clete told him.

"I always order the rack of ribs. What do you suggest?"

Clete improvised with scraps of conversation he'd collected while waiting in the lobby. "Ostrich is delicious, although heavy.

Venison, wild boar, pheasant under glass. I've never tried their grilled shark steaks with raspberry Drambui sauce." After they'd settled on what to eat, Clete placed their orders. They lit cigars and smoked silently. Age-old mountains folding in on themselves beyond the bay window gave guests the impression that they were far from Jacuzzis, refrigerators stocked with caviar and smoked oysters, and beds bigger than Clete's bathroom. A protracted crack of a giant tree limb breaking free from its trunk echoed through the forested gorge below them.

"We heard it, so I guess a tree really did make a sound," Krumrine said.

Clete curled his lips, approximating a smile and began running his hands along the window frames and doorframes. He checked under tables and examined the bed headboard.

"What are you doing?" Krumrine asked.

"Checking for bugs."

"In a place like…. Oh, that kind of bug." Krumrine searched the wet bar and bathroom.

An attractive woman wheeled a cart into their room. They ate their meals and talked about the stock market, ostrich farms and Krumrine's new granddaughter. Clete could not remember ever feeling this comfortable around the senator before. Perhaps the man was human in spite of being a politician.

"Enough pleasure. What's your business?" Krumrine asked.

"I think you'll agree that this business opportunity I'm going to propose will be a pleasure too. Hear me out on this before you say anything." He declined the offered drink because he wanted to stay sharp. Krumrine could become a bastard in a heartbeat. "My men are this far away," squeezing an inch of air between thumb and forefinger, "from building a prototype system that will solve the water crisis."

"Bullshit."

"You'll say bullshit when you've realized you've missed the chance of a lifetime."

"Wait. I get it. It all falls into place now: At the Apex club you were jabbering about a government grant and pretending you had no personal stake in water remediation. You silver fox, you. How much up-front capital do you need?"

"Not penny one."

"Where do I fit in?"

After he explained as much as he could about how the Aquamira works and Krumrine's role in the plan, he mixed a stiff martini for himself.

"Who else have you presented this business opportunity to?" Krumrine asked.

"Not one person. These types of enterprises are best kept small and manageable."

"Keep it that way. Exclusivity and anonymity, it goes without saying, are non-negotiable conditions for my participation." Krumrine took one last bite of crème caramel and said, "Please thank Mr. Gourlay for the use of this magnificent suite and for the fine meal."

"It's his pleasure, I assure you, Senator."

They shook hands and the senator left. Clete walked around the room, flicked light switches on and off, turned a pillow and plumped it, opened the fridge and closed it immediately. The adrenaline that he'd had to control during his meeting with the senator was coursing through him. My god, it had been too easy. He punched the air with his fist. He didn't know what to do with himself. He whipped off his tie, kicked off his shoes and fell spread eagle onto the bed. He put his hands behind his head and felt the smile stretch his facial muscles. The smile encompassed his entire body. Funny, his heartburn wasn't acting up after his gorging on shark meat and rich sauce. A knocking at the door.

"Come in."

It was that pretty girl who'd brought their meals. "Excuse me, Mr. Gourlay, I can return later to collect the dinner trays."

"Now is fine."

"Was everything to your satisfaction?"

"Dear lady, I cannot begin to tell you how fine it is." On her way out of the room, she turned around at the door and bestowed him with an inviting smile. He wiggled his fingers and said, "Bye bye." The hotel staff would have a tough time getting money from a Mr. Gourlay. He'd checked in, but was going to slip out the back way.

The hands of the dusty clock in the lab showed eleven o'clock. Statistically it probably didn't pan out, but the adage If you want it to rain, plan a picnic, contained some folk wisdom. What could he do to make Henry (the rain) walk into the lab right now? Sit on the toilet? Light a cigarette? Make a phone call? The lab was getting stuffy and hot. He propped the back door open and looked for Henry Healy's car, but it wasn't in the back parking lot. He counted out enough change for a Java Break Tablet. The tablets were worse than the tar Lucinda brewed, but counting out the change and inserting the coins in the vending machine slot in the canteen did the job of passing time. He crunched the bitter caffeine tablet, strolled through the factory (not much work in progress there) and continued on through the offices thinking maybe his supervisor had gone there. Then he went to the men's restroom. When he returned to the lab he saw Henry going out the back door.

"Henry! Where are you going? I've been waiting for you."

"Have you been waiting long?" Henry asked.

Only three hours. "Well?"

"I thought no one was here."

"I'm here." Was irritating people something they taught Henry in college or was he naturally talented in the art of making you want to shake him. Rusty paused to get control of his temper. He affected a cockney accent and said, "Top of the morning to ye."

Henry sucked hard on his cigarette. "What's your brilliant idea?"

"You contact your scientific buddies and ask them to help us with the Aquamira."

"Bloody hell!"

"Why not? Don't you have friends or associates who can understand Thane's work?"

"It's not so difficult. Quite simple actually." He poured a cup of tea for himself from his thermos.

"Yeah? What? What do we do next?"

"Naught. The Aquamira, she's belly up. Pull up the stumps, chaps. Back to the drawing board."

"How can you give up so easily?"

Henry screwed the cap onto his tea thermos and grabbed his satchel.

"There goes Henry Healy, the man who let the Aquamira slip through his fingers. Just a few phone calls. That's all I'm asking. Ten phone calls."

"I don't know ten scientists well enough to call them out of the blue and the time zone differences between here and England—"

Henry had stopped speaking because Rusty's face was a hand span away from him. The whites of the Brit's eyes were bumpy. Burst capillaries laced the beaky nose. Eau d' ashtray reeked off his raspy breath. And years' of tea breaks stained that sickening yellow tie. Rusty poked his index finger into the tie. He said evenly, "We'll find ten scientists."

"That's all there is for it, then," Henry said weakly.

"There's gotta be a list or an index. How about the 'Who's Who' book you said you're listed in. How about some of those guys?"

They e-mailed past Nobel Prize winners, the chairman of physics at MIT, an independent water remediation research facility in London, and other scientists of various stripes. The responses arrived sporadically for the remainder of the day. Some of these guys apparently worked Sundays. (It was already Monday for the Far East Asian scientists).

"Although the theory holds water," one wag wrote, "in practice, it's impossible. Good luck."

"Preposterous! Current technology bars molecular transformation using the methods you propose," wrote another. "Get this gibberish off the Internet and let us scientists who are truly dedicated to our field of water quality protection work on the water crisis."

One respondent requested a download of the Aquamira's engineering drawings and software program. The requestee was twelve years and five months old.

Rusty's mouth still tasted bitter from that Java Break Tablet. "There's no hope, is there, Henry?"

"Don't be so despondent, old fella. Monday we'll pick up where we left off with my polymeric filter."

"You are so dense. It's down to you and me, Henry. Clete laid off your staff. The only reason he hasn't fired us is because we started making demonstrable progress on the Aquamira. Thane's version of the Aquamira. If we give up, we're finished. It's over. Nice working with you! Ho! Wait. I think we've got a bite." He scrolled through a seventeen-page e-mail message crawling with formulae. "Henry, what do you make of this?"

"Print it out. I'll fuss with it at home. Moira's cooking a Sunday roast. It'll be drier than a tinker's boot if I dally."

Rusty gripped Henry's shoulders, those slopped shoulders. Between clenched teeth he said, "What's this e-mail about? Can they help us?"

Henry poured another cuppa as he pored over the message. "Oh, yes. Quite interesting, actually. Two wogs from a British lab, Belvessier, it is, are working on neutralizing phenols discharged with wastewater from oil refining processes." He lit a cigarette and began struggling with the file cabinet drawer.

"And?"

"Oh, right. Their studies indicate their methods effectively stabilized waste and they wanted to know if we could recommend a symposium in America where they could present their findings. It's nothing new. They did it back in Oh-three."

"Can we apply their methods to the Aquamira?"

"Have you gone daft? They've stabilized wastewater, not purified it. It's still toxic to humans."

Clete straightened his tie, composed his face into what felt relaxed and pleasant and entered the lab. He wanted to give them a Monday morning pep talk, tell them how important they were to the company's future, tell them they were his most important assets and mumbo-jumbo like that. He was going to say anything they wanted to hear as long as it would insure that the Aquamira would be operational before Krumrine contracted an unfortunate dose of ethics. "What's cooking?" he asked as jovially as he knew how.

Henry and Wade looked at him, their faces blank as stones, causing him to wonder if his question had betrayed his anxiety. He jammed his hands in his pockets.

"Sir," Henry said, "I hate to be a wet blanket, but we've got to rationalize Mr. Gabler's project and go back to my original plan of developing a superior polymeric filter."

What's this rationalize bullshit? Clete wondered. He turned to Wade who nodded glumly and said, "We've hit a dead end."

"So? Why the long faces?" Clete asked, fighting a panic that was stealing his oxygen. "Reinstall your polymeric filter. Use that instead of vibrations. I'm surprised at you, Henry. I thought you'd rather work on filters." Then he remembered the old project master plan. "How long do you think it will take?"

"Oh, dear, I'm in for a bollocking," Henry said, nonsensically.

Clete could have sworn the Brit had said ball licking.

Pulling the corners of his lips down like Henry's, Wade said, "A bollocking. That's British slang for disciplinary action."

"A year. . . Two," Henry said, answering Clete's question.

That tore it. He opened a ring-binder notebook, sprung the rings apart and shook the papers out onto the floor. He opened a file cabinet drawer and threw files at Henry, all the while yelling, "No way. You've got till August. August you hear me? That's it."

"A year or two," Henry said, "until we have a viable prototype. Then months of testing—"

"I don't have a year or two!" The lab phone rang and Wade answered it. Clete checked himself. It had felt as if he'd come undone, there. He adjusted his tie, shot his cuffs out and straightened them.

"Try Extension 23 in production," he heard Wade telling the caller. "We don't have anybody named Gourlay working here."

Clete ripped the receiver from Wade's hand. "Don't muddle this deal," came Krumrine's voice, "the repercussions will be excruciating."

"Wrong number," Clete told them. Krumrine had him by the short hairs and these two gomers were telling him the Aquamira prototype was a long way off from completion. He looked around. He didn't think he could make it to the lav in time. He broke into a trot and went out the back door. He dry-heaved beside the trash container. Another spasm convulsed him. He clung onto the metal trash container and spit out thready acid. The mucus plopped onto dormant grass bristles between his leather shoes. Bleary eyed he appealed to the sky. *I'm disintegrating, help me.*

Laborers enjoying lazy smokes on the truck dock didn't grant him the dignity of looking the other way.

"This came in the morning mail," Lucinda said. She handed Rusty a white envelope addressed to Wade Rhodes and waited for him to do or say something.

He opened it and found a get-well card addressed to Grandpa and signed in childish print. He turned the card over. The rickety message read: "When I awoke from my nap, you were gone." Teetering block letters read: "Energy Neutralizing Formula." Two cramped columns of programming instructions filled the back of the card.

He gave Lucinda a bear hug, dashed down the hall and through the door marked "Research and Development Laboratory Employees Only."

"Henry, old chap, we're back in business!"

CHAPTER 12

"Drive faster! We'll lose Clete!" Henry said. His voice was girlish with uncontrolled excitement.

Rusty knew exactly how his supervisor was feeling. It was that euphoric, tickly feeling your insides get when you're about an hour into a really decent chocolate mesc high, or that jellified, warm sensation right after a gusher orgasm. Over the past nine months and some spare change, he'd imagined this day, but he never imagined that taking the Aquamira prototype out for her first field test was going to fill him with this unbearable pride, joy, fear, name the feeling, he was feeling it.

"Don't panic, Henry." Rusty slowed down to stop at a railroad crossing. The red lights were flashing. Ahead of them in his gas-guzzler, Clete Shatz gunned his car through the railroad crossing gates that had begun to close. The Pontiac bottomed out on the macadam. The undercarriage threw sparks.

"Faster!" Henry whacked the dashboard.

"No. The railroad tracks will jostle the system." He checked the rearview mirror where the reflected Aquamira was strapped under a tarpaulin on the flatbed trailer.

"I don't know where bloody Arrowroot Lake is," Henry said. A summer snow of Benson & Hedges ashes blew back into the truck cab.

"Arrowhead Lake. It's about three miles beyond the tracks." Rusty waved to the train engineer and read boxcar graffiti: Tim luvs Shakala. Save Water. Skin Tribe. He wished Thane Gabler was seated between them, but the old man would have to wait until visiting hours to hear about the Aquamira's field test.

"Wonder if the heat will affect the system's performance," Henry said for the fifth time. "Indian Summer."

Spewing plumes of dust, Shatz's car turned onto a dirt road and scared up pigeons that'd been scratching at the roadside. He blared his horn at two bicyclists. In the sideview mirror Rusty saw the cyclists dismount in a dust cloud and rub their eyes. The Pontiac's taillights flashed and Shatz parked under a beech tree. Rusty backed the flatbed onto a tab of hard-packed dirt next to the lip of Arrowhead Lake. The sun burned in a flat white sky. Shadows of heat waves banded the lake surface.

Shatz grinned and rested his arm on his opened car door. "Guess I drove a little too fast." The engine murmured as cool air rushed out. He sucked on his water bottle, rinsed his mouth and spat, splatting a brown Rorschach in the dirt. "How long to hook her up?" he asked Henry.

"How long do you reckon it's going to take?" Henry asked Rusty.

Rusty peeled off his borrowed blue coveralls and addressed his response to Shatz: "About ten minutes to connect the intake and exit tubes and maybe ten to re-check program parameters. Twenty minutes."

"Twenty minutes," Henry echoed, dabbing his temples with a handkerchief.

Shatz returned to his vehicle, shut the door and leaned his head against the headrest.

While Henry set up the water test kit, Rusty attached the Aquamira's intake tube to the bladder with a liquid measure capacity for 935 gallons. If the black toaster's software programs worked according to plan and obeyed the men's unleashed dreams, lake water passing through the bladder would be transformed into H_2O safely without energy surpluses and deficits.

Satisfied that the seal between the intake tube and the bladder was watertight, he carried the mouth end of the tube to the edge of the lake. Blue iridescent dragonflies darted from him. His boots slid on furry green pebbles as he waded into the lake and fed the tube out a few feet. Arrowhead Lake, although beautiful, was teeming with impurities both natural and manmade. A breeze swished through hemlocks on the opposite shore, but died before crossing the lake. When he stood up, he felt dizzy. He stripped off his sweaty T-shirt and tied it turban-style on his head to block the sun's rays.

He began fitting the exit hose to the Aquamira. Fishermen who'd left snarls of line, cigarette butts and Budweiser cans underfoot had packed the dirt down hard. Three cabbage butterflies flapped like tiny sheets on a clothesline over a damp spot in a baked tire track. Rusty saw that Henry had the water test kit ready and, for some reason, his tea thermos.

Success guaranteed Henry Healy lifelong celebrity in rarified circles that normally excluded nerdy scientists like him, and success meant no more worries about the exorbitant medical costs his wife's treatments incurred. For Clete Shatz, the Aquamira's success meant he'd enter the exclusive club whose roster included the Bill Gateses, the Sultan of Bruneis, the Lillian Chungs of the world. Somehow Rusty was going to ensure that Thane was rewarded too. He barely dared to contemplate what the prototype's success meant to himself. For when he did, he felt like a sham. Even he found it hard to believe that all he wanted was to leave a legacy of pure water. It was more personal than that.

"For posterity." With his Nikon, Henry snapped a photo of Rusty checking the seal on the spigot attached at the end of the egress tube. "Wait until I put my gear on and then snap one of me." Henry put on a British World War II helmet and gas mask. "In the event of an explosion. Cheese." His voice sounded hollow and far away.

"If she blows, that helmet will melt into your brain," Rusty told him.

"I was only joking." He removed the mask and helmet and mopped his forehead. He fingered the keypad, turned on the Aquamira.

Rusty didn't hear the plaintive minor chord the Aquamira had hummed during dry runs in the lab. "It doesn't sound right."

"Sounds spot on to me," Henry said.

Water and pebbles gurgled up the intake tube. The tube's belly sagged to the ground. The payload weight tore the tube loose from the bladder. Water puddled on the dirt.

Shatz yelled, "Fix it! Fix it!"

"I knew it. I knew it," Henry whined. "My polymeric filter would have bloody well worked."

Rusty checked the clamp. It had snapped in two. "Henry, find another hose clamp."

Henry held up two inch-and-a-half diameter clamps he found in the toolbox on the truck bed. The intake tube was five inches in diameter.

"Use duct tape," Shatz screamed.

"We're out."

"Right, then." Henry whipped his yellow tie from his collar and tied the tube to the Aquamira's bladder with it. The tube was ridged like vacuum cleaner hose and a synthetic tie wasn't up to the job of creating a tight seal. "Won't work, will it?"

"No. Nice try though," Rusty replied.

They ransacked glove compartments, the toolbox, Henry's satchel, the car's trunk, but found nothing other than cause to sweat more profusely than before.

"What, you fancy a swim?" Henry asked Rusty.

"That's an idea." He unlaced his boots, dunked his rawhide laces in the lake and wrapped them around the tube, tying them off with double knots. The laces fit snugly in the valleys between the tube's ridges. As he did this he asked Henry, "Where'd this ridged tubing come from anyhow?"

"Me wife's Hoover."

"You're kidding. Next time, let's use FRP Epoxy plastic piping, OK?"

"Aren't you the cheeky one," Henry said.

"It's very high in strength and has excellent chemical resistance. It's good up to 220 degrees Fahrenheit."

"Why you Yankees persist in using Fahrenheit and yards and

pounds when the rest of the universe uses Celsius and meters and kilograms."

Rusty had been acquainted with Henry long enough to know that as soon as he turned his back on his supervisor, he was going to jot down FRP epoxy in his memo pad. While the men were speaking, the bootlaces had dried and shrunk, creating an effective seal around the intake tube.

"Let 'er rip," Shatz barked.

Again the intake tube undulated, ingesting water, aquatic vegetation and pebbles. It held. Again the hum wasn't quite right. In the time it takes thunder to rumble after lighting strikes nearby, a sequined twist of water flowed out the open spigot.

"What's happening?" Shatz shouted, even though he was standing right next to Henry. "Does it work?"

Henry held a beaker under the water that had traveled through the Aquamira. He held the clear water heavenward, catching a sun shard. With shaking hands and no cigarette, he tested the sample for contaminants.

"The results? What are the results?" Shatz hovered at Henry's damp shoulder.

Rusty knew it wasn't right. The sound wasn't right.

"The results indicate that...." Henry's droopy eyes refused to meet theirs. A smile flickered over his face. "No go. Both gross matter and microscopic matter that should have been transformed by vibrations are present."

"What the fuck's wrong? You said it would work!" The vein in Shatz's forehead swelled.

"Let's run a systems check," Rusty said. He knew his arms and back would sting with sunburn tonight. Somewhere in the trees, cicadas drilled away. After checking over the system he said, "It's the pump. This seal is damaged. See right here. Untreated lake water leaked through here, bypassing the bladder, and was pumped into the egress tube and out the spigot. That explains the presence of contaminants." And that was good news. Had it been a problem with the hardware or software programs, well, they would have had to ask Thane for more help and he wasn't always available or entirely lucid.

"Put on a new pump seal." Shatz's voice cracked adolescently.

"We don't have another one," Henry said.

"Well, where did you bloody get the first bloody one?"

"Builders' Supply. Er, they close in twenty minutes." Henry swallowed on the bad news.

"Henry, stay here and guard the Aquamira. Wade, you know how to make fast getaways. You drive us in my car to Builders' Supply." Without waiting for Rusty's response, Shatz dove into the passenger seat and punched the number on his car phone for information to get Builder's Supply's number.

Rusty backed Shatz's gray barge away from the lake and spun onto the dirt road. What was that crack about fast getaways?

"Clete Shatz here. Shatz Company CEO. Don't close till we get there. Do you have a…" He turned to Rusty. "What do we need?"

"A K3-4 seal."

Shatz repeated the part number into the phone. "Our accountants won't what?" He disconnected and punched another number. "Where is Ingle? Christ! Transfer me to Lucinda!

"Lucinda. I can't get Ingle. He's on the stinking phone. Tell him to transfer payment to Builder's Supply right now for whatever we owe them from outstanding invoices. We can't? Then tell him to hand deliver the goddamned cash now. It's got to be there before five o'clock. I know. I know. Tell him I said his ass is on the line. What? Yes, he's with me. He's driving." Sheepish, he handed the phone to Rusty.

"Just answer yes or no," she began. "Will you come over to my place for supper tonight after work to celebrate the Aquamira?" He careened around the bend and passed the two cyclists they'd passed on the way to Arrowhead Lake. In the rearview mirror, the bicyclists shook their fists at the reckless driver.

"Sorry," he said to their diminishing reflections. "No, sorry. Can't do that." He handed the phone back to Shatz.

"What'd she want?"

"She asked if we'd be back at the office yet today."

He felt uneasy. Maybe it was telling the petty lie to a man in a suit that brought on an unpleasant rush, not unlike the way he'd felt long ago sitting in the family sedan with his dad who'd collected him from the police station after a stern lecture about under-aged drinking. "You oughta be glad it was only beer and not drugs," Rusty had said, his logic further infuriating his dad. From the corner of his eye, he could see Shatz chewing his lips and micro-adjusting the air-conditioning. You can't tell control freaks that thermostats, like many things in life, work best if you give them a chance to reach their full effect before you cranked on the knob or pushed the button again.

"We're lucky actually. It's only a broken clamp." Rusty plowed ahead, ignoring Clete's condescending sneer. "If it'd been a microchip or programming bug, it'd take hours or weeks to fix."

"You're lucky to be working in a small company where a data analyst can work outside his job description. Job enrichment."

"I do what needs doing." He slowed for the railroad tracks' blinking red lights.

"A stinking train. Floor it!"

No way would the car make it through the gate before the arms came down. Rusty tapped the brake pedal.

"Floor the bitch!"

He did.

The train whistle filled their ears. The headlight caught their stares like spotlit deer at night. The car bucked as the inevitable sounds of crunching metal traveled with bovine slowness through the car's interior.

"Keep going," Shatz commanded, unfazed at the damage the gate was causing to his roof and trunk. "Turn here." He leaped out of the car before it came to a full stop and tore into Builder's Supply. And tore back out.

"You see Ingle anywhere?" he asked Rusty.

"Give him a few minutes to cut the check and drive here."

"I hate waiting."

"Relax. Wait slower."

Shatz grunted. Ingle slalomed into the parking spot next to them and bolted in the front door of Builders' Supply. Bickering. Swearing.

Waving the box with the seal in it, Shatz jumped back into his car. "Got it!"

Rusty gunned the engine.

"What salary grade are you?" Clete asked.

"Four."

"If the Aquamira works, I'll give you a three-grade promotion effective Monday."

Rusty just shook his head and glanced out the window at the dun-colored tableau. Shatz probably forgot his promise before the warm breath of it grew chilly in the air-conditioned interior.

"If the Aquamira works, Mr. Shatz, you'll get book offers, you'll be given keys to cities and granted professor emeritus-ships. You'll be installed on prestigious boards of directors. You'll be an obscenely rich, rich man."

He expected the tweak about "obscenely rich" to goad a retaliatory response, but Shatz apparently had been thinking about something—the Aquamira, or how he would spend his money—and let it pass. After a while Shatz said, "There's easier ways to get rich. You could go to rural India, exchange a few of your paychecks for suitcases full of rupees and live like a king."

Rusty started to form his rebuttal, but a slight change in register, a relaxing of the shoulders? A softening of the lips? The, for once, immobile hands? of the man beside him told him to be silent.

"The same time my daughter was born," Shatz began almost inaudibly, "a neighbor's kid was born with congenital defects. He had stumps instead of hands. Didn't stop him. He was the high school's star athlete and never made anybody feel pity for him. He went on to get a football scholarship. My neighbors," he began enumerating on his fingers, "Jim Montrell, Margaret Brown and David Falcon got cancer. In the back of my mind, I'd thought it was a strange coincidence, but I brushed it away. It was too horrible to think about for very long. If anybody'd collected data, they'd have realized that the rate of diseases and deformities was above normal."

I realized, Rusty thought. *I realized*. Shatz's soliloquy seemed so out of character. Either the bullshit was getting very deep or Shatz was revealing a facet of himself that Lucinda had hinted at. Rusty stared ahead, locking his eyes on the double yellow line. If he looked at the man sitting beside him, speaking unguardedly, he would lose it, for sure and begin speaking unguardedly too. The ache near his heart stirred and told him to listen. Listen without judgment.

"We were all pretty stupid back then," Shatz went on, "which suited a lot of people. Our town was situated downstream from a paint manufacturer. More than once my wife insinuated that mental retardation was in my family's genetic makeup. I'm no Mensa candidate, I guarantee that, but I've had years to mull this over and I think the contaminated water did it. I'd do anything in the world to change that. It's not just the money I'm interested in." He placed his fist over his heart and tapped his chest. "It was."

Rusty slowed at the railroad crossing. The parallel rails, gleaming in the late afternoon sun would never meet, apart from the momentary illusion of perspective that merged them to a golden point in the distance. "You're going to change people's lives, Clete."

Shirt soaked, waistband sweat-stained, Henry returned from consulting with Shatz at his Pontiac window and told Rusty, "The gaffer asked how long. What do I tell him?"

"Tell him to—" Rusty crimped his words. "Tell him soon." Runnels of perspiration crept down his chest and back. Thoughts of Lucinda and annoying sweat bees swarmed his head. He'd been abrupt, cruel with his rebuff. But she'd picked a helluva time to invite him to dinner. Why get entangled with someone if you really don't want to? If you're not really serious? Going in halfhearted, now that would be cruel.

The lowering sun flashed on the lake. A solitary goldfinch dipped and rose, dipped and rose above a stand of cattails. His Grandma Beatrice used to call the small yellow and black creatures lettuce birds. More like banana birds or black-eyed Susan birds, Rusty thought. "Lettuce birds," she'd say, her voice creaky, "means we're gonna have a spell of drought." He would smile and watch the birds flit like yellow confetti over the blue-green alfalfa field. "Lettuce birds," she'd say another time, "means corn will be sweet." Different omens every time. Sometimes the winged harbingers were foreboding, sometimes promising. He'd figured Grandma was trying all angles to see which forecast bore out. When he became an adult, he'd noticed that goldfinches didn't travel in flocks like they used to. They flew in ones, sometimes twos. And later he'd understood the message: A lone goldfinch is its own prophecy.

He finished replacing the faulty seal with the new one. Everything looked set. "Let's rock and roll!" Rusty hollered. He signaled Henry to activate the system. This time the Aquamira's distinctive D minor chord hung in the air. The tubes held tight. The bladder filled.

Henry tested a beaker of water and looked pleased with the results, judging by the way his nose and mouth almost met. "Cheers!" Henry's Adam's apple worked in his throat as he held the beaker to his lips and drank Aquamira water. "Mmm. Mouthwatering." He cackled.

"Hold it. Let me see." Shatz blitzed Henry with questions and Henry, wiping his brow with his wet kerchief, interpreted the water test readout to his boss.

Suddenly, Shatz filled Henry's thermos with water from the Aquamira's spigot. He held it aloft over his head. His grip around the thermos was loose. It wobbled, drops splashed over the thermos rim. Henry raised his arms to ward off the dousing, but it didn't come. Shatz tipped the thermos, sluicing silvery water into his gaping mouth, drenching his white shirt and tie. Smiling maniacally he filled the thermos again, ran to Rusty and dumped water on his head. Rusty inclined his face and let the water stream over him. The water revived him. It felt and tasted wonderful. Then Shatz hurled the thermos into the cattails, dislodging their gossamer beards.

The idea popped into Rusty's mind as if spoken by someone else. Do it as an experiment. Attraction was a form of energy. Lucinda was attracted to him. He knew that from the first day when he'd applied for a job at Shatz Company. Resisting Lucinda was sapping too much energy. Creating a deficit. Neutralize it. Neutralize her surplus energy. A female lettuce bird swooped over the cattails. A male gold finch followed it. Hands clasped above his head, he shook his head like a wet dog. Diamonds flew into the thirsty air. He hollered "Eeeeeeeyah!"

Shatz joined in and they both shouted, "Eeeeeeeyah!" Their faces contorted with lunatic joy.

Henry's Nikon clicked.

CHAPTER 13

Rusty drove directly from Arrowhead Lake to the Fort Trust General Hospital. People milling about the hospital's over-landscaped front entrance paid no attention to the odd shape strapped down under tarpaulin on the truck bed. Henry took over the wheel and drove off.

When Rusty walked down the hospital corridor, he felt like a wild colt that had to be reined in, but not broken, no, not broken. Nurses smiled at him, apparently in response to the shit-eating grin on his face. He forced himself to stand still at the doorway. Thane Gabler, looking especially lucid and alert, turned off the TV. A lawnmower droned outside.

"I swear," the old man said, "I can feel my brain cells devolving, turning reptilian when I watch TV."

Rusty handed him a drink in a paper cup.

"I was hoping for Scotch," the old man said, eyeing the cup suspiciously.

"It is liquor."

"Aqua vitae."

"Aquamira water."

Thane's eyes filled and the water in his cup almost spilled over the lip of the cup. "The nurse won't come back for half an hour. Hows about a celebratory cigarette?"

The Marlboros lingered in his shirt pocket trying not to be smoked. "I left them at home." Rusty touched his cup to Thane's. "Congratulations. The field trial was a success." And he performed a jig while holding Thane's gnarled hand in his.

The stroke-slackened left side of Thane's face exaggerated his right-eyed wink. He asked technical questions and was obviously nettled with Rusty's unscientific answers, but visibly proud that the Aquamira had performed to spec. "We used to have a joke in the lab. 'Sure, it works in the field, but does it work in theory?' I first had hunches about altering matter by changing the vibration rates and modes when I was a junior at MIT."

"A junior," Rusty repeated as if in a trance. The old man had been working on the problem for half a century, if not longer. A rush of awe, veneration, and fear, the kind of fear people experience in the presence of the leviathans of civilization, flooded through him. He pulled a chair to the bedside and sat down.

"It kept me awake at night," Thane went on, "writing frantically. I strapped a small light on my head so I wouldn't disturb Ginny. She always woke up. We got married while we were both juniors. She's a trooper, I tell you. I did the early theoretical work on our kitchen table—a door on orange crates. We'd eat on the studio bed. It took over my life. She said I was a fiend. I'd yell at the kids if they disturbed my papers to do their homework at the table. I don't know if they've ever forgiven me for that."

"Now your efforts have paid off."

"Shatz will do well, I suppose."

"He didn't do squat. You should be rewarded."

"I'm decrepitating," Thane told him. "My share would only be fought over by my heirs. Better that those who made her come alive enjoy the rewards."

Lucinda's buttery bungalow reminded him of a fairytale cottage. White geraniums spilled out of window boxes hanging between redwood shutters decorated with shamrock cutouts. Late-summer informality thrived in the garden. Tall hollyhocks formed a natural backdrop for tiger lilies, red-hot pokers, ferns, portulacca, and impatiens. Sweet peas climbed a trellis attached to the stucco house. Being careful not to step on sedum pillows growing between the flagstones, Rusty approached the redwood door. He lifted the knocker and let it drop on its strike plate.

She was wearing a surprised expression and peach terrycloth sunsuit tied at the shoulders with thin, frayed straps. An ammonia odor swelled out from behind her. Cat piss.

"Your garden is a masterpiece," he said.

"I use wastewater to water it," she said defensively. "Get in, before the cat gets out."

"I would have called you back but I stopped to visit Thane, and cleaned up." And he knew if he put too much forethought into this meeting, or whatever it was, it would turn sour. He had, however, taken a quick shower and put on fresh underwear, T-shirt and jeans. The cool shower water had temporarily relieved the sting from spending the entire day in the sun.

"So 'no' means yes," Lucinda said, referring to his curt refusal to her invitation.

"No."

Lucinda laughed and padded barefooted to the kitchen. Feathers, geodes and anthropomorphic pieces of driftwood were arranged casually on the tables. A triptych of Georgia O'Keeffe prints hung on the one wall under soft track lighting. Giant pillows covered with African textiles were strewn about the sofa and sisal floor. Apart from the piles of magazines, books and papers stacked against the far wall behind the dining table, the room had an earthy feel to it. She returned with a mug of dark beer with a creamy head floating on it. "Here you go."

"Damn, that's good. It tastes like Watney's. What is it?"

She gave him an off-center grin.

"Really? Where'd you find it?"

"I'd noticed you drink European beers. I'm friends with the owner of an import beer warehouse. I ordered it special."

So, she had been planning on his coming here. . . for how long? He felt flattered and then ashamed for feeling flattered.

She sat on the floor facing him. "I designed the garden and selected all the plants myself. Some were already in the yard when I bought the place. The neat thing about a cottage garden is, you don't have to keep it neat. I've tried to create organized disorder. A lot of work up front but now that it's established I can enjoy it. Something blooms every season. Except winter. Hungry?"

"I don't expect you to feed me. I'll call for a pizza or Chinese take-out." A cat slithered next to him and he wondered if Lucinda's last question had been directed to him or the cat. He petted the black and white female. Her spine felt as ridged as an old steam radiator, shoulder blades peaked like a tin roof. The cat purred.

"We can whip up something, can't we Q-tip?" Lucinda asked the bony cat. "Boy, you're red, Rusty. What happened today?"

"Nothing much. I'll tell you later." Q-tip shed hairs on him. He carried his beer mug to the stacks. She had five years' of journals published by the International Association of Water Quality, a 1993 National Geographic Edition of "Water," newspaper clippings, brochures from the EPA, WHO, the American Water Works, the Water Environment Federation; scientific papers read at annual World Economic Development Congresses and Earth Summits, marketing information from water pollution control technology suppliers and clippings from radical magazines like "The Fifth Estate." He turned and asked, "What is all this?"

"My apocalypse file. I read everything about the water situation I can get my hands on, mostly because I'm concerned, partly to keep Clete informed. The odd part about it is, that," she pointed to the stacks, "isn't what convinced me how severe, how real the water crisis is. My dad did that."

"Yeah?"

"He's an avid angler. Was. He doesn't fish these days. He used to take my sisters and me on fishing trips starting when we were as young as four years old. When I was a teenager, I suddenly became too cool to go fishing with my dad. When I got older, I was too busy. He started complaining that the fish weren't as big as they used to be. I didn't believe him until he gave me a copy of 'Field and Stream.' It's in there somewhere," she gestured at the stacks and with a continuous fluid motion pushed a frayed strap back up on her pearly shoulder. "The article was an eye-opener. Fish were smaller. There was also an article about male fish developing female sexual organs in the UK. A similar study confirmed the same phenomenon occurring in North American waters."

"Yeah, I read about that. Did you find anything in all those papers about anyone working on a project similar to Thane's?"

"No." Lucinda cleared her throat. "What happened today? Clete dropped off this paperwork for me." She hooked her bare foot in the straps of her black tote bag leaning against a huge pillow and dragged it across the floor toward her. "He said this paperwork has to be done by Monday. I don't get overtime pay for this. I don't mind really. It's the least I can do to keep his head above water. Get it. Aquamira. Water."

Obliged to, he smiled.

"You're not going to tell me what happened today, are you?"

"No."

"No as in yes?"

"No." Q-tip dug her claws in his sunburned arm. "Shatz made it explicitly clear," Rusty said softly, "that Henry and I are not to, 'breathe a stinking word of the Aquamira's results to anyone.'"

Lucinda gathered her cat in her arms. "Even me?"

"He didn't mention names."

"He'll tell me. Shall we eat soon?" She nuzzled the cat's pale pink nose and bare-footed to the kitchen. Rusty dozed on the domestic sound-mattress of pans scraping on the burner and dishes and silverware clinking on the dining table. A dreamless, hot nap.

During dinner (toasted cheese sandwiches, green beans and pickled beets) she explained that the papers Clete Shatz had dropped off at her house were a rough draft of a grant the State government was thinking of spearheading, and that someone pretty high up had asked Shatz to give the draft a once-over and add comments and suggestions. Shatz had requested Lucinda to write the Aquamira's specs between the lines and in the margins as ideas for government grant-writers to play with. "Anyhow," Lucinda said, carrying their dirty plates to the kitchen, "I'm relieved you'll help with this technical paperwork. I should have asked, did you want more to eat?"

"No, thanks." He went to her bathroom. The fixture that sat where one normally finds a commode contained no water. He stood in the doorway to the kitchen. "Uh . . ."

"Oh. I'll give you a demonstration."

He panicked. He didn't want to observe her peeing. "I'll figure it out."

"Have you seen one of these before?"

"Huh-uh. I've never seen a," he read the label on the strange fixture, "'Dry-Doo' before."

"After you're done your waste goes into the decomposition tank. Throw in a spoonful of this organic compound. This gets mixed with the chemicals in the tank. In about six months, I'll scatter your biofertilizer on my impatiens."

He chuckled.

"They've been using similar systems in Mexico City for thirty years. The lakes there were poisoned with human waste. The lakes are still contaminated but less so thanks to the Dry-Doo. A woman designed it. Our government should make them mandatory."

"Yeah, starting in government washrooms."

After using the Dry-Doo he said, "I'll take a look at those grant papers now." The terminology, design parameters and specs looked familiar. He flipped through the rest of the pages. Delete the government-ese and it was obvious: Clete Shatz was trying to rig a grant so Shatz Co. would win. Someone in the government would definitely recognize the attempted fraud and stop Shatz from hiding his own Easter eggs. Maybe it was a joke. No. Shatz wasn't a joker. He was a tactician. A manipulator. Rusty had a strong desire to tear the papers up into tiny bits and throw them in the Dry-Doo tank.

"Did Shatz ever say anything to you about that night we went to the lab and set off the alarms?" Rusty asked her.

"No-ooh." She picked at a stapled corner of the grant papers, making a clicking sound with her fingernail.

After two hours of transcribing detailed performance criteria onto the draft grant, as Rusty explained them to her, Lucinda said, "Thank you, thank you, thank you."

He'd considered giving her false information, but was afraid she'd take the hit for it. "We're not done," Rusty told her.

"I'm too beat to do anymore. Aren't you?" She crossed her eyes.

"Let me borrow these papers. I'll complete Part C this weekend. I can't remember the specs for it, right now."

"No problem. I'll call Henry. He'll know."

"No, don't bother him!" Too late. She was at the kitchen phone, punching in a number.

"Hi, Moira. It's Lucinda…Is Henry there?…Rusty, uh, Wade and I have a question about a work project…What?…Oh, uh, maybe the Giant store has leeks…That's right…OK. Uh, no. I'll ask Henry on Monday…No. No message. Bye."

"I'll take the papers with me," he said as casually as possible. She shook her head.

"Don't worry. I'll slip them in your mailbox sometime Sunday." *After I photocopy them.*

"You don't need to take the whole thing. Just take Part C."

"I need to read A and B for the sequence so I can fit in what goes in Part C."

"I have your word you'll give it all back Sunday?"

"What have I done that you don't trust me?"

She squashed a crumb on the table. "I have to think about it. Let me think."

"Yes. Think. Think about what you're doing."

Q-tip jumped on the papers and washed herself. "I named her Q-tip because of the white marking on her nose. I've had her since I was sixteen. She's an old lady, for a cat: fourteen years old. You're not too old for me, you know, Rusty." It sounded like a reprimand.

"Too old for you for what?" Maybe she'd back off if he made her say it.

She disappeared into a room at the back of her house.

The lights dimmed. Rusty turned around and felt himself respond to the figure in front of him. Although the gown covered more of her body than the terry sunsuit had, it was cut in a way that hugged her figure. Slashes in the fabric revealed keyholes of flesh that one didn't normally think erotic.

A chasm of silence yawned between them. He'd underestimated the escalation of her intent. The surplus/deficit energy experiment was spiraling out of control. She'd out-flanked him. He'd dreamed of floating in tandem with her, on inner-tubes on a languid river, dipping his toes in the silky water, feeling his essential juices undulate sympathetically with the movement of the underwater grasses, until the sun wheeled to its zenith baking his skin sensitive. They'd slide into the river for relief. Hot skins sizzling on contact with coolness. But now, in that elusive here and now, he wanted to strip on shore, their clothes flying off their limbs like flags, and cannonball into the current, stirring up mud.

"I've stayed too long." He gathered the grant papers. "I'll drop these off Sunday."

"Do you know how much guts it took for me to do this?" She waved her hand in front of her, indicating the clothes she'd changed into. "I never do stuff like this. This is from a schlocky B movie. I'm so embarrassed."

He laid the papers on the table and walked to her. He placed his hands on her upper arms in a comradely manner. Her eyes reflected light from somewhere. "You didn't have to do this," he said. "I really appreciate it."

"You 'really appreciate it'? Now I'm intensely embarrassed." Peeved, she plopped down onto a big purple cushion on the floor. "I own a mirror. I know I'm not beautiful. My boobs are too small. My skin is too white. My hair is frizzy. I'm skinny."

"None of that has anything to do with beauty. Beauty is what two people allow to happen."

"That's a load of biofertilizer."

He re-collected the grant papers.

"Can we? Allow it?" She looked at the grant papers in his hand.

"That's how you see it? Quid pro quo? I do these papers for you and you—"

"What? No! What's wrong with you?" She followed him to the door.

"I didn't ask you for anything. I'm not expecting any favors, any payment." Although whispered, his words flattened the cat's ears.

"I apologize for my effrontery. I thought we had some chemistry, some sparks going between us. I don't want to force myself on you. It felt natural to me."

"Natural to me means we both feel the same way." He held the papers in front of what betrayed his words.

"You're afraid to allow beauty to happen. Rusty." She reached for the papers.

He held them tight in both hands. "Well," he said, and let it dwindle off, offering her a chance to say something else to him, something that would ease her embarrassment and his turmoil. But she shrewdly remained silent.

He was a man with the normal desires and urges men get. He hadn't remained celibate during the past seven years. Sure, he slept with women, the kind of women who seemed cut out to provide relief, the kind of women you knew weren't going to suggest you meet the parents, the kind of women who never asked what was on your mind, the kind of women who never commented on your moods. He knew where to find those women. And he knew Lucinda was not of that breed. He owed her some sort of explanation. "I could love you," he said. "That's why I can't."

"You are one hurtin' cowboy," she said sadly.

Knowing she was right, but not knowing how to cope, he screwed on his black hat, clamped the papers under his arm and opened the front door. Q-tip escaped between his legs and into the red-hot pokers.

CHAPTER 14

On Saturday morning, Clete Shatz was sprawled in his favorite chair in the den with a mug of black coffee steaming on the armrest. Halloween was a month away, even so, last night hooligans had soaped the French doors leading from the den to the patio. *Probably the kids from next door,* he thought. He'd heard their footsteps and laughter, but hadn't bothered to chase them away. Alita could clean the glass doors. Hell, they were already conveniently soaped for her.

Shatz Company was going to go bankrupt in two months, just as Fred Ingle had predicted last November. Naturally, Ingle had changed his tune when Clete shared his grand plan with the head of accounting. Since then Ingle had forgotten how to mold his features in that hangdog expression he'd perfected at Columbia or Wharton or wherever the hell he'd picked up his sheepskin. A quaint grin lifted the lines around his mouth, and he had said, "The number one rule of government spending is why be thrifty when you can be spendthrifty?"

The TV in the Victorian bar mumbled to itself. When the peacock logo appeared on the screen, Clete turned the volume up. A sky-camera beamed the image of thousands of protesters thronging the grassy area between the Smithsonian museums. The multitude resembled colorful pebbles paving the mall. Another camera showed a newscaster reporting live from D.C. standing in front of the oft-televised iron gates at 1600 Pennsylvania Avenue. He announced, "The chairman of the National Water Remediation Grant allocation committee said a winner will be announced October sixth. The grant will be awarded to the company which designs and builds a water remediation system meeting strict specifications. Alice Thistlewaite has more. Alice?"

The camera cut to a pasty-skinned, fervent woman standing among a crowd of people. The World Trade Center at Baltimore's Inner Harbor loomed behind the reporter and the crowd. "Thanks, Bret. Yes, excitement is high here at the International Association of Water Quality convention. I have IAWC representative Professor Murray Jenks here to comment on the significance of the grant. Murray, what does this grant mean to Americans?"

"We, uh, are pleased to see a, a, a joint effort of this magnitude to advance the science and technology of the collection and treatment of water and wastewater."

"How does this grant differ from previous water remediation grants?"

"Never before have so many diverse groups—EPA, IAWC, Sierra Club, the Sea Shepherd, Earth First and others—contributed funds toward one water remediation project. The specifications are naively optimistic, in my opinion. I think—"

"Thank you, Professor Jenks. Bret, our sources tell us the dollar amount is unprecedented, not only for water remediation grants, but for grants of any kind in North America."

"How much is it?" Clete shouted at the TV. "How much?"

The reporter didn't answer the question that caused Clete to slosh hot coffee on his thigh. He brushed his thigh absently, not feeling the heat soak his slacks. He turned the volume up another notch.

The reporter went on, "Groups who are normally at odds with one another agree the grant program is a giant step in the right direction. Bret."

Bret appeared on screen, unaware the camera was rolling. "I'm on? Hello. Maria Salvador chairperson of Water Now is on standby via satellite link in Los Angeles. Maria, Maria can you hear me?"

"*Si.*"

"What is Water Now's reaction to the grant?" People crowding behind her thrust fists at viewers in TV land.

"We're angry. We were not invited to participate on the allocation committee. We were not consulted. Our organization is 3,000,000-members strong, sixty-three percent are registered voters. This is another indication in a long line of halfhearted attempts. The grant is too little too late. The Government of the United States has had its head up its—." A high pitched whistle bleeped her words. "Rachel Carson, God rest her soul, is spinning in her grave. She told us decades ago about the problem. We have documentation proving the government withheld the seriousness of the water crisis from the American public for many years."

The camera zoomed in on Bret in D.C. "Regardless of politics and sour grapes, October sixth will be a momentous day in American history."

Too unstrung to drink his morning coffee, Clete turned off the TV. October sixth was going to be a momentous day in his life.

The next week crept by at a glacial pace. On October fifth, Clete watched the reflection in the rearview mirror of the automatic garage door opening its jaws. He tilted the mirror forward and unnoosed his tie. He'd told Alita to throw the gaudy thing away, but she'd laid it out this morning and helped him dress, picked lint off his pants, smoothed his shoulder pads and made the quick grope. The novelty tie of silk-screened money from different countries had been Darla's idea of a gag gift. A striped tie, a dry-cleaned shirt and suit hung on the back of the door in his private restroom at work. He'd put that tie on before meeting Senator Krumrine at the Apex Club. Krumrine had left a message to meet him. Early. Krumrine never left messages.

He guided the Pontiac up his S-curved driveway slithering between a lawn encrusted with frost, and past the For Sale sign the realtor had plunked next to the Japanese maple. He pulled out of the Oak Heights housing development and immediately had to stop behind a school bus. Kids he didn't know wearing baggy bright parkas and fluorescent sneakers, swaggered onto the yellow bus. Part of him was sure Krumrine had news about the grant. Another part cautioned him, *Don't get your hopes up too high.*

The bus gathered power and slowly pulled away. He turned the heat down and the radio up, trying to find the station that carried world business news, but some grease monkey had reprogrammed his tuner for fragsounds or whatever Alita called that nerve-shredding racket. He turned the heat up a notch and hoped the bus would get off the road real soon. It stopped. He nudged his front bumper up tight.

Everything hovered in a tight holding pattern. Everything. He'd given Henry and Wade a battery of tests to run the Aquamira through to stall for time, kept them busy, but non-productive. Henry was jolly glad for assignments he could handle. Wade, well, Clete had him where he wanted him for now. The lab was off-limits to everyone but himself, Henry Healy, Wade and Lucinda. He needed to time the Aquamira's unveiling perfectly, so it looked as though the system were built after he'd won the grant, not before. Clete hoped Krumrine had news about the grant, then he'd assess his position, proceed as planned or drop back. But if he were forced to wait too long, darling Darla was going to ram their divorce through, demand her half of their marital assets and sell Shatz Company. Little did she know: by that time Shatz Company would be sinking in a sea of red. Without his company, he'd be unable to proceed with his plan. And no fucking way was he going to bring Darla in on his scheme. She was more ruthless than he was. He didn't trust her. Especially not now with her on the warpath. Twin boys at the back of the bus flipped two birds. Clete returned the salute with a vigorous thrust as he wheeled onto the bypass.

He re-adjusted the rearview mirror and engaged the cruise control. And disengaged. Too much traffic on the bypass. The car phone rang.

"Shatz here."

"Listen. My lawyer says your lawyer keeps postponing their meetings." Darla was using her prosecuting attorney's tone on him.

"Don't even entertain the notion of reconciliation. I want to be free and clear of this by Christmas. This has been dragging on for almost a year, Clete. These dilatory tactics only serve to antagonize me. I highly suggest you avoid antagonizing me."

He thought he'd done a superior job of that already. A black cat flashed from the edge of a fallow field and under the car. He felt an insubstantial bump.

"Ah, jeez!" He'd hit a skunk. "Why Christmas? Are you planning a winter wedding?"

"The best gift I will have ever given myself."

"Where are you calling from?" He sure as hell hoped she wasn't on her way home. He enjoyed having the house to himself. And Alita.

"I'm in my office. Tell your lawyer to meet my lawyer, or I'll—" She changed to a satiny voice. "I'll not tell you what I'll do." Her lead crystal laugh always irritated him. Her tough guy talk. Her big lawyer words. The same take-no-prisoners thinking that had attracted him to Darla also repelled him. She was incapable of flipping the toggle switch from big guns female lawyer to female. All decisions were brisk, rational as they usually were for him, but protected by her portcullis of reason, he became more exploratory, trying out other ways of thinking on the home front because he knew it would be safe. He could count on Darla to maintain order. Perhaps that's what drove her away. He made her enforce the rules and order while he played the softy.

"Darla, you can threaten me all you want but you don't scare me. Do you want to buy Shatz Co?"

"No! I have no interest in running that dying dog. But I will if I have to to get my half. I'll suck out the assets and sell the carcass to the highest bidder. Two companies are already sounding me out for the asking price."

"Bear with me and you won't have to worry about it."

"And pigs'll fly."

"If things swing my way, I'll buy out your half and give you a hefty—" A truck stopped suddenly in front him. He hit the brakes and cut the wheel hard.

"A hefty divorce settlement? You bet you will!"

"I'm in a hurry. I don't care to discuss this now."

"I talked to Janice." Her voice became spherical and fluffy to talk about their daughter. "I didn't tell her anything about us yet. I don't know."

He let her twist.

"I don't know if she'll understand," Darla continued. "She'll know something's wrong when she has to visit us in two separate cities." A long pause. "I'm going to pick her up now. We're having our own private 'Take your daughter to work day.'"

Her gooey maternal tones, her cuddly concern for their daughter taunted him, and he knew somehow she'd make him pay for what he was going to say next.

"Let me remind the jury," he said, palming his hairline in the rearview mirror, gathering reassurance, "that it was Mrs. Darla Shatz who insisted Janice be placed in a home. It was Mrs. Darla Shatz who insisted Janice get an abortion." He'd never uttered that word in the context of a conversation about his daughter before. "It was Mrs. Darla Shatz who filed for divorce."

"We've been through this," Darla said tiredly. "Statute of limitations has passed. But if it pleases the court, may I remind the jury that those decisions were made in her best interests."

"We'll talk when I pick Janice up at your office tonight." He disconnected and slowed to turn on to Apex Club Road. A lawn tractor was sucking up chestnut tree leaves and prickly hulls. Clete had held his daughter's hand while life was vacuumed from her uncomprehending womb. The dashboard clock showed he had a few minutes to spare before his meeting with Krumrine. He parked next to Krumrine's car on the back lot.

"Goddamn!" On automatic pilot, he'd driven to the Apex clubhouse instead of his office where he was going to change his tie. No time now. A tie with currency printed on it was better than no tie. He blamed Darla's phone call for this lapse.

His car phone trilled. "Shatz here!"

"Clete. It's me. I've been called on an emergency trip to Connecticut. A defendant with deep pockets. I have to go."

"So? Go, Darla."

"You'll take Janice to work."

"What? No. I'll pick her up at your office after work."

"I won't *be* in my office. I'm on my way to the airport now. Take her to Shatz Company for her take your daughter to work day." Your daughter, not our daughter.

"Not today, Darly. Not today." He punched the raucous radio music off. He didn't have time for this shit. Krumrine was expecting him. Janice's home was on the east side of town and he couldn't bring her to the Apex Club. It wouldn't fly.

"I already told her you're coming to pick her up."

"Jesus, Darla!"

"She's really looking forward to it, Clete."

"Goddamn. Why couldn't you pick another day?"

"Clete."

"I'm not doing this for you, Darla. I'm doing it for our daughter."

Tires squealed when he backed out of the lot and sped toward the home where his daughter lived. The rising sun glared, forcing him to slow down. He could smell himself sweating on his shirt. At the least, he'd be thirty minutes late for his meeting with Krumrine.

He brushed a wisp of hair off his daughter's forehead and assessed her appearance the way he thought a stranger, a man, might. She was beautiful like her mom, and well dressed. Darla spent a wad on Janice's wardrobe. It wasn't until she started talking or moving that you knew something was different. Words seemed to fall reluctantly out of her slack mouth. She was blessed with none of the physical élan or wit her mother possessed. *If Krumrine says one crude thing, I'll deck him.* The sound of the door lock releasing pulled him up straight. He adjusted his garish tie in the foyer mirror and entered the clubhouse lounge, pulling Janice by the hand behind him.

"Janice. This won't take long. I want you to sit quietly and wait till I'm finished talking. Kapish?"

"Kapish."

"Sit here, honey." He handed her a "Newsweek" magazine.

"Shatz, you're late." Krumrine's expression was illegible, obscured in oleaginous shadows.

"This is my daughter." It dawned on him that he'd neglected to teach her rudimentary social skills such as how to conduct oneself during introductions.

"Well, I'd keep my daughter a secret too if she was a looker like you. I'm Senator Krumrine and you are?"

"Janice Shach-eh." She never could enunciate their last name properly. Clete was relieved, though, to see Janice hold out her right hand to let Krumrine shake it. He watched Krumrine's eyes linger on her.

"All right, all right." Clete broke them apart. "Enough glad handing. She doesn't vote. Against her religion." He ordered orange juice for Janice and sat to the left of Krumrine who reigned at his usual position on the sofa. The ornamental birch logs in the marble fireplace had been replaced with perfect gas flames. The heat toasted Clete.

"The governor and I have a press conference tomorrow morning," Krumrine finally said. He turned toward Clete and studied him at length, as if searching for a hairline crack.

Clete's ear itched. His tie was too tight. His socks accordioned. His shirt stunk. He willed himself not to move, not to blink too frequently. He waited, watching the groundskeeper shroud the patio barbecue with canvas.

"The rival contending companies will no doubt scream of racketeering. A fix. With your cash flow hemorrhages, they'll say you couldn't have afforded to retool your company from a materiel recycling systems manufacturer to a state-of-the-art water recycling and purification research and development concern. Not with your run-of-the-mill staff."

The only people who voted for Senator Krumrine are the suckers who'd never met him, Clete thought. He envisioned kicking the bastard in his pitted face. Get to the point. Did Shatz Company win the multi-million dollar grant or not?

"Phew!" Scott Billet rushed into the lounge. "There must be a skunk on the property." He stopped short when he saw Janice paging through a magazine. "A lady!"

"Billet! Come over hear and watch Shatz shit his pants," Krumrine said.

Billet glanced at Janice once more and then frowned at Krumrine. He sat on the edge of the chair opposite of Clete and Krumrine, "Did you tell him?"

"I'm prepared to state with utmost confidence and sincerity that it's ludicrous to think Shatz Company could have pulled a fiddle. The other companies' grant applications were way off the beam. Their cost estimates were from la-la land and their science was riddled with flaws." Krumrine could no longer contain his glee. He broke into a smile and said, "You won."

Shatz ran his finger under his collar and thrust his chin out. It fucking worked! It fucking worked! The grant panel was handing over the key to the vault for money to fund a project he'd already completed. A cake walk from now on. A gimme. Winter rules. He'd buy Darla out and still have millions left to play with. Calmly he told the senator, "Everybody wins. Not just me."

Senator Krumrine stood, approached Clete with an extended hand. It felt damp. Spongy. Krumrine knelt in a suppliant yet threatening position. Reflected gas flames licked his irises. "Between you and I," Krumrine whispered too loudly, "I think something smells rotten in Fort Trust." He glanced at Janice picking at upholstery tacks on the leather chair.

Clete prepared himself to be drawn and quartered. Cold fear climbed his vertebrae.

Krumrine stood, tapped Billet's shoulder and said, "I'll be back. Shatz and I have to talk dirty."

They stood on the other side of the patio fence and surveyed the fare way and the mountains which the sun, a wen hanging on the face of the sky, had drained of color. Neither man looked at the other. Except for the skunk stink, they could have been anywhere—a Rotary outing, a ribbon cutting ceremony, a funeral.

"What the hell you trying to do, talking like that in front of Billet?" Clete asked.

"I want forty percent. That's not an offer. It's what I'll get or I'll blow down your house of cards."

"No you won't. You're already having wet dreams about schmoozing with the president, being the country's savior. We agreed you'd get twenty-five percent. That was the deal."

"Forty-five. Keep at it, I'll take it all. I can."

"Forty and—"

"Fifty," Krumrine said firmly.

"Forty-five and you do not tell the press the identity of the winning company. I, we can't afford the risk of industrial spies infiltrating my company and duplicating our work. If that happens, our future profits will be decreased."

"I get fifty percent of the grant monies. You get anonymity. Plus I get twenty percent of all related pre-tax income from production, licensing agreements and spin-off projects in perpetuity."

Clete's heartburn heated up beneath the currencies of the world. He couldn't afford many more deals like this. Anybody else in on it would have to accept percents of percents. He lifted his hand out of his pocket to shake Krumrine's rising hand.

Krumrine ignored Clete's offered hand and clapped his handkerchief to his face. "That piss kitty is nearby."

Clete jammed his hand in his pocket and jingled spare change. Soon he'd be so rich he wouldn't have to carry any money at all. Janice came to the door with a questioning look on her face.

"Come on, honey! We have work to do at daddy's office."

"Did your daughter buy you that tie?" Krumrine asked. "It's quite the tie."

"It is something, isn't it." Clete held on tightly to his daughter's hand. For the moment her trusting grip was the only force keeping him from soaring off the planet.

CHAPTER 15

Work was at a virtual standstill lately so Rusty didn't feel guilty catching a few Zs. Like a cat stretching after a nap, he sat up and, from among PVC pipes stored on a high shelf, he peered down at the lab. Henry was pouring tea down his gullet like illegal hooch. Motes of Henry's daily tea break phone conversation with his wife Moira caught light in the beams of Rusty's indifferent awareness or had he dreamed the conversation? "You alright, love?…the doctor say, then?…Sod the treatment cost…Give it a go…and Yorkshire pudding…Cheerio, duck."

The phone on the lab desk rang. For real. Henry's voice hardened, "Right. I'm on my way." He returned five minutes later. "Wade! Get your bleedin' arse over here!"

Rusty jumped down from the shelf and landed inches from Henry's Brogans.

"Bloody hell!" Henry dragged both hands through his feathery hair.

"Don't get your knickers in a twist," Rusty said, borrowing Henry's colloquialism.

"It's Shatz." Henry's droopy eyes darted from the Aquamira to Rusty and then battered against the translucent windows. While under acute pressure to complete the Aquamira, Henry had been, for the most part, a study in passive resistance. Now he was chomping at the bit. Maybe Shatz, encouraged by the Aquamira's successful field trial at Arrowhead Lake had tightened the specs, upped the gallons-per-minute flow requirements.

Rusty prompted his supervisor: "It's Shatz ."

Henry yanked his tie, popping a shirt button. They watched

it bounce on the concrete floor and settle in a miniature pyramid of dust and stainless steel filings under the Aquamira prototype. "Never mind that," Henry said, "we're to mothball the project. The gaffer assigned you to knock it down and store it in the back warehouse. Time to pull up stumps, old chap."

"Why?"

"Ours is not to question why...." Henry scrubbed his hands over his face and went out the back door.

Rusty punched the Aquamira, denting part of the frame that contained the bladder. Pain concentrated his thoughts. *One, shelf. Two, stool. Three, telephone. Four, ashtray. Five, pencil.* He counted objects to force himself to stay in the here and now, stay away from thoughts about wasting so many months on the project. Damn Shatz for lacking executive foresight. Damn it. Dragging Thane Gabler into this. Damn this false pride. If not for his persistence, the Aquamira would still be dreams pressed between Thane Gabler's lab books. *Six, thermos. Seven, Aquamira. Detach,* he counseled himself. *Detach from results. Avoid disappointment.*

The project had been a priority for a long time before Rusty was hired. And Shatz had approved overtime, crunchtime, checking twice a day on progress, asking redundant questions he should have known the answers to from reading Henry's lab reports. He'd been obsessed with completing the Aquamira. He'd breathed fire down their necks, and today, according to Henry, he'd ordered them to disassemble the system.

What changed? Why did Shatz want them to mothball the Aquamira? Potable water was a human requirement, a valuable commodity. Whoever unveiled the Aquamira was guaranteed herohood in his or her own lifetime. A Pasteur, a Salk, a Curie. *How,* he wondered, *did Shatz's order to abort tie in with the grant he was trying to force-fit onto the Aquamira?* Rusty guessed that Shatz's hoax to collect grant money illegally must have failed. Good. That meant Shatz couldn't afford to convert the material recycling production line on the other side of the lab wall into an Aquamira assembly plant. Bad.

He gripped a socket wrench and fitted it onto a bolt on the Aquamira. With a sharp twist, he began dismantling the water recycling and purifying system. He felt as if he were tearing off his own limbs. His elastic conscience couldn't stretch far enough to encompass any reasons, no matter how eloquently stated, for withholding purified water from the world.

The back door banged shut on a draft of autumnal air. Henry entered holding the kind of blue envelope Shatz Company used for high priority deliveries. His tie was snug against his wattles. "Don't be bothered with dismantling it now," cigarette bobbing, "Shatz says you're to deliver this packet to EnviroZone. He reckoned we'd need to get out to cool off, as it were."

"I don't have a car. Is the company van available?" Shatz's concern for their mental states was considerate and suspect.

"I'm to give you a lift." Henry patted his pockets for another cigarette and found a flattened pack on the workbench. He stroked the white cylinder, restoring its carcinogenic roundness and lit it with the one burning in his lipless mouth. "Face it, old chap, we're dog's bodies. From chief engineer to chauffeur in one swell foop." His laughter was artificial. He smacked Rusty in the chest with the blue packet emblazoned with Shatz Company's green and white triangle logo. "Proprietary" was stamped in two-inch letters on both sides of the packet. "I don't know what's to become of you."

"I guess that makes me mail boy." He smiled, knowing what was to become of him. He'd accumulated plenty of walking money over the past year. He was going to ask Mrs. DiMartino to refund his deposit.

Henry opened his satchel and rooted around the various sections and pockets. "Here, an illustration for when you write your memoirs."

It was the photograph Henry had snapped of a jubilant, wild-eyed Clete Shatz cavorting in the rivulet of water poured from Henry's thermos the day they'd tested the Aquamira at Arrowhead Lake. In the background, Rusty stood, hands raised overhead like a champion boxer. He slipped the dated photo into his coverall breast pocket.

"Bollocks!" Henry stomped the accelerator pedal of his compact car. "My heart was in that project. What am I to do? The worst part is, the gaffer forbid me to apply for patents." He pronounced it pay-tents.

"Let it go," Rusty advised, letting go of the desire to reacquaint Henry Healy with facts: Thane Gabler was the engineer who deserved patents and if it hadn't been for Rusty's tenacity, the Aquamira would not be. He let Henry blather on as he watched terrain sail past the window. Factories were cleverly camouflaged behind low hills. Stands of defoliated locusts and silver maples and clumps of indigenous sumac bushes growing along the berm gave shallow credence to the oxymoron term industrial park. They drove past a housing development. Oak Heights the counterfeit rustic sign announced. Elegant Executive Housing for Sale. Water US Gov't Approved.

Henry jerked his car through an intersection, muttering something about "roundabouts like in England," turned off the main road and drove down a lane with flat-roofed, charmless buildings bunkered on either side.

Maybe Shatz sold the Aquamira production rights to another company. Maybe another company won the grant and Shatz was throwing in his towel. That meant Shatz Company was going to go under for sure. Maybe Lucinda knew what was going on.

"I think we're driving in circles," Henry said. "We've passed that warehouse twice."

Mouse, the self-described futurist, had once told Rusty that too many unscrupulous people and organizations profited from the water crisis for anyone to seriously want to attack the problem. All show. No go. At the time, Rusty had thought that was too scandalous to believe. He cracked his window. Cigarette smog streamed out. The here and now sucked.

"EnviroZone is in this cul-de-sac." Henry squashed a butt in the overflowing ashtray and slowed down, squinting at signs on the buildings. He parked in front of the EnviroZone building. Henry was winding down, having the last word with himself. "It's Shatz's company. He can do what he bloody well pleases. Yes, sir, yes, sir, three bags full. Shall we apply for jobs at EnviroZone?"

"Maybe."

"They're expecting the delivery. Stand at the front door and someone will fetch the package from you."

Rusty waited at the door beside the EnviroZone sign. Buzzards circled lazily under cirrus clouds. Grandma Beatrice used to tell him, with a bright, creaky voice, "Buzzards gliding overhead means something died." He'd figured out later that the birds coasted on thermals, waiting for something to die. A rabbit darts into oncoming headlights. A groundhog licks salt off the centerline. A fox gets caught in a trap. Buzzards rip, peck, and bury heads into viscera. Nature abhors sentimentality. Grandma was right about some things, though. She'd said, "If you see a great blue heron in the fall, it means you'll always be on the move." He was sure a heron wasn't far from view.

An EnviroZone woman opened the door. "I get so stressed out in there." She hesitated taking the packet from Rusty. He felt Henry watching him from the car. He relaxed his eyes to soft focus, listened. At the moment the woman accepted the packet from him, Henry's Nikon shutter clicked three times. "Back to the mushroom cave for me," she said, evoking the joke about being kept in the dark and fed shit.

In the car Rusty asked, "What's in your satchel? Your camera?"

"No." Henry laughed self-deprecatingly. "Oi got me thermos, pork pies and me fags."

Wind teased out clouds where buzzards had coasted seconds ago.

Moist aromas from the cafeteria mingled with the hospital's antiseptic odors. Thane Gabler's bed was cranked up from its normally flat shape into three segments like a lawn chair. This sign of improving heath lifted Rusty's low spirits. The roommate was zipping through the TV channels. All 108 of them.

"He flashes through the stations so fast, I get see-sick," Thane joked.

Rusty smiled and set the handcrafted wren house, a miniature white Georgian-style home, on the bedside table.

"Maybe Ginny will soften up when I tell her you made it," Thane said.

"Let's hope so. I made it months ago before she despised me, back when she merely disliked me."

"He has the attention span of a gnat," Thane said, referring to his roommate.

"Whoa!" Rusty shouted. "Flip back!" The roommate either didn't hear or didn't understand what Rusty said. "Go back to the news. Flip back, man."

A newscaster stood in the midst of a mob in front of the iron gate at the White House. The Washington correspondent said, "Describing the protesters as irate is an understatement. The mood is incendiary. Sir, sir! What group do you represent?" He held a mike in the face a man carrying a sign that said, "The conspiracy stops here!" Others carried signs with the same message, as if they'd been mass-produced in a factory.

"I don't represent nobody. They say someone's getting all that money to make a water machine, but now they won't tell us who it is. How do we know it's true? I wouldn't put it past politicians to pocket the money themselves."

"That seems to be the consensus among the protesters," the reporter said. "Mbotu Akanzi, the White House press secretary said although the Executive Office is not involved with the grant, Madam President supports the grant allocation committee's decision to withhold the name of the winner, but her press release doesn't explain why the secrecy is necessary. A source in the Department of Defense agreed to talk to us only if we didn't reveal his name. He said an invention of this much importance to America and indeed to the world could become an issue of national security if it fell into the wrong hands. He wouldn't elaborate. Back to you, Alice."

"Thanks, Bret. In a related development an attorney representing the unsuccessful applicants for the grant are suing the National Water Remediation grant allocation committee. The attorney declined to comment on what grounds her clients are filing the suit. The governor of Pennsylvania who is credited with spearheading the grant also mentioned security as the reason for the grant panel's silence. It was less than two years ago when three Libyan scientists stole secrets from Aquarius, a California-based water remediation company and that was on the heels of the astounding story of a ring of thieves transporting water stolen from Canadian reservoirs. So secrecy is understandable. Among those plausible theories for secrecy, here's another view. This was taped earlier today in Salt Lake City at a meeting of a group calling themselves God's Warriors."

Rusty wanted to scream, to holler. He didn't know what was happening exactly, but his instincts told him it was not good. Thane sensed corruption too, for his face was drawn and his white eyebrows pulled down to a scowl.

A picture of a man in a hooded black robe, pacing from one end of a stage in a sports arena to the other, flashed on screen. He was speaking to 500,000 avid listeners. The screen split to multiple images. His ranting hologram was being broadcast live to packed stadiums across the nation. "Satan is among us, brothers and sisters. He wraps the American flag around him. He speaks with forked tongue: 'I must protect you. I will give you pure drinking water.' Yet what does the devil do? Lucifer hordes water, the pure water the Lord God created for us to bathe our tired bodies, for us to drink after a hard day's work, for us to baptize all God-fearing souls in. I promise you, we are God's Warriors. God is my refuge and my fortress. We shall arm ourselves for the righteous battle against evil."

Thane batted his ear. "Turn that crack-pot off. If Shatz Company had won, you'd know, I suppose."

"Yeah. Clete would have gone ape shit."

Clete looked up from buffing his fingernails. Lucinda had entered his office without rapping on the door. She handed him a piece of paper with the great seal of The United States of America hologram in the top left corner. This was one document he didn't need her to read for him. The corners of the room disintegrated. A film of water blurred his vision. His hands tingled. A loud buzz extinguished all thought except one: I'm having a heart attack.

Holding the check tightly with both hands, he mustered a semblance of composure and said, "Thanks. Go."

He mentally deducted Krumrine's lump, and he earmarked Lucinda's, Henry's, Funk's and Ingle's cuts. He'd call their bribes performance bonuses. He'd open an offshore account with the remainder of the check. No yachts, no summer houses in Tuscany, no gold pinkie rings, nor private jets for him. Not yet. Perhaps he'd spring for a set of titanium clubs. That'd be it. Whispered wealth, he hoped, wouldn't raise suspicions.

The phone rang. He jumped and knocked the receiver out of the cradle before getting it to his ear.

"Shatz Company. Shatz here."

"Call your bitch off!"

"What are you talking about, Senator?"

"Your wife represents the grant applicant losers. She's filing for disclosure of the grant winner and all related documents under the Freedom of Information Act."

Rusty carried two grocery bags to the small kitchen. He tried to avoid stepping on the cat weaving between his boots, rubbing her scent on his jeans. He laid the ingredients for pizza out on the counter and placed another bag in the corner of the living room next to a candle stand. For Christmas Lucinda had hung real holly sprigs on the lampshades and the picture frames. Pinecones filled a red clay bowl on the dining table. He shucked his duffel coat.

"Wow. You look great," Rusty said. Lucinda had looked striking at work today too in a blue suit that nipped in at her narrow waist and emphasized her petite curves.

"Thanks. I never thought I'd hear you say that. To me."

Why do women say shit like that? Well, probably because the last time he'd visited her they'd parted with acrimony, that's why. She could have given him a royally tough time the other day when he'd happened to see her in the company parking lot, but she'd only mentioned that Q-tip returned four days after Rusty had let the old cat escape. Then she had invited him over. Why should two people who enjoy each other's company have such a difficult time together? They were adults. They could do this. "No big deal," she'd said. He agreed, "Yeah, no big deal."

"I feel so free and comfortable wearing these. Look." She turned up the hem of her beige wool pants, showing him the silky lining. She or someone with fine taste had selected a necklace of freshwater pearls and cabochon faux pearl earrings. Her normally fuzzy hair hung in smooth cello curves against her jade mohair sweater. "Feel me." She held her arm out for him to stroke.

"You're softer than Q-tip."

"But just as bony."

Rusty laughed, surprised by her sense of humor.

"What's for dinner?" she asked.

"Miso pizza." He went to her kitchen and began chopping green peppers, mushrooms, onions and black olives.

"Did you see Henry's new car?" She grated mozzarella and cheddar cheese into neat white and yellow mounds.

"Yeah," he said, and began spreading brown miso on the pizza crusts. "He puts a car cover over it during work so the pigeons won't crap on it."

"No shit?"

Trying oh so hard to just get along, they both laughed. Henry Healy's car. A green late model Jag. The company canteen gang pitched loud comments about winning the lottery or killing off a rich auntie, but Henry ate his sardine sandwich with regal indifference. Later he told Rusty he'd "gone skint saving for yonks to buy the car of my dreams, but no one wants to hear that, do they?"

"Let's stop with the juvenile jokes," Lucinda said, "before you tell me you're at my disposal." She pointed to the garbage disposal in her sink.

They sat on the giant cushions in her living room, Lucinda with her feet tucked under her haunches and Rusty, beer mug in hand, with his legs stretched out under the coffee table. Q-tip sat on the table, her ellipsoid green eyes following every move of Lucinda's wineglass to lips, wineglass to table, wineglass to lips. Yeasty, garlicky aromas from the oven aroused their appetites.

"Would you like to accompany me to the Christmas Eve service at my church?" Lucinda rattled her fingernail against a strand of pearls.

"I think the pizza's done."

"How can you tell? You didn't set the timer." She jumped up and followed him to the kitchen. Q-tip ran ahead, tail a hopeful question mark.

Seated at the table, she peeled cheese off her pizza wedge and dangled it, making Q-tip prance on her hind legs and snap it out of her fingers. "Will you come to church?"

"Thoreau said, 'Beware of all enterprises requiring new clothes.'"

"It's a Unitarian Church. You don't need new clothes."

He dived into a sermonette about how religion was public; spirituality private, and wondered what she saw in him. What kind of man was she accustomed to dating? He tried to imagine how another man might treat her and if it was different than the way he was treating her. She'd never mentioned a boyfriend, or girlfriends either.

"Do you believe in God?" Lucinda asked.

"No, but I'm still ascared of him," he drawled in a ridge-runner accent.

"Have you ever been to a Unitarian church?" Narrowing her nail-head eyes at him, she finished her wine.

"No." He matched her hard gaze.

"Then you don't know what you're talking about." She tore off a large chunk of pizza, dropping a glob of cheese on her sweater. "Oh, fudge!"

"Not fudge. Pizza." He drizzled more habanero sauce from his silver flask onto the pizza.

"Do you put chili sauce on everything you eat?"

"No, not everything."

"This wasn't authentic pizza," she said testily. "It didn't have tomato sauce or pepperoni on it." She dumped the cat off her lap and tramped to the back of the house to change out of her cheese-schmutzed sweater. That could be dicey. He placed their dishes in the sink and sat on the living room floor waiting to give her her Christmas present and boogie on out of there.

She returned wearing the same pants but with an aqua cable-knit sweater. "What's in the bag? Dessert?"

"Your present."

"Oh, no." She looked crestfallen. Little peaks formed in the green eye shadow on her upper lids. "I didn't get you anything. I thought it'd be the wrong thing to do."

"You thought right."

She opened the bag. Allowed a blinkered smile. Q-tip sniffed fastidiously at the birdhouse in Lucinda's hands. "It's cute."

"It's supposed to look like your bungalow."

"Oh."

"It's a wren house."

"Oh."

Christmas was a nuisance. You shared something that delighted you, something you thought would delight the recipient, and as thanks people looked at you like you'd sprouted an extra head. Not that he was angling for gratitude. "Hang it about nine feet up on your trellis or the mountain ash or donate it to the Salvation Army." He pulled his boots on, stood and punched his arms into his duffel coat.

"I love birds. That's why I don't have a birdbath or birdhouses in the garden. Q-tip thinks they're kitty fast-food restaurants." Lucinda remained seated, head bowed, finger stirring the hole in the birdhouse. She looked up, forsaken. "Let's face it. I'm Leibenfraumilch. You're Watney's."

He knelt beside her and felt his nautilus of hurts twist open a notch.

"I give up," she said, flatly.

"Don't do that." He petted the cat purring in her lap. Lucinda's musky perfume cocooned them.

"I mean I'm giving up on you."

"I mean, don't do that." He placed his finger under her chin and turned her face to him. She tasted like lipstick and wine. She returned his kisses tentatively, yet didn't give any signs that he should stop.

"Are we safe?" he asked, before removing his jeans.

"We won't make babies, if that's what you're worried about." She watched, almost detachedly, as he removed her sweater, pants and stockings. He kissed her through filmy underwear. Inhaled her heady tang. He felt huge. His red, helmeted cock looked like a grotesque sea creature beached against her slender, white thighs. She remained passive, his punishment possibly for making her wait so long for this. He plunged in more roughly than he'd meant to. She grunted with each impact, her neck taut, eyes clinched shut, head wrenched sideways as if he'd backhanded her. He had thought she'd respond athletically but her body was limp, slack. Her hip points, shoulders, and collarbones reminded him how fragile she was. This roused him to churn deeper, to provoke a resounding response.

He felt alone whisking himself to a solitary frenzy, vainly seeking mutual release within her self-protecting coolness. He came, shuddering, shooting anger into her. Anger for doing it. She'd not participated. Anger because he burned to do her again. He rolled off her. It happened so quickly. "Sorry. That snuck up on me," he said.

"You're different than other guys," she said without emotion. "I guess I thought you'd be different at this too."

"Maybe it's you who's the same."

"What are you insinuating?"

He flailed into his clothes. "It means what it means."

She jumped up, tripping on the bottoms of her pants. She tugged at his coat. "Don't leave yet! I need help!"

"I can't help you."

"Yes. Yes, you can. You have to. Clete says it's got to be completed by the twenty-seventh when we go back to work after the holidays. Promise you won't go." Genuine emotion flushed her face.

Rusty held his hands up, surrendering.

She returned from the back of the house carrying an Office Works paper box. The box thudded on the sisal carpet. "He told me to finish all this."

He leafed through the papers: timecards, Aquamira drawings, schematics, programming instructions, Henry's lab reports, invoices and suppliers' receipts from the past months. "What does he want you to do?"

"Change the dates."

"To what?"

"To make it look like we're doing the work now."

Rusty wasn't surprised by what he was hearing, but he was irritated that he hadn't done something to stop it. He first suspected Shatz was cooking a mean brew when he'd ordered Lucinda to scribble Aquamira specs onto a dummy government grant, a task in which Rusty had assisted, but only, he argued with his conscience, in order to give him an opportunity to photocopy the draft grant pages. And then do what?

Apparently Shatz had pulled it off, which explained why Shatz had not announced the Aquamira to the world and had asked Rusty and Henry to mothball it. He was planning to unveil it after he'd received all the grant money. "Have you retro-dated forms like this before?" he asked.

"Last month."

"And voilà! The government sent Shatz Co. a fat check."

"How'd you know? The amount had two commas."

"Lucinda!" She cringed. "Can't you see? Your boss is embezzling government grant money. We did all that work over the past year and Thane spent years, fifty years, on the preliminary work. You're falsifying government documents. You are already implicated if you altered the papers for last month."

"I know!" she screamed, fists clenched at her sides.

"Why are you doing this?"

"Clete can't read or he would do it himself. He's lysdexic." A ghost of a smile passed over her face. "He's dyslexic."

He ignored her ill-timed stab at levity. "But he has no trouble adding and subtracting, does he?"

"Clete's always been good to me and people need the Aquamira. Big deal if the government is paying for it! Someone *should* pay for it."

"You're wrong. No one should pay for it, not like this. The Aquamira is ready now. It's unethical to delay it. It's immoral." He thought he'd better leave before he picked up one of those geodes off the table and hurled it at something, or someone.

"It's only for another eleven months," she said.

He was speechless, beyond counting one, table; two, cat; three, sofa, to regain control. The sum Shatz was bilking off the government must have been enormous—two commas' worth just for one month's no work. Henry had bought a Jag outright and he was undoubtedly low man on the misappropriation totem pole. Lucinda, even lower, had been bought off with a string of pearls and a few upper-casual outfits. Thane?

"No one is getting hurt," she said, laying her fingers on his sleeve.

He backed away from her touch and accidentally tromped on the cat. Q-tip howled and slunk away. Rusty felt depleted. Energy deficit. His groin felt moist, warm, bruised. He ached to ram it to her, to wake her up and make her see how wrong she was.

"You're wrong," he said. "I'm not like other guys. I am different."

The telephone sitting among Darla's dusty makeup bottles on the Louis XVI vanity rang.

"Let it ring." Alita's voice was muffled between his thighs.

"It might be important," Clete told his housekeeper. He groped through a tangle of white satin sheets printed with gold fleur-de-lis to answer the phone as he pushed Alita's bottom away from his mouth and wiped his face on the sheet. When he picked up the receiver, he gestured with a giddy hand for her to continue her work.

"Shatz here. Ouch!" Alita had bitten him.

"It's Lucinda. Sorry to call you on the weekend, but I don't think I can get all the Aquamira re-documentation done as soon as you want it. I tried to get Rusty to—"

"Wade? You asked Wade?" Alita was bearing down on him, getting down to the root.

"Wade. I tried to get Wade Rhodes to help me, but he's too busy."

"You showed Wade that box of documents?" Alita worked hard, competing with the phone for his attention.

"I don't think you have to worry about him, Clete."

"Why not? Ah, jeez. What did he say? How long ago? Jesus, Lucinda. Why'd you do this?" He hung up.

The dam holding back the wall of water was about to burst and carnally irrigate his core, sweeping his bones and lucidity with it. Clete punched in a telephone number he'd hoped he wouldn't need. A bottom feeder's number.

"Listen, Funk." He sucked in air, trying to hang tight. "You know where Rusty Sinclair lives? Good." She kneaded his buttocks, vermilion nails scratching his dissolving hide, twanging tributaries deep in his groin. "Find out what he knows. What he has." Her tongue fluttered, erasing the boundary between inside and out, he; not he. "Right, right, right! Disguise the intent. Bring it to me. Bring it to me."

The phone fell to the carpet. Someone who didn't know, could have mistaken his moans for moans of ecstasy.

Rusty sat on the silvery park bench in a world the street lamps limned with shades of blue. Snow mounds, melted at the edges, lay like polar bear pelts on the grounds around the pond. Wind bit his cheeks. His stomach felt tender, empty, his insides unanchored, swinging free. He didn't know what to do.

The right response would be to report Shatz's swindle to the government. He could dig up the appropriate government officials and show them Thane's notebooks and photocopies of the grant draft with Lucinda's wide, loopy writing in the margins—proof that the Aquamira had been designed over the course of years and tested recently and proof that Shatz had written himself a blank check. Rusty would be required to testify and he'd most likely be viewed as a suspect himself. But he'd risk that in order to kick the mechanisms into motion to set things aright. The government would put the Aquamira on the market and Shatz would go to jail, as would Henry and Lucinda. But that didn't seem entirely fair. They were pawns more than cons. Shades of gray. He'd been in this box before. Whistleblowers don't fare well.

Freezing wind drove tears from his eyes. He headed toward the garage apartment.

The simplest, safest thing to do was boogie. Leave Fort Trust. Keep his mouth shut. Avoid a snafu. In another eleven months Shatz Company could unveil the Aquamira amid the requisite fanfare. Henry could wallow in borrowed glory. Lucinda could strut her stuff in designer clothes and French perfume. Shatz could retire a millionaire and restrict his benighted operations to the golf course. The government would have spent the grant money on something anyhow, so why not let the fantasy that the government's enlightened grant program brought water to the people reach its happy conclusion? If Rusty squealed, it'd be a coin toss whether he'd be providing testimony as the defense's witness or as prosecution's. Either way it'd drag on for years or however long Shatz Company's defense attorneys could protract the case, raise objections, submit appeals. No, thank you.

As he approached the street the DiMartinos lived on, he noticed that something was wrong. The DiMartinos' outside lights were ablaze. Rusty ran. Icy air serrated his lungs. He slipped where snow had melted and refrozen in their driveway. Mrs. DiMartino, wearing a housecoat and slippers, ran toward him, her arms pumping awkwardly from side to side in front of her. Lights glared from their open garage door like a drive-in movie screen. Len stood staring at the paint-splattered keepsake of himself. Jigsaw-puzzle shapes of yellow, green, and white paint splotched the Toronado's glossy red coat. The same vandal or vandals, only moments ago, had poured a bucket of black on the expansive trunk. The paint was spreading like a mitotic organism.

He heard a crunch. Splintering wood. A man's loud cry. Rusty bounded up the stairs, skipping over the rotten step. Someone had crashed through the wood. Rusty's clothes lay about his room like deflated body parts. Stools upended. Sheets tossed willy-nilly. He searched in all his kitchen drawers. The bedside table. The bathroom. The countertop.

The vandal, someone with a broken or sprained leg now, had known exactly what to steal. Thane's lab books and the draft grant photocopies were missing.

Rusty ran down the steps and through the DiMartinos' back yard. He whipped his head from left to right. A car approached. He sprinted down the back alley chasing a limping man. The figure hobbled into the car. It tore out, chucking rooster tails of gravel. Two red eyes retreated in the frozen black. The license plate number was obscured with mud.

It became clear to him what to do.

CHAPTER 16

It was the first time Rusty had entered the CEO's office. He was certain it would also be his last visit to Shatz's domain of polished surfaces and barred windows. A credenza devoid of officious accoutrements, stood behind the desk that was bare except for the communications system, a doodle-free blotter and Shatz's heel marks. A black and white photo, the composition top-heavy, the background busy, the figure blurred, hung over the credenza. He approached the vast desk and the man who seemed to be in reverie, gazing at the photograph.

Shatz uncrossed his legs from the top of his credenza, spun around and sat upright in his high-backed office chair. "Who let you in?"

"Lucinda wasn't at her desk." Rusty cased the office in the event a goon jumped out of the executive john. The sofa facing Shatz's desk left only a narrow passageway to the door, requiring the occupant and office visitors to sidle in and out. A long meeting table and chairs filled the remainder of the office. A video monitor was set up on the table. If he needed to escape, he could use the sofa like a staircase, run across the table and leap out the door. He wondered if Shatz controlled the door with a discreet button under his desk.

"I was going to send for you anyway." Clete Shatz smoothed his tie and folded his hands on the desk.

Rusty stepped up to the desk; pressed against his reflection at the edge of the protective plate glass. The black and white photo titled simply "Paris 1932" was a repro of Henri Cartier-Bresson's man leaping from a recumbent ladder into a mirror of water. His leading foot was a millisecond away from meeting its reflection and shattering the water's surface. Cartier-Bresson's exemplary brilliance or luck lay in capturing the decisive moment when the subject had committed himself to accept the consequences of his black and white action.

Rusty said, "I know you're embezzling government money."

"You think you've got me cornered." Shatz's fingers strained to break free from their own grasp. His lips pressed down a smile.

Rusty rubbed his forehead with his hands and wiped them repeatedly on his coveralls, trying to make Shatz think he was nervous and intimidated. "I, I, don't get it. Why would you, Clete Shatz, owner of Shatz Company defraud the government of millions of dollars?"

Shatz erected a steeple with his hands. "Why? Because I'm greedy and I can't lose. You can't run interference in this game. Sit."

He remained standing. He had been afraid Shatz would deny the scam, but he hadn't. The man's pride superceded his caution. Shatz hadn't seemed disturbed by Rusty's confrontation. He acted as if he'd almost expected Rusty to find out. The corners of Shatz's mouth trembled; he had more to reveal. Shatz opened a desk drawer, pulled something out and burned it at Rusty who caught the object with a deft twist of his palm. An old golf ball. Wm. Gourlay 26. He chucked it back so Shatz could easily catch it.

"You're quick," Shatz conceded, "but not innocent." He squeezed the ball in his hand. "I know all about your misfortune with Statonics. You're on the lam." He tossed the ball from left hand to right, left, right, left, right. "But I'm a fair man, Rusty Sinclair. I don't plan to reveal your whereabouts. What do you say to a piece of the action?"

"No."

"That's what I thought you'd say. You're predictable."

The office door shut softly behind him. His muscles tightened, waiting for a blow to the back, ready to accept pain of an unknown intensity. He shifted his weight to one leg, preparing to fire his boot heel behind him into someone's knee. Shatz opened the desk drawer again. Smiling broadly, the outline of his lips more rectangular than curved, he placed an eight by ten color photo on his desk. It was the photo Henry had shot of him handing the proprietary Shatz Company package to the EnviroZone woman. Rusty checked the coveralls he was wearing in the photo first. The stitched name Thane Gabler wasn't visible. His shoulder blocked it.

Shatz handed the photo to him. "I have more of these. You can frame it." Laughing, he stood, hid his hands in his pockets and spoke in the tone of a newscaster. "Corporate espionage involving government projects is a federal offense. This snapshot shows you delivering proprietary, confidential information to our competitor. Aquamira specs, blueprints, test results, blah, blah, blah. It's called technological theft." He turned to contemplate the cars passing by on Point Street. Finally he said, "Turn on the TV and hit play."

Electronic rice scattered on the screen and then formed images of a white car parking in front of Shatz Company. Rusty watched Thane, Lucinda and himself enter the building. He turned the monitor off and looked outside. Crows mobbed a hawk beyond the barred window.

"That recording doesn't mean anything. I'm an employee. I was working late. Lucinda too. The police let us go that night."

Shatz brandished one of Thane's lab books and Rusty's photocopies of the grant. He ripped out several pages from the lab book and fed them to the paper shredder. He continued ripping and shredding until the shredder had destroyed Rusty's tangible evidence of foul play.

Rusty knew if he blew Shatz's cover, Shatz would counterattack by turning in cooked-up evidence proving that Rusty was an industrial spy. What dullard would believe the words of a part-timer with a shadowy past over the story from a corporate citizen?

"You breathe a word about my game," Shatz dropped his voice, and stood, "and I'll have the law on you like flies on shit." He zinged the golf ball against the back wall. It bounced on the table and he caught it on the rebound.

Rusty consciously kept his breathing steady, bridled the adrenaline urging him to lash out. "You're an outstanding con man, Mr. Shatz. You thought this through to the last detail."

Shatz stroked his tie, sat in his chair and sighed as if he were a genius instructing a moron. "Stealing from the government is easy if you know what everybody wants and give it to them. The people get clean water. The politicians are heroes. The environmental zealots are happy. The White House is happy. I'm happy. It's win/win/win/win."

Rusty had heard enough. He edged his way to the door and tried the knob. He let his hand fall to his side and waited for Shatz to release the lock.

"Don't go AWOL, Sinclair or Rhodes, like before. That'd be a bad move. Important people would be a tad miffed if the party ended." His smile splintered.

The office door opened on well-oiled hinges. Lucinda shrunk into herself when Rusty walked by her desk on his way out the front door. *So this,* he thought recalling an afternoon sitting in Kokus' Pool Hall, *is the reason Thane told me that saga about Lesher and the turncoat soldiers. It was a cautionary tale.*

As Rusty approached the old folks home, nestled in the apple treed foothills of a mountain, a cliché movie scene came to mind. The scene takes place in the mid-west in the vast desert and there's a lone gas station. The faded sign swinging in the gritty gusts says Last Chance for Gas, or something similarly frightening. Old folks homes were the last chance for, for what? Reconciling the mistakes of a lifetime? Putting one's affairs to rights? Asking for and bestowing forgiveness?

Thane Gabler's nursing home roommate, a man with oily black hair, was reading an old Jeffrey Archer potboiler. The author's gold name outshone the title. L-shaped Christmas cards stood on the bureaus and bedside tables. One of Thane's kid-made cards depicted an old man's tonsured head above a blue bowl labeled "Purina Pappy Chow." The card was signed with a dog's footprint drawn in magic marker and the closing, "Love, Nancy, Terry, Kira and Kyle and Sooty, Jr." The poinsettia on the bedside table was parched. The toilet flushed in the small bathroom and Thane entered the room. He wasn't surprised to see Rusty standing by his bed, reading the Christmas cards.

"After the hospital released me, Ginny sent me here to Orchard Village to get me out of her hair, I think," Thane said. He lowered himself, grunting softly, on his bed.

Rusty could barely stand to witness the slowness with which the old man moved. Outside, a boy, someone's grandchild possibly, packing snow in his hands, squatted behind a boulder capped with an icy antimacassar. Another smaller boy ran past, head twisting left and right, both hands charged with snowballs. The boy behind the boulder popped up and blindsided his brother.

"You were barking up the wrong tree," Rusty blurted. "You should have been asking Clete Shatz what his motivation was, not mine."

Thane raised his hand, gesturing weakly for him to slow down, what's this about?

"You made me tell you about why I left Statonics and I told you stuff about my wife that I haven't told anybody else."

The old man's eyes were watery and distant. Was he listening? Was he comprehending? Thane said, "I had to assess you. Tampering with vibrations causes explosions. Giving my system to the wrong person would be like handing dynamite to a baby." He blinked slowly, parted his lips to say something else but changed his mind or had forgotten already what he had wanted to say.

Rusty couldn't stand still, but the room was too small to allow him to do much more than sit in the chair or stand and look out the window. He was restless, wanted to go, get out of this room. And then he realized he wasn't restless. He was angry at Thane. "You should have asked Shatz his motivation," Rusty said.

"I'm not senile. I heard you the first time."

"He's withholding the Aquamira from the public."

"Why?"

He didn't know if Thane was in on the scam or not. If so, Rusty had been doubly duped, played for the gullible, willing fool, as naïve and as shocked as he'd been when he'd read that Jefferson kept slaves, fathered mulattos. What the hell. He began revealing what he knew to the old man. "Shatz admitted to me that he's accepting government grant money for the supposed design and development of the system, the system you've worked on all your life." The roommate stole a look over his book.

Thane's face melted into the pillow. His eyes looked askance. "I'm a bad judge of character, I admit. I didn't want to give you the instructions, remember? You bribed me with Scotch and cigarettes. If you would have recognized Shatz's motivation, this wouldn't have happened this way."

"Get off that tired horse. It's not going anywhere. What about your motivation?"

"'The cosmic religious feeling is the strongest and noblest motive.'" The old man closed his eyes, pale lashes resting against his crepe skin.

If Mr. Gabler were asleep, so much the better. Rusty didn't want to battle with him, not now, but he felt cornered. Quietly: "You wanted the Aquamira to work as much as any of us did and now you blame me for what Shatz is doing, as if I could have foreseen it. It's not your fault. It's not mine!"

"The fault was mine. I didn't heed my instincts."

"Quit dabbling in voodoo. You're a scientist. Stick to empirical evidence, scientific methods."

"Scientists are the worst offenders, Rusty, the biggest practitioners of voodoo, as you say. They claim to use empirical methods, basing their premises on concrete evidence perceived by the senses, yet scientists are the ones who speculate that things exist that we cannot sense, cannot prove. Antimatter. Black holes. Infinity."

It tore his heart out picturing a cadre of plank-shouldered, mustachioed cops bursting in on Thane and Ginny Gabler during Orchard Village visiting hours. They'd be playing a pinochle game to the strains of an easy-listening station. Mrs. Gabler would lay her meld face down, wring her hands, offer the policemen some of the raisin cookies she'd brought, as the men handcuffed her unresisting husband and arrested him for conspiring to defraud the government.

"Are you in on it?" Rusty asked.

His lids dropped concealing the story his eyes held. Rusty pulled his chair closer to the bed and laid his hand on Thane's forearm and squeezed encouragingly.

An orderly entered the room and all business-like straightened his sheets, scanned his charts, checked his vital signs without registering any giveaway expressions on her blasé face. Thane was old. If his pulse had been faint, his heart winding down, it would be as she expected, nothing noteworthy, no need to summon the doctor. She repeated the routine at the next bed.

"I'm not a businessman. My goal was to invent something useful, leave a legacy."

"If you say you are involved, I won't," he whispered in Thane's bangle ear, sickening himself with his obligatory compromise. "I won't turn Shatz in."

"Your morals are more flexible than I thought."

"My morals are more flexible than *I* thought."

Thane continued, "I didn't start the experiment for financial gain, and I didn't help you complete them for financial gain. I'm an artist, a creator. I am the hands of God, as we all are."

Rusty Sinclair let himself bend double in the chair and he rested his head on the bed. A warm hand stroked his head.

Rusty had heard from TV and radio reports that the water grant was the brainchild of the governor of Pennsylvania, but regular citizens can't drop in on the governor just like that, so he kept pestering clerks on the phone until he was granted an appointment with the governor's aide. His appointment with Scott Billet, scheduled for two-thirty, was to end by two-forty. Ten minutes should be long enough to halt Shatz's crime.

He hitched a ride north on Route 83 with a loquacious boy suffering the tail-end of a forty-eight-hour New Year's Day hangover. The boy said he was on his way to a construction job interview. Rusty passed on a tip he'd learned the hard way. "I didn't get hired for a roofer's job one time," he explained, "because I made the mistake of wearing spanking new clodhoppers."

"Dang!" the boy said. "I'll scuzz mine up before my interview."

As he walked along the berm of the road, thumb extended into frigid slipstreams for another pickup, he realized he'd ratcheted like a speed-fiend with the boy. Rusty was anxious. They might not believe him. They might arrest him. They might kill him. Any number of scenarios could play out, depending on how convincing his presentation was and how far and wide the embezzlement clique spread.

The second ride, an elementary education student from Shippensburg, tailgated a Green's Dairy milk truck, letting the white vehicle clear a slow path for her.

"What do you get out of teaching?" he asked the young woman.

"That seems backwards."

"You wouldn't teach if you didn't get something out of it, something back for yourself."

"I come from a family of teachers." The Green's Truck turned off the highway and the woman found an electric bus to tail.

Watching on-coming traffic and thinking that if everybody exchanged jobs they'd all live where they worked, but they'd find somewhere else to go anyhow, Rusty asked, "If your folks were hog butchers, would I be riding in a farm truck full of fat hogs instead of a future teacher?"

She chewed her cheek pensively. "My grandfather was a teacher. My aunts. My dad. It's in my blood." She turned on the radio and said nothing for the remainder of the drive, which was as far as the west shore of the Susquehanna River. The quartz-like formation of commercial and government buildings in the middle distance across the river where the golden statue atop the capitol dome held a hand high, looked majestic, impregnable.

He was grateful for the opportunity to walk across the bridge. It gave him time to collect calm from the slow river. If he believed in a god, he would have prayed. Instead he tried to empty his mind. That he was also crossing a metaphorical bridge was not lost on him.

A clot of people circumscribed the pavement in front of the state capitol steps. They were tramping their feet and carrying signs: "You Need Farmers. Farmers Need Water." "Increase Farm H_2O Quota." "No Water-No Fodder." Amid a circle of God's Warriors, a man in a black robe bellowed the story of Genesis. "'And God said, "Let the water under the sky be gathered to one place."'" God's Warriors sang the refrain: "And God saw that it was go-od!" to the tune of "And Bingo was his name-o!"

Stepping inside the capitol rotunda, Rusty recalled the woman from Shippensburg remarking that the university's Heiges Field House gym was so huge that condensation formed on the ceiling and dripped on the Raiders' basketball games. He had misgivings being inside a building large enough to generate its own weather system. Heavy weather. The marble staircase led his eye to the triple arcaded gallery. Woodwork on the arches, eaves and the dome itself resembled Goliath diatoms. Framed in large medallions were four painted figures representing Religion, Law, Science, Art. The ideals were tested and sometimes pulverized in the day-to-day machinations required to run a government.

"Mr. Rhodes?" A harried-looking woman held out her hand. "I'm Mr. Billet's assistant, Ms Dodd. He's expecting you." She walked ahead of him with a sureness he found alarming because he knew she knew he was watching her buttock muscles dance under her skirt. Once out of the rotunda area, they entered a hall that smelled and sounded like school halls from his childhood. Powdery, hollow, reinforced. She held open a dark wood door with a pebbled-glass window and told him to please have a seat. She ran to answer a phone. People tossed papers on her desk, she took phone messages, typed from a thick document and answered staff's impatient questions.

"The assistant needs an assistant," Rusty commented.

"You're telling me." She smiled gratefully. "Mr. Billet will see you now." She ushered him into Billet's office and introduced the two men.

"Nice to meet you, Mr. Rhodes." Scott Billet stepped from behind his desk, not slouching as many tall men did, and nodded Rusty into a chair beside the one he sat in. Billet's long limbs reminded Rusty of a grasshopper's and he wondered if he had a thing going with his assistant. He wouldn't blame either one, on a physicality basis.

"You said you have a tape with information on it which you believe impacts the water recycling and purification system grant." He sounded interested but not aggressive or skeptical as Rusty had assumed someone in his position might sound.

"Yes. It's in my pocket."

They listened to the two tinny voices Rusty had taped in Shatz's office with a voice operated micro-cassette recorder hidden in his coverall breast pocket. A waterfall hissed from the cheap recorder.

I know you are embezzling government grant money.

"That's me," Rusty interjected.

You think you've got me cornered.

"I recognize Shatz," Billet said, eyes on the cassette player.

I, I, don't get it. Why would you, Clete Shatz, owner of Shatz Company defraud the government?

Why? Because I'm greedy and I can't lose. You can't run interference in this game, Rhodes. Sit. Stealing from the government is easy if you know what everybody wants and give it to them. The people get clean water. The politicians under the dome in Harrisburg are heroes. The environmental zealots are happy. The White House is happy. I'm happy. It's win/win/win/win.

Billet covered his face with his hands. "Jesus wept!"

He told Billet that Shatz had a film of him, a secretary and a former employee working in the lab after hours and that they'd set off the alarm. "Shatz didn't reprimand me or the secretary. He never mentioned it. He's using the film to set me up as a corporate spy so I won't squeal. Plus he has a picture showing me delivering a packet, supposedly of Aquamira blueprints and technical papers, to EnviroZone. I called EnviroZone. The woman there told me I'd delivered the Fort Trust phone book."

"I see. I have another appointment." Billet ejected the cassette tape and slipped it into an inner pocket in his jacket. "You're a good man, Mr. Rhodes." He held out his hand.

"I need a favor."

"I can't promise anything. What is it?"

"Take it easy on the secretary. She's only following orders."

Billet seemed to be weighing the request. "I'll do what I can, but that line doesn't absolve anyone of illegal acts. The governor will be in later this afternoon. I'll call you tomorrow at…" He pressed a button flashing up tomorrow's agenda on his watch. "Give me a number where I can reach you at ten forty-five. I'll contact you after I get instructions from the governor. Do not tell anybody you talked to me. Don't tell anybody else what you know. I'll take it from here. I promise."

They shook hands. He felt like a slimy snitch but didn't know why. A bolus of nerve ends knotted in his stomach.

CHAPTER 17

Hake Point, located on a semi-tropical island, only a water-taxi ride away from Hilton Head, South Carolina was an easy drive to tits-and-ribs Myrtle Beach which Clete had told Alita didn't interest him, unless they were her tits and ribs. The course designed by Gary Gibson, a protégé of Rees Jones, challenged him sufficiently, but he kept his score under ninety and hoped to shave off a few strokes before the end of this two-day boondoggle with Senator Krumrine. Well, yes, they did talk business. "Monkey business," Krumrine had snorted.

For as much as Krumrine paid for his Hake Point membership, it seemed like a waste. The man couldn't golf his way out of a wet paper bag. Earlier in the game Krumrine had hit the ball too soft, aiming it dead straight toward a creek. The ball had bounced on a footbridge and traveled another fifteen yards, landing on the green. Lucky bastard. It suddenly dawned on Clete: taxpayers unknowingly picked up Krumrine's membership tab at this exclusive golf club and probably several others, too.

The five sand traps in the green grass resembled a giant dog's paw print on the seaside course. Clete resolved to play golf down here whenever the mood struck. He could easily afford it now, unless Darla mucked things up. He tried her number again. Busy. Clete had been calling Darla's number hourly for days, but her staff always gave him the runaround. He couldn't leave a meaningful message: it would incriminate him. He had to talk to her personally, convince her to back off pursuing the grant winner with her clients' lawsuit. She was going to sever her own purse strings and strangle him with them if she wasn't careful.

Standing with one foot in the sand and one on the grass, he choked his sand wedge and sprayed the ball onto the green. It button-hooked around the hole.

"That's a gimme," Senator Krumrine allowed begrudgingly. He cocked his seven iron and tried to pop his ball out of the rough, but awkwardly skinned its dimpled face. His ball waddled an inch in the tall grass. Wasted shot.

Taking up golf had been Darla's idea and damn if Clete didn't enjoy tooling around Hilton Head from one ritzy club to another, playing two rounds a day, smelling the sea-salted air, eating gourmet food, making love to Darla in a fancy bed. Other couples they'd known split after building a house, a miscarriage, financial straits. Janice, the fruit of their triumphing over all of that, was the cyclone that drove a sliver of straw into the bedrock of their marriage. He'd really wanted his third marriage to last. He really had.

Krumrine selected his seven iron again and with stiff wrists, shifting his weight from one foot to the other, as if it made any difference, walloped the ball too hard. Following a miraculous parabolic path, it bounced against the pin and dropped in the hole. "The sun shines on the righteous," Krumrine cawed.

Clete was thinking about the double martini that he was going to order in the antebellum clubhouse after finishing this round.

Krumrine's phone bleated, as unwelcome as an alarm clock in a sleep-deprivation lab.

"Those things ought to be outlawed on golf courses," Clete said. He trotted to their golf cart parked under a tupelo tree. Whoever had phoned Krumrine had him riveted on the green. He didn't notice or was ignoring the foursome waiting to play the hole. Krumrine hooked his phone onto his belt.

Clete waved him over. "Let's knock off. I need a drink. We tee off tomorrow at six-fifteen. We can get two rounds in before we fly back."

"We've got a problem, Shatz." Krumrine's pocked face and the sand traps collected elongating shadows. They took a shortcut through the woods, bags jouncing in the cart.

"What problem?" They had too little in common for shared problems. "The grant? Did Darla do something?"

"Yes. The grant." The senator refused to be drawn out any further.

They parked the cart in front of the clubhouse where deciduous trees reflected nakedly on the onyx lagoon. Inside, Krumrine told Clete to order their drinks, and without warming into it, said, "The party's over." White spittle collected at the corners of Krumrine's lips.

"Who called you?"

"Nope. Forget that. What are you going to do?"

"I don't know what you're talking about." Clete forgot about his martini. He tried to make sense of what Krumrine was telling him. And not telling him. A waiter asked if they'd like to order dinner.

"Our special tonight is goose a l'orange, green beans almondine, and rice pilaf."

"I'll have the special," Clete answered. He'd eaten only a shrimp salad and beers for lunch.

Krumrine pre-empted him. "We don't want to eat."

The waiter looked at Clete who said, "Maybe later." When the waiter left Clete asked, "What the fuck's going on?"

"Your boy taped your confession. He played it for Billet."

"Ah jeez!" The asshole had taped their conversation in his office. Clete knew he'd been cocky. Hadn't denied a thing. He remembered offering Rusty a piece of the action.

Krumrine's forehead reflected the winking fairy lights taped to the ogee ceiling molding. "Who else did you brag to, Shatz?"

"Nobody else. Only us." Clete was pretty sure that was true. He didn't think he'd mentioned it to Darla or Alita. Lucinda and Henry knew. And Funk. And Ingle. "Only us and Wade Rhodes. I can't believe he did that. I have him framed."

"Not tight enough. Not tight enough. I'll handle my side of it." Krumrine tossed his drink down, crushed ice between his teeth and leaned halfway across the table. Clete could smell his breath. Medicinal. "You take care of your boy before he takes care of you."

"What about—"

"Don't make me say any more."

"No. No. Don't say any more."

"We're checking out and catching a late flight to Harrisburg. Go pack."

In his room Clete wadded his golf togs into his bag. He felt as if he were in one of his nightmares where a curtain of cellophane or water distorted his vision and he had difficulty moving his arms and legs. His limbs were heavy, he tried to walk in a gluey tunnel. He turned on the TV, a beacon to direct his runaway thoughts. This was too unreal. Like a stinking gangster film. But he wasn't a bad guy. He'd done it for the good of humanity. Prestige and money were side benefits. Money: that's what all the bad guys wanted. He couldn't imagine himself in a role where he'd have to, in Krumrine's words, "take care of" Rusty Sinclair.

The weather girl was forecasting a brutal cold snap courtesy of a Nor'easter. Clete re-opened his overnight bag and unpacked his Scottsdale golf sweater and windbreaker and ticked off his options: He could disappear for a while, get a new identity from Krumrine or someone, and never see his daughter again. No good. Make Henry Healy the scapegoat. Nah, no one would believe the fusty lab supervisor could've pulled off a coup without his CEO's cooperation. How about Ingle in accounting? Let him be the fall guy. No. Clete's crabbed signature embellished every damning document, prosecution's Exhibits A through Z. Any halfwit jury and judge would know that no man could have pulled the grant scam off single handedly.

Rusty blew the whistle and now they were all going down. Henry, Lucinda, Ingle, Funk, Krumrine, the governor. Maybe he could convince Rusty to leave town, give him a golden handshake and a plane ticket to Bali. No. He'd already tried that more or less by offering him a slice of the pie. Eliminate him. It was the only way out of the nightmare.

Clete slumped on the bed. The rerun theme song of "Spin City" came on. He turned off the TV with the remote control.

How do you eliminate someone? Call a number in the yellow pages and ask a guttural voice to rub him out? He started giggling. Products to fill this specialized market niche materialized in his imagination: Snitch Guard, Stooly Off, Acme Rub 'em Out Kit, Squealer Eater, Lip Seal, Raid Silencer. *Jesus H. Christ,* he thought, *what's happening to me? I'm going fucking loony.* "I don't want to hurt anybody," he croaked. What then? Face the music?

His stomach gurgled and his slippery bowels uncoiled. He stooped to peer in the mini-fridge. Chocolate bar, salted beer nuts, Miller Lite, Bud, Smirnoff. He bit open a foil pack of nuts and tore three mini-lids from their mini-Smirnoff moorings. *If this place is so stinking lavish, why is everything miniature?*

Chilled alcohol slithered down his throat, esophagus and through his intestines. He thought he remembered hearing that spouses were barred from testifying against each other in a court of law. He hoped that wasn't only TV fiction. Feeling nauseous, he punched his home number on the phone.

"Hello, Shatz residence."

"Oh, good! You're home!"

"Who's this?"

"It's me, Darly. I need help."

Darla made a dismissive noise.

He saw the man in the mirror whose face was tight and sallow, like something breakable. Searching for his normal voice, he cleared his throat and turned his back on the queasy man in the mirror. "I'm in trouble."

"Save your tale of woe for your attorney. It doesn't concern me. A Maryland couple is interested in buying the Oak Heights house. Let's expedite the divorce process."

"Darly! I'm in trouble. We'll lose everything. Everything. I don't know what to do."

"Get a grip, Clete. What is it?"

He told her how he'd hustled Henry and Wade on the Aquamira, influenced the grant requirements to match the Aquamira's specs and had been accepting monthly checks from the grant allocation committee, allegedly for labor and expenses incurred while designing a revolutionary water recycling and purification system. His mouth was dry, his bones going soft. "We've altered all our supporting documentation to make it look like we're doing the work now," Clete said.

"But you finished that Aquatron a while back."

"Aquamira. Exactly!"

"Oh, my God. You won the grant! It's your ass I'm after. I can't believe this. That's why you stalled our divorce. You wanted to rake in enough money to buy me out. And here I thought you were dragging ass for romantic reasons."

A machine-gun knock resounded in the room. "Shake a leg, Shatz," Krumrine boomed from the other side of the door. "The limo is waiting."

"Is that Krumrine?" Darla asked. "What a slime bag. What's the problem, Clete? Now you can buy out my half of the company. Let me worry about the lawsuit. I'll think of some way to waylay it. You're shrewd. No wonder I married you."

His heart fell into a gorge.

"Shatz," Krumrine bellowed, "quit playing with yourself!"

Clete looked up. The man's chin in the mirror was crumbling into the phone receiver. "One of my employees taped me saying incriminating things. He played it for someone high-up in government."

After a pause Darla said, "You are in trouble. Even I can't help you with that."

"I love you, Darly."

"Puh-leaze, Clete. No you don't."

"Haul ass, Shatz!" Krumrine pummeled the door.

Clete rushed to the bathroom and retched. "Stinking shrimp."

CHAPTER 18

The only reason Rusty had given Scott Billet the lab phone number as the way to contact him was because he knew Shatz was off on a business trip for two days, and he didn't want to raise anyone's suspicions by not reporting to work as usual. The bubble of time was shrinking, though. The dusty lab clock read ten fifty-five, which was ten minutes past the time Billet promised he'd call Rusty. Something must have come up. But Billet had been precise: Ten forty-five.

The phone rang. "Shatz Company. Wade Rhodes speaking."

"Where's Henry? I have a question about his wife's health claim form."

"He's not here," he told Lucinda.

"Oh." She hung up.

Henry entered the lab.

"Lucinda's looking for you."

Henry patted his empty shirt pocket. "Do you have a fag?"

"I thought you quit smoking."

"I'm right good at quitting." He flopped his satchel and set his thermos onto his desk. "Someone in accounting probably has smokes." He left. Henry's aloof, distracted manner had returned when he began driving the green Jaguar to work. He wore down shoe leather trundling to the production area and over to the process engineering blokes getting niggling, petty questions answered so he could write work instructions for future production runs of Aquamiras. Rusty thought about luring him with a Benson & Hedges, cornering him and asking, "Hey bro, how's the ol' payola comin' along?" or whatever they call it in England, and then driving the heel of his palm into the man's nose before he had a chance to answer.

Eleven-fifteen. He called Billet's office. "Mr. Billet said he'd call me this morning. I was wondering if I missed—"

"Call back tomorrow." Ms Dodd's good-hearted temperament from the day before wasn't carrying through the phone lines. Sounding troubled, her voice straining to be civil, she said, "He didn't come to work and he has scads of appointments and I need his signature." Her voice grew faint when she spoke to someone in her office.

"Ms Dodd, did he mention a tape?"

"A tape? No! His office was burglarized and no one knows where he is. His wife said he left for work this morning as usual. Call back tomorrow." She hung up.

He stepped outside. Cold air filled his lungs. Someone didn't want Billet to play that tape again. Someone didn't want Billet to repeat what he'd heard on that tape. That someone had to be the governor. Or, no, Billet was in on it too and had faked it to look as if his office had been burglarized and the tape stolen. Rusty had made only one tape. He smacked the maple tree with his open palm. He focused on the sting. How could he be so stupid? He hadn't made a copy of the tape. He'd lost his original evidence—the lab books and photocopied grant papers—because of this same mistake. *I'm not cut out for this shit.*

When he returned to the lab, Rusty strode over to Henry and ripped the phone out of his hand. The receiver chirped when he slammed it into its cradle. "Come out here."

"Bloody hell, I was talking to—"

"Come on!" He gripped Henry's upper arm and dragged him outside.

"Blimey, it's cold." His scalloped teeth chattered.

"Henry!" Rusty grabbed his arms. They were flabby like an old lady's. He let go. "I know how you paid for your Jag. I know Shatz is defrauding the government."

"What are you planning to do?" Cigarette smoke came out in short bursts.

"Not me, Henry. You. If you come clean now, they'll be lenient. If you wait until they come after you, the state government and the federal government will prosecute you to the fullest extent of the law." He was bluffing. How the hell did he know how hard they would press on Henry?

"Oh, right." Henry tossed his half-smoked fag between his shoes and crushed it. The fatty pad on his chin was a determined white. "Let the limey fry whilst Clete and the others walk away clean as a whistle." Tobacco breath billowed in Rusty's face when Henry stepped closer and whispered, "My job is secure. My wife is in remission. We can afford nice things that we never could before, fly the grandchildren over from Sheffield. Well," he yelled, "you can jolly well eff off." He opened the lab door, crashing it against the cinderblock wall.

Rusty walked past the loading dock, past the garbage bin and into the field of corn stalk stubs. He walked away for good. He'd tried, but it hadn't been good enough.

Although the rotten stair step to the garage apartment had been replaced, but never painted, Rusty still stepped over it out of habit. He buttoned the one flannel shirt he was not wearing, folded it and all his other clothes into precise segments. He packed his mess kit, Swiss army knife, maps, soap, razor, towel, ditty bag and other traveling paraphernalia into his new backpack.

Preparing for a journey was like opening a book he hadn't read before. Hope that this book would surpass the last one battled with skepticism that it wouldn't. He recalled snippets of past books, remembered a well-turned phrase or two, a character with whom he'd developed an imagined intimacy. He had read some books slowly, rationing his reading spells to only half an hour at a time to make the story last longer even though he knew there were always more books, better ones possibly, and books as engrossing as the ones he'd already read, and some less absorbing. Fort Trust had been a slow read with a surprise bad ending.

The linoleum floor creaked behind him. Mr. and Mrs. DiMartino had never entered the garage apartment since the day he'd occupied it. They would have knocked or he would have heard their footsteps on the stairs. Without turning to see who it was, he kicked backwards and caught someone in the groin. Twisting around, his fist connected with a man's shoulder. Had Rusty been taller he would have smashed the man's ski-masked face. The man didn't present a weapon or assume any particular offensive stance. He stood breathing heavily and lunged like a football tackler. Rusty stepped into the tackle, pulled the man past him and elbowed him in the back.

The man grabbed the bedside lamp and swung it down on Rusty's shoulder, sending a dull pain through his collarbone. Rusty thrust his palm toward the man's nose. The man ducked and pulled Rusty's legs out from under him. His head bounced on the floor. The man sat on Rusty's chest and punched his face. He tried to let the pain flow through him, through and out. Before the next blow mashed his nose he caught the man's wrist and with his other hand yanked the ski mask over his assailant's eyes. Rusty bucked, arching his back and when the man threw his hands to the floor behind him to regain his balance, Rusty grabbed the back of his thighs and flipped him on his back. He rolled him over and pinned him to the floor. As if observing himself from an objective position on the low ceiling, Rusty saw a stranger who enjoyed fighting. He'd been preparing for this day all his life.

With one hand, Rusty pulled off his own belt and used it to lash the man's arms behind his back. He tied his feet together with the lamp cord. Lastly he pulled off the mask. Both men blinked. Rusty didn't recognize him.

"You better let me go. If I don't check in, someone else will come after you in two hours."

"Thanks for the tip, pal." Two hours to put as much distance between himself and Fort Trust as possible. He poured habanero sauce on a dishcloth and crammed it into the man's mouth. The captive's cries were smothered, his eyes and nose streaming mucus. His skin turned red as his body commandeered all its forces to expel the spice.

Rusty daubed his finger with red sauce and held it in front of the man's crossed eyes. "I'm going to ask you some questions. If you don't answer..." He wagged his finger. "They say this stuff can blind you. Did Clete Shatz send you?"

The man's head shook vigorously, jarring teardrops off his jaw.

"Someone connected to the Aquamira?"

He shook his head again. Rusty believed the man because, for an instant, a quizzical expression clashed with fear and agony.

"Someone from the capitol?"

The man grunted affirmatively. Rusty lugged the man down the steps, through DiMartinos' backyard and out to the alley. No cars or neighbors were around. He carried the man over his shoulders a few houses down from the DiMartinos', and dropped him beside a rank of garbage cans. The thug's eyes were white-rimmed with fear.

"One man's garbage is another man," Rusty muttered. The laughter of a stranger bubbled out of his mouth. He wiped his brow and when he looked at his hand he saw blood. The sight of it caused a stirring in his genitals. *So this is who I've become?* Rusty asked himself.

"Come in, come in. Join me in a cup of coffee." Mrs. DiMartinos' mouth hung open. "Your face is bleeding!"

"I was in a fight."

"Why? Who with?" She led him to a stool at the breakfast nook. Santa's elves, perched on the corner shelf, leered at them. She wet a tea towel and pressed it against his lips and eyebrow. She rattled around in the freezer and gave him plastic balls containing frozen liquid to hold against his cuts.

"I came to tell you I'm leaving."

"Let me write you a check. I owe you your deposit. Remember?" She dug through her gargantuan carryall that contained a pocketbook that contained a wallet that contained her checkbook. "It's none of my bee's wax, but why are you leaving?"

"Looking for better weather." He didn't have time to dally getting a check cashed. His lips throbbed. "Keep the deposit to fix your lamp. I broke it."

Her hands didn't know where to go, so she finger picked her white halo of hair. Her jaw hinged open and closed, somewhere between laughter and confusion. "It won't take the whole deposit to fix the lamp." She dug through the carryall and mined several wrinkled bills, which she smoothed out beside an array of coupons arranged on the counter like cards for a solitaire game. "Oh. Hey. Lookie here!" She reached into the depths of the bag again. "I found it in your coverall pocket when I did the wash. Lotta times I find money in Len's pockets! I found this picture ages ago and kept forgetting to give it to you."

The sight of the photo was a salve to his bruised body. Henry had snapped Clete Shatz and Rusty celebrating the Aquamira prototype's successful field trial out at Arrowhead Lake. The date on the bottom right corner of the snapshot proved that the operational water recycling and purification system had preceded the grant award by almost a year. He hugged Mrs. DiMartino and asked her, "May I use your phone?"

"Be my guest. If I'd a known the picture meant so much to you I wouldn'ta been so forgetful."

Lucinda answered on the second ring.

"Lucinda. You have to decide right now if you're going to go down with Shatz and everybody else or if you want to run away." He didn't add, with me.

"Rusty! Where are you? You left work early. Henry and Clete have been asking for you. Are you leaving? You're leaving. You're used to leaving, you have no ties, tell me what I should do."

Given different circumstances he would have challenged her "no ties" remark, but his time bubble was shrinking ever faster. He realized with self-honest clarity that she was right. He had no ties. "I won't decide for you."

Mrs. DiMartino hummed ostensibly to cover the fact that she was eavesdropping.

"Tell me where you are," Lucinda said. "I've got to see you before you leave."

"No can do. I'm hanging up."

"Don't! I know what I'm going to do. But I need to talk to you."

He checked the clock. The thug's backup thug wasn't due for another hour and forty minutes. He sighed and gave her directions to the garage apartment. "If you're not here in ten minutes, I'll be gone." He hung up.

"Gonna say goodbye to your gal?" Mrs. DiMartino's eyes were lively.

"Yeah. Thanks for everything. I'll leave the key in the mail slot." He kissed her powdery cheek.

Lucinda's knock on the door was surprisingly forceful. He didn't answer. He didn't know if he could trust her.

"Rusty. Open up! It's me."

"Who's with you?"

"No one. Why would I bring anyone?"

It was a gamble, he knew, but he rolled the dice. He opened the door and quickly locked it behind them.

"What happened to your face? Your place is a wreck."

"Someone tried to get me. There's more where he came from."

"Get you?"

"Yeah, what do you know about it?" he asked, not caring what the answer was, but finding that he cared if she knew the answer.

"Nothing, I swear. I never thought it would get ugly like this."

He was relieved to hear her say that even though it was ridiculously naïve of her. Her life was going to be ruined after he turned in the photo. He showed it to her. "I'm taking this to someone who can use it to blow the lid off Shatz's scam."

She sat down on the cot. "I fully understand why you're doing this, but can't you let this one go? No one's getting hurt." She stopped herself. The red badge on his eyebrow began dripping. "I'm sorry," she said.

"What did you need to see me for?" he asked. "I'm running out of time."

She took a tissue out of her black patent tote and pressed it gently to his brow. Suddenly she pressed her hands onto her tummy, and bit her lip.

"What's wrong?" he asked.

"It's my friend."

"Wait here." He ran to Mrs. DiMartino's, disentangled himself from her questions and returned with a small bottle of castor oil. He lit a candle and set it on the bedside table. "Lie down," he said with a clinical tone. "Roll up your sweater and pull your waistband down a few inches."

"I didn't come here for that." She touched the broken lamp with her shoe toe. "What happened to your lamp?"

"This will soothe the pain. I used to do it for my girlfriend."

She lay back and exposed her stomach.

"Is this where the cramps are?"

She stared at the sloped ceiling and pulled her skirt, pantyhose and panties down to her pubic hairline. He heated the bottle of castor oil over the candle flame and poured the heavy, warm oil onto her belly. He laid his hand on her tummy and gently massaged her, smelling the papery odor of castor oil, as viscous as swamp mud, menstrual blood.

"Your hand feels warm and big, like it's rubbing me all over. Like it's a balloon sinking into my body."

"Breathe without expanding your chest. Send fresh white air down to the cramp and breathe it out as a gray cloud. Gently, deep. Breathe in. Breathe out."

Her was voice low and soft when she asked, "Who was in your car when they firebombed it?"

The air was sucked from his lungs. The ache swelled painfully behind his heart. He fought for control by breathing the way he'd told her to, and by concentrating on swabbing the oil off her stomach with the hem of the sheet and wiping her makeup off with it too. Her clean face glowed like mother-of-pearl. He felt he'd known her as a child, the little one who fished with her daddy, who collected pinecones and geodes. The little one inhabiting the woman with doubts and desires. The little one who just wanted to be loved like we all do. He kissed her belly, smearing his blood on her pale skin.

Pantyhose had pressed her reddish pubic hairs flat against her all morning. He fluffed her hair with his fingers, releasing the musky aroma he'd hold to his nose hours later like an elixir. He pulled his hand away, worried that residual habanero heat might burn her. His tongue traversed the folds, crevices, bud. Her body tensed, arched, vibrated. She pushed his face away and caressed his brow. When she held her hand before him, he saw blood. His own. She licked her fingers and worked him with her hand.

"Does this hurt?" she asked after kissing his split lip.

He found his voice. "I'm used to hurting."

"What are you going to do?"

"Take the photo to the political journalist at the 'Fort Trust Standard.'"

"I'll take you."

She crouched on her heels and squatted over his prone body. She slammed her weight against him, around him. He held onto her petite hips. The one time that he had justification for hurrying, he didn't.

The parched poinsettia had been removed from Thane's bedside table, and the Christmas cards were gone, recycled, thrown away or packed in a cardboard box in the Gablers' attic. The roommate was out of the room, either participating in the handicraft class or participating in the life beyond. Thane rolled his red-rimmed eyes slowly to the doorway without turning his head. His careworn voice was barely audible. "Look. My bolo. Ginny brought it." He tightened the asymmetrical turquoise against his pajama collar and made a small noise of surprise as Rusty and Lucinda came closer to the bed. "I hope the other fella looks worse than you do."

"Someone didn't like my tape recording." Rusty pulled two chairs next to the bed and sat on the one nearer Thane. Lucinda sat next to him. He kept his eyes on the door.

"Well hell!" the old man exclaimed, watery eyes dancing when he saw Lucinda hold Rusty's hand. Thane's chin dropped to his chest briefly. He raised his head, keeping his eyes closed. "You're here to say goodbye."

"He's going to give a photo of the Aquamira to the press. It's all over for Clete and everybody involved." Her voice gurgled. She whipped her hand out of Rusty's. "What about Thane? Will he be implicated?"

The roommate returned, making no signs that he was aware of anyone's presence in the room. He lay on his bed and fell asleep instantly.

"He said not." Rusty bit off the words. He stood quickly. The stammering scrape of the chair legs on the wooden floor woke Thane's roommate. He checked the hallway and walked to the window. A woman and a little boy were catching snowflakes on their tongues.

"What's eating you?" Thane asked.

Lucinda said, "Of course he's jittery. Someone tried to beat him up."

Rusty pictured the pond where he'd sat tying up loose thoughts from time to time. Round and round and round. The pavement, weathered benches, shrubs, gingko trees and road formed concentric circles. The pond was the bull's eye. In a plight again, he'd have to book. Boogie. Split. Move on. Shove off. Hit the road. Pull up tent stakes. For how else could he stay ahead of the truck bearing down on him? How else could he survive? The hunted, haunted feeling was as familiar as the feel of the cowboy hat resting on his head.

"A life of running is no life," Thane said.

Lucinda shot Rusty a questioning look.

How did the old man know? Rusty retreated to gazing out the window. The woman outside adjusted her son's knit scarf and held his hand as they walked toward the main entrance of the nursing home. Another boy wearing a red cap, standing by the boulder on the front lawn dredged with snow, watched the mother and son enter the building. Rusty removed his duffel coat and laid it on the windowsill. He kept his hat on, the wide brim sheltering him. *Integrate*, the dream interpreter had told him. What was he afraid of in this warm, safe room with his friends, his only friends, Thane and Lucinda? Snowflakes silently floated on the other side of the cold pane.

"Did you guys really believe Rusty Sinclair had become Wade Rhodes because he was afraid of getting fired from Statonics?" he asked. Lucinda started to speak, but decided against it when he said, "Read the footnotes, boys and girls. I didn't blow the whistle long or loud enough. The EPA published the bogus data. You're looking at a perfect son of a bitch here. A son of a bitch." His voice broke. He swallowed down the lump in his throat.

"Why?" It was Lucinda.

"She's gone! Don't you get it?" It was the night before New Year's Eve, the night he'd told his girlfriend Kim about the bogus data. The night the correct data was hacked off his computer's screen and replaced by a black skull and the images of flames. "She wanted to carpool to work with a friend, but I made her take my car. She turned the ignition and…" A blast shook the house. The bedroom took on an orange glow. Rusty ran to the window. Kim's burning body toppled against the steering wheel of his flaming car. The revelers in the street below began screaming and running away from the flames, yet the screaming didn't stop. It went on, an unpunctuated howl. The screaming was his. The screaming was coming from his every pore.

"And you think she was killed because of you," Thane said.

"I roamed the streets all night going out of my mind. I came back the next morning long enough to pack some gear and I left. I haven't seen or communicated with my family since that night."

Lucinda said, "You're not responsible. You didn't plant the bomb."

"The bomb wouldn't have been there if I hadn't told my boss I was going to blow the whistle. It's happening again. Scott Billet is missing. I told him how Clete got the grant money. They might be after you too. I'm sorry. I'm sorry."

Thane's blue eyes locked on Rusty's. "The bomb was meant for you. Are they still on your tail?"

"I don't know. Someone's after me." He touched the blood encrusting his brow. "I've been so spooked. Staying in Fort Trust this long, I may as well hang a target on my chest. Shoot here. Open season on whistleblowers."

"My God, Rusty." Lucinda reached for his hand.

"Don't. I'm hazardous to your health." He turned away from her. Lucinda wrapped her arms around his waist, pressing her head against his shoulder blade. She tightened her grip. He relaxed a bit.

"That explains your avoidance behavior with me." He felt her voice vibrate and her warmth against his back. "You were afraid to get close again. Afraid you'd get hurt. I thought there was something wrong with me. You could have told me about Kim sooner. I think I would have understood."

"I'm sorry. I know you would have. That's what scared me."

He knelt beside the bed, cupped Thane's gnarly hand in both of his and hoped his eyes were conveying all the gratitude and love he didn't want to belittle with inadequate words. Thane smiled. His smile reached inside Rusty and spread like a soothing balm on the raw spot they'd scraped open.

Rusty opened the passenger door of Lucinda's car and said, "Wait here for me. I'll be back in five minutes."

"I'll wait." She kept the motor running.

He stepped into a phone booth across from a neo-Colonial building with Fort Trust Standard Newspaper written on the façade in foot-high gothic font that merged like a double exposed photo with his reflection in the telephone booth glass. A homeless man standing beneath the letter U of Trust held up the January issue of "Rough Voices" the magazine published by homeless people. By any name—vagabonds, hobos, bums, gypsies, nomads, migrants, transients, a Problem—Rusty didn't consider himself to be one of them, although he knew how they lived, rummaging in grocery stores' trash bins, scouting for food samples at open houses and gallery openings, lurking outside restaurants. He knew, as they knew, that if you looked long and hard enough you'd find a gap in the fence that someone traveling ahead of you had pried apart. Convenient escape. Two women spilled out of the Fort Trust Standard building. They ignored the man selling papers.

Rusty pushed coins into the telephone slot and turned his back on the street.

"Fort Trust Standard. How can I direct your call?"

"I need to talk to Nora Li."

"I'm afraid she's on assignment. May I take a message? No, wait. She's here." Some catchy tune came through the receiver, but he couldn't remember the title. Perhaps he'd never known. A man in a suit walked by the "Rough Voices" vendor and shook his head no. Clouds stacked up, seedpods ready to burst and spill more snow.

"This is Nora Li."

"I have some information."

"So does the Encyclopedia Britannica. Why are you calling me?"

"Because you've been covering the water grant story."

"The highlights, please."

He told her about the fraud, mentioning Clete Shatz's name, and no one else's. He told her that the lab books and photocopies of the draft grant scribbled with Aquamira specs were stolen and destroyed and that he'd given a tape recording of Shatz bragging about his handiwork to the governor's aide Scott Billet. "Mr. Billet said he'd call me. He didn't. His assistant doesn't know where he is."

"Ai ya! Billet's still missing in action," Li exclaimed. "Give me something to go in on. So far all your evidence has been conveniently destroyed."

"Except for one piece."

"How can I get it? Where are you?"

He pulled his black hat down and turned his coat collar up. "I'm in the phone booth across the street. Look out the window." Rusty saw a woman come to the first floor window. Reflections of traffic slid over the figure of Nora Li.

"I see you," she said, "but I can't see your face. Take your hat off."

He waved the receiver in the air.

"Don't hang up! Leave the hat on. Are you involved?" Nora Li added, "No one's innocent in these things."

"You're not the police. Do you want this story or not?"

"What do you have?"

"Go to another room away from the window for two minutes. Then come out to the front of the building and give the 'Rough Voices' man twenty-five dollars. He'll give you a dated photo of the Aquamira. The photo proves that the system was operational months before the grant was awarded."

He hung up and watched her leave the window. Chin tucked deep in his collar, hat brim low, he crossed the street and approached the homeless vendor. "Hey, bro." He bought a copy of the magazine and handed the Aquamira field test photo and a five-dollar bill to the man. "When a Chinese lady hands you twenty-five dollars, you give her this pic."

The man stroked his grinning mustache.

"You don't remember what I look like or where I went," Rusty told him.

"Don't remember who?" The man started counting out Rusty's change, but he was crossing the street. From the inside of Lucinda's car, he watched Nora Li run out of the Fort Trust Standard building and exchange cash for the snapshot. He saw her mouth open and her black pageboy swing as she looked up and down the sidewalk. She didn't spot him across the street in the bank parking lot sitting low in the front seat. She said something to the vendor. He pointed down the street toward the square, making hand motions indicating a right turn. Rusty threw "Rough Voices" on the back seat with his backpack.

"What happened?" Lucinda asked.

"I gave her the photo. If she runs with it, Clete Shatz and—"

"I will be arrested for defrauding the government." Tears glazed her gray eyes.

"Maybe if you cooperate they'll make considerations. I'm sorry." He'd adopted a personal policy years ago not to put himself in a position requiring him to say, "I'm sorry." Now he was saying sorry again. He was sorry he'd stayed in Fort Trust as long as he had. Sorry he was leaving so soon. Sorry he'd become curious about how he and Lucinda might be together. Sorry he'd grown to like her eagerness to be loved, her small breasts, her cottage garden.

"Henry too," she said, referring to others who'd be arrested.

"Yes, 'Enery too."

Lucinda laughed weakly. She laid her hand on top of his and squeezed. "I've never been more terrified in all my life," she said.

"Shut your eyes and breathe like I told you before." He held her hand in both of his, sharing his heat. He began a litany his grandmother had used when he was too excited to sleep. "We are holding hands and we jump, and whoosh, we're flying." His voice resonated behind his closed eyes. "The air is warm, stroking our bodies like feathers and we look down. See. There's the lake and there's a herd of deer running. We see golden fish in the water. It's a deep azure color that never ends and we see our own reflections on the lake. Two people soaring, arms out, hands linked. And you get fancy and do a loop-de-loop pulling me along with you."

Lucinda laughed lightly.

"A hawk," Rusty continued, "flies beside you for a while and you talk to him. What does he tell you, Lucinda? What does the hawk tell you?"

"She tells me to be strong," Lucinda said softly. "She tells me to be light-hearted so I can always fly. She tells me I'll be all right."

They opened their eyes and saw snow falling.

She backed out of the parking spot without checking the rear-view mirror and took the back roads out of town.

"Let me out here," Rusty said. Even though it was a little past one, some drivers had turned on their headlights. Feathery snow twirled in the on-coming beams. Snow clung to black tree branches.

"It's coming down fast." Lucinda pulled off the road next to a woods several miles south of Fort Trust. Her car skidded on the snow. "Stay until the weather lets up."

He reached for the door handle.

Lucinda suddenly hit the steering wheel with the heels of her hands and said, "This doesn't make sense! You don't have to leave. No one is going to try to harm you now that you've already informed the press. Stay! You can stay. We can give each other moral support."

He'd thought the same thing but, "There's too much bad history here. The town is not a pleasant memory." He reached over, turned the ignition off and said, "For the most part."

"You think you can change the past by re-directing your future?"

He settled into the seat. "No, that's not quite it. But I don't know what is it. I don't think people's lives, their fates progress on a strictly linear cause/effect basis. I'd never planned to be a data analyst. I don't know if there even was such a thing when I was in high school. I just happened to be working a summer job at a lumber company when they introduced computers. Who knows where we'll end up?" He could hear the minute sound of snowflakes hitting the windshield. "The first thing I'm going to do is pay a long-overdue visit to my family."

She looked away from him, fiddled with a loose button on her coat. "So what do you plan to do after that?"

In her ear he whispered, "Nothing. Nothing. Nothing."

"Sweet nothings. You have a new adventure ahead of you with all sorts of opportunities and interesting people to meet."

"Thanks for the lift."

"I'm sorry it had to be done, but I'm glad to be the one who did it."

"Listen. You be real careful." He kissed her wet cheek. "I'm going to miss you, Lucinda."

She shook her head and turned the ignition key. The windshield wipers ticked, swishing snow off the window. He retrieved his backpack from the back seat and began hiking south, leaving boot prints in the snow.

CHAPTER 19

Clete Shatz came out of his office looking for Lucinda, but she hadn't returned from running an errand. He paused again in front of the large window and watched the snow accumulate, blanketing his car and the rest of the world. It had been coming down since yesterday. The cars passing by slowly on Point Street sounded distant with the muffling effect of snow under their tires. A white car crawled into the parking space and stopped beside his car. Clete watched Lucinda mince through the snow in her high heels.

"Where've you been? I need you to take dictation!"

She shrugged her coat off and shook the snow off it. "I stopped to buy ink cartridges for the printer. We're out."

"It took you that long?"

"The roads are terrible. Snow's drifting now." She blew her nose.

He remembered crawling out of bed on winter nights during snows like this. He'd been extra careful not to wake his older brother. Sitting by his bedroom window, cold air leaking through the casement, he'd watch snow tumble down as if angels were sifting flour. Snow looked so busy and diligent but it never made a sound. If it snowed enough school would be postponed. In classes Clete could remember nearly everything he'd heard and parrot back Paraguay's chief exports and the times tables. The written tests, the tests his teachers believed in, were his nemesis. He failed every test and was tormented by teachers, parents and the other children.

At the one parent-teacher conference his mom and dad had attended, the confounded fifth grade teacher, Miss Fornadel, admitted Clete had won the class spelling bee, getting through s-a-n-d-w-i-c-h and A-l-b-u-q-u-e-r-q-u-e, but he'd failed for the year and would have to repeat fifth grade. "We'll see that he studies harder," his dad had promised. The promise became a fulfilled threat. But Clete still could not distinguish e-v-i-l from l-i-v-e no matter how many times his dad tanned his hide. The letters swam on the page.

Lucinda threw the "Fort Trust Standard" on her desk and said in a scathing voice he'd never heard her use before, "You don't even have to read to comprehend this story."

A studio photo of him taken three years ago was placed beside one of Krumrine and the state governor shaking hands. The dated color picture of Rusty and him celebrating the Aquamira's successful field test took up one-fourth of the front page. The photo of him acting like a crazy man on the shore of Arrowhead Lake mocked him. Acid burned the back of his throat. It took several moments for him to be able to speak. "Who sent that picture to the paper?"

Lucinda bowed her head so he could not see her face. Surely she didn't betray him.

"Henry did!" Clete yelled, incredulous. "That prick! Why? I'm paying him."

"The end begins," Lucinda said. She swept papers off the surface of her desk and into the wastebasket. She yanked the computer's many plugs out of their many outlets. She opened the middle drawer of her desk and threw nail polish, a pair of pantyhose, a candy bar, a nail file and a box of tampons into her black patent tote. Tears streaked her face.

Clete retrieved the papers from the waste can and replaced them on her desk. "You can't quit," he said. "You're my best employee."

"Please, shut up."

Clete looked out the window again to see what her eyes were fixed on. A State police car cruised slowly, windshield wipers brushing snow off the window. Two more cruisers and two unmarked cars followed that one. The first car turned left into the Shatz

Company parking lot. The other cars followed, two driving on around the building to the back.

His blood solidified in his veins. He could not move. Outside the silent white world flashed intermittently blue.

Henry burst into the office. "Where's Wade? He hasn't returned since morning tea break yesterday."

Clete punched Henry in the mouth. He knew he'd broken a knuckle, but wasn't feeling the pain right now. Henry bawled, his unintelligible words coming from behind his hands now dripping with blood.

Clete felt the air pressure change as a state trooper opened the foyer doors. Uniformed officers walked in briskly. Thinking that leniency might be awarded him for maintaining a sophisticated, regal demeanor he considered going willingly, with dignity. Don't act like a crook and you won't be treated like one. Stinking Krumrine and the governor couldn't help him. They were all going to fall. Hard. Clete shoved Henry out of his way, and ran past him toward the hall leading to the research and development laboratory. He slammed into an officer who had entered through the lab.

An officer read them their rights while another cuffed Clete Shatz. His hands manacled behind his back pulled his shoulders back, which made his jacket lapels spread farther apart. His chest felt exposed, laid bare. "I'm a good guy," he told no one in particular. Another trooper cuffed Henry and a fourth officer handcuffed Lucinda. Employees peered over the tops of office cubicle walls when the troopers escorted the three to the police cars out front. Clete bowed his head.

And in the dream he's in California, driving a truckload of beehives up to Oregon. And in the language of dreams, it is logical that it's his ninth grade art teacher riding shotgun with him. She shows him a small sketchpad. On the page is a mathematical equation written in black grease pencil. The equation proves that our heart's deepest desire is within our capability. It's a natural law. It is God in action.

When he woke up, Rusty couldn't remember the equation shown to him in the dream. He recalled only that it was very short and that the first number was squared. It didn't matter if he remembered the equation or not. It only mattered that he felt lighter and rejuvenated, as if a tumor had been dissolved and sloughed away.

*cbc.ca/dragonsden

Printed in the United States
1087400002B